THE GAUDY IMAGE

THE GAUDY IMAGE

William Talsman

MUSWELL
PRESS

First published in France by The Olympia Press, Paris, in 1958
This edition published by Muswell Press in 2022

Typeset in Bembo by M Rules
Copyright © 2021

Every effort has been made to trace the current copyright holder of
this title. The publisher would be glad to hear from them.

Printed and bound by
CPI Group (UK) Ltd, Croydon CR0 4YY.

A CIP catalogue record for this book is
available from the British Library

ISBN: 9781916129238
eISBN: 9781916129252

Muswell Press
London N6 5HQ
www.muswell-press.co.uk

Acknowledgment

The line from the song which appears on pages 120, 124 and 192 is from "Going to the River" by D. Bartholonew and A. Domino, an Imperial Record (Commodore Music Corp.), 137–139 North Western Avenue, Los Angeles 4, California.

An Introduction to Titania

"Nothing so flagless as this piracy."

White Buildings.
HART CRANE.

I regret that I shall be unable to spend my eternity listening to the rain as it falls upon my casket roof. I am fond of rain, but it troubles me, for its beat suggests an order which I have never known. It's high-speed chattering implies a friendliness which is foreign to me; and its dampness, as soft and comforting as a caress, is a gentleness which escapes me. I sit in the attic room and listen to the rain, but I am not consoled, for a deceit overshadows me which is more urgent than the need for heaven. Yet, it is related to that eternal yearn, for how can one contemplate his future life until he is certain of his present life? The question enrages me. The answer overwhelms me.

That I shall be unable to hear the rain for all eternity is my one big regret, but Titania has no regrets, no large

1

regrets. She is too thin to carry the weight of regrets on her person. She may store them in her closet, if her closet is not too full of dreams already, but she wouldn't be caught dead with a regret on her. But I must get on with this introduction.

"Titania, you're on!"

She is not ready. She makes the most elaborate preparations for an appearance of any kind. She is as vain and as particular about her entrances as a celebrated actress, but her vanity is unreal. Her vanity stems from her pride, but it is an offshoot of that pride and operates in a fashion which is similar to the growth of an ingrown toenail. As the nail grows inward, Titania grows down. Heights dizzy her, but depths soothe her as refreshingly as cool water rippling the foot of a clam.

Her vanity originates in her gestures. That glissando of arm, punctuated sharply with a stare and followed by a nervous flutter of eyelids, releases a flurry of little vanities which she sheds to the passing breezes. The operation is known as wind-pollination in some circles, air pollution in others, but it is more closely associated with the excited sparks which are given off by a fire under pressure, as though a wire were overloaded with electricity. She is knitted together by an electrical current which is over-volted. Tension is tantamount. Her nerves share their sheaths with a current which swells her ganglia outrageously.

She is powdering her behind. She calls it "dusting" her behind. Flagrantly, she swishes the puff in the powder box and ladles the contents on her bottom until white clouds envelop her.

At first, I think, her bottom is smoking, but she assures me that it is more than that.

"My ass is on fire," she says. "Quick, the extinguisher!"

She grabs the bottle of perfume with the atomizer apparatus on top and squirts it in the vicinity of the smoke, the source of the confusion. The perfume does not blanket the smoke, but it does render an ass vapour harmless. I swear that the odour was irrepressible, but Titania just swears.

She sneaks her legs into a pair of slacks. She doesn't forget her underwear. She deliberately omits it. She wiggles into the sheerest of her sheer silk shirts, the light, high blue one which she calls "a vaporous blue." Then she slips her feet into sandals which are really moccasins of soft, white leather. Since she got them on sale, they are too big for her, but they don't flop, for she curls her toes in a gesture of narcissism which she does not understand but which holds them securely on her feet. When she uncurls her toes, she creates a flap, a little noise which announces her approach or adds a flounce to her attire.

She places two pendant earrings of immodest size in the centre of a hankie. She folds the hankie and tucks it in her pocket. "For later," she winks, "so I can dawdle in the john."

"Going reckless tonight," she says, slipping her wallet in the hip pocket without the button, "to court a feel."

Then she gives her coiffure a tiny fluff, gazes into the mirror on the door of the medicine cabinet, takes a leak, smells her fingers, and heads for a bar, just the right bar, the one which she calls "her club," Sparafucile's Bar and Grill.

On the street she slinks. She passes a drunk, then a merchant seaman. She knows he's a seaman by the roll of the ship in his walk. When this same seaman is drunk, his walk pitches. Titania ignores a woman in a yellow dress. She watches a shuffling, male negro instead. Then the summer uniform of a chubby sailor turns her head. His ass bounces. She thinks. The night is drunk with possibility.

3

As I sit in the attic room and stare at the ceiling, the shadows unfurl, and I listen to the rain. The scene is lovely, the music sublime, but I am not consoled.

I review some comments on Titania. They come from many sources, friend and foe:

"That one? He's a she-he!"

"She's the sloppiest slut who ever slinked down a side street."

"A heavenly piece."

"I had her in a john."

"Always the lady."

"They say her ass is lined with mouton lamb."

"Did Tit ever get into that boxer?"

"Of course not! Not until he was punchy."

"As I recall, she married rather late in life."

"Yes, to that pool-hall greaser, Bengal."

"She couldn't expect to do better. By that time her ass was so full of holes no self-respectin' cock would have a thing to do with her."

"Her philosophy was short but sour: If given the right amount of demonic encouragement, every man is a woman in the ass."

"Do you think she'll ever make the team of saints?"

"Frankly, I don't think they'll give her a hard flat mat on a strato-cloud."

"I don't know, I guess you'd say she had technique. She'd drop that double reverse twist on a stiff dick and do the impossible: give a prick a conscience."

A fleeting sense of quietness creeps over me. My thoughts rush back to Titania in order to retain that calm which she has imposed upon my chaotic interior. Titania returns from afar, from the depths of that abyss which is my mind. For Titania to put in an appearance is to console me in part, but only a small part. In the same way as a child creates an imaginary companion on which to lay the blame for his own misdeeds, Titania is a creature who purges that which she reveals sordidly.

Titania is at the club. You consent to follow her in – but only because you are with me. You bump into me. You graze my shoulder accidentally.

"O, pardon me," she says insincerely, but your eyes accuse me of speaking. As if by some witchery, Titania has materialized in my place.

You hesitate, withdraw, wish you hadn't come. A sense of decency retards you, and ever so slightly, you suspect dirty work afoot.

Titania breaches the awkwardness with, "Lo."

She sees me. She turns upon herself.

"O, so it's you," she snarls. "You cheap, slimy, yellow son of a bitch!"

You're struck numb. But not for long, not for long, that is, as long as you read this novel.

The First Declension of the Flesh

When Titania came to the pool hall, her name was Thomas, not Titania, but she went by the name of Schwartz so that she would not have to commit herself to her surroundings. That way she could maintain her deception in a state of rare purity. Not revealing her name gave her a freedom of action which was useful in her work, and she did not want to restrict that freedom or contaminate that purity in any way. She had dropped into the pool hall to run a few balls, kill some time, have a look-see, and wait for evening, which was the proper start of her day. It was five o'clock in the afternoon, so the proper start of her day was just around the corner.

The pool hall was scabrous. Schwartz saw the hall as an old beggar woman who had fought many diseases, all infectious, and had fought them with little hope of recovery. She imagined the rain streaks on the walls as runny sores, but the streaks were not all rain, for there was a dance casino above the hall, and spilled beer had seeped through the dance floor and had stained large circles on the pool hall ceiling. The peripheries of the circles were trimmed with a heavy lacing of dried foam. Schwartz thought the circles might have been urine stains, but the impossibility of the angle robbed her of her supposition.

When she noticed that all the tables were taken, she chalked her cue obscenely. Not being able to play immediately did not disappoint her because it provided her with an excuse for hanging around the hall. When she sidled up to a group who were watching a game, her nostrils widened to capture the heady stench of virility.

"You shoot?" a little runt asked her.

"I play it," Schwartz answered.

"That's what I mean. You play?"

"After a fashion."

"Want to have a game after?"

"After what?" Schwartz asked, elevating her eyebrows. This was going to be easier than she had ever imagined.

"When a table's free, natch," he said. "What's with you? You square or somethin'?"

"Not where it counts,' Schwartz quipped. "No, just new."

"I could tell that the minute you breezed in. Ain't ya a little south for you?"

"I migrate naturally to the warmer areas."

Schwartz took her gaze off the shrimp and placed it on the bass, the player who was shooting. The bass sprawled on the table with his back to her. She noticed how his t-shirt sprang out of his pants and hugged the small of his back, exposing a trail of coarsely knit black hair which, she suspected, led to a wonderland of desire.

"That's Duck shootin'," the runt told her.

"O," she drawled, implying an indifference which she didn't feel. "What's his surname?"

"Don't be square."

"O, pardon me."

"The guy he's playin' with is Bruce."

"Just Bruce?"

"Yeah, Bruce."

"I see," Schwartz said.

"That's Jo-Jo over there. He'd be playin' only he's broke."

Schwartz had met Jo-Jo in her imagination, but only when her imagination had been operating in its greatest heat. Jo-Jo's hair lounged on his forehead. It blackened his forehead. The perfect curves of his arms were veiled by a blue nylon shirt, and his legs were poured into the mould of his levis. His smile challenged the worst words to defile the desirous curve of his lips. And other erotic things.

"That's Slim," the runt said as he pointed to a thin body.

"What's a matter?" she asked flatly. "Are they all bastards?"

"Lettem hear ya callum that. They'll lump ya up good."

"What I meant to infer was just this. No last names. How do they call each other up?"

"Who's got a phone?"

"Well, that takes care of that."

"That's Ducky No. 2 chalkin' up."

Ducky No. 2 bore no resemblance to Ducky No. 1.

"There's Bengal the Greaser."

Bengal exhibited all the accoutrements of desire, but his equipment was distorted as if it had been squashed in a box, as if he had grown up in a room which had been too small for him. His hair was black, but greasy black, and he needed a widow's peak to break the monotony of his hairline, but his forehead was too low, so there was no room for the widow's peak. His nose overlapped his mouth like the beak of Jupiter. He was built low to the ground and solid, too solid for his height which had been bent by an obvious deformity of spirit. He looked Middle Eastern, and that was too far off centre for him to qualify for the first rank of Schwartz's taste which was Mediterranean.

As she was given the one-way introduction to them, she

glanced at each one, but, always her glance returned to Jo-Jo to refresh itself. Finally, after desire had parched her, she told the runt that she was going for a beer.

"I was just thinkin' about a beer myself," he confessed. "You treatin'?"

"I hadn't thought about it "

"Don't be cheap."

"Here's a nickel. Get a coke."

"Gee, thanks, man," he said with surprise.

They walked through the entrance which was near the back of the poolroom. After Schwartz ordered a beer, the runt guessed he'd have a coke.

"See that guy at the bar with his hand out? That's The Mooch. Steer clear of 'im."

"You could hardly do better than that for a first name. That 'The' is magnificent. But 'Mooch' is a trifle too revealing. It strikes at the core of the personality so."

"Huh?"

"Yes, that's what I said."

"O, yeah," he said, implying comprehension, a halfway sort of thing. "That's Crazy Al actin' up in the corner." He had returned to that which he had been good at, remembering names.

"O, two names," Schwartz said with glee. "Crazy Al must be a brave soul."

"He's crazy, that's all."

"Obviously."

"I got two names myself."

"I suppose you have, but, naturally, I'm not supposed to ask what they are. I'll overlook the remark.'

"You can ask me," he said. "It's my handle."

"O? And why are you so free with your names? Don't you think two names is overdoing it a bit?"

"Naw, like I say, it's my handle."

"Well, what are they?"

"Passion Rat, they call me."

"Sounds interesting."

"I use it for protection. To keep the fuzz guessin'. Queers, too. Then they can't pin anythin' on me. Every guy does."

"There's something delightfully hostile about it, if not downright anonymous."

"What's yours?" Passion Rat asked.

"My handle?"

"Yeah, I told ya mine. What's a matter, you chicken?"

"I've been known to hen it up a bit."

"Well, give. Every guy's got one."

"Why not go all the way and remain completely anonymous?"

"I don't follow you."

"I usually have that trouble, but, if you must have a handle, call me No Name."

"Come on, that ain't a name. I thought we was pals. I told you all the guys' names, and now you pull this. What kind a creep are you? "

"It was a funny, that's all."

"I don't dig your jokes. You been goin' to college or somethin'?"

"That tense!" Schwartz shuddered. "Don't use that tense in my presence again."

Schwartz hated verb tenses in general, but she hated the past tense most of all, especially one whose action continued into the present as if it refused to be forgotten.

"College? I?" she asked. "I'd rather not say."

"Okay, but what's your handle? "

"Just call me Titania, Titania Schwartz."

Titania raised the bottle of beer over her head and tipped

it, ceremoniously. The beer bubbled and splashed on her tight little brown curls and cascaded down her face and front. Passion Rat snatched the bottle out of her hand and drank from it. After he had emptied the contents of the bottle, he laughed at the sight of Titania who was soaked by her own desire to be wet.

"Why Tit?" he asked, choking on some giggles. "Why Tit?" he asked again, swallowing the last giggle.

"'Cause I'm a fairy, that's why, a queen who falls in love with ass!"

Nickie Machete was out to impress Gunner. Gunner had been to the state prison, and Nickie had only known the comforts of reform school, so he looked up to Gunner in full reverential awe.

Nickie reached halfway up the height continuum. He was slim but hard and wiry, like a cat which had been nourished on cement and the sinewy boards of back fences. His brusque manner suggested that he possessed a forceful personality which he invoked when he felt like it, and, when he felt like it, which was most of the time, he was pure power. The blood drained from his face and was replaced with a nerveless substance, black diamonds. At which time he appeared as a silhouette to Titania. His emotions were composed of stone from gargoyles, but, when he was with Gunner, who had more rock in his body and more black in his veins and had spent more time around cement, or vice versa, Nickie enacted the compromise which his hair colour suggested. The deep rich mud brown indicated that he had more than black in his veins.

Nickie and Gunner stood at the bar, jawing about this and that conquest. They spoke in brag. Titania huddled with herself nearby. She was dying to meet Nickie because he qualified. He had eye appeal. But Titania didn't know his name, not even his handle, and she was inexperienced in the protocol of introduction, so she waited for a chance to crash the conversation.

Nickie flashed his wallet to prove that he had some green, and he offered to buy Gunner a drink, but, as he flashed the beat-up leather, Tit sneaked a peek at his ident card.

"O, so it's Nickie Machete, is it?" she squealed. Never had she been more indebted to Fate.

Nickie knew that his act of carelessness might bring on serious consequences. Since Titania knew his name, she had something on him, and, as he stole for a living, he liked to keep that information to himself. He had to get something on Titania in order to keep her quiet. There was only one thing, short of knocking her off, which would silence her, and that was to knock her up. So, he did just that. He gave her a shove so she was forced into a vulgar position in the men's room. She fell on her face.

Then Nickie and Hot Hole retired to the club to consecrate the coupling. They didn't invite Titania. They let her come. Hot Hole bought a drink for Nickie, and they talked of other things. They ignored Titania until she started to drift away. Then they called her back in order to buy the next round of drinks. Once, in a fit of generosity, they let her buy a drink for herself.

When Hot Hole said that he didn't have a place to flop for the night, Nickie told him not to worry. He didn't either, but Tit had a place, some hole, and they both could crawl in.

Titania's evening was over before it had begun. The climax had occurred at the beginning of the evening instead of at the end. She grew morose and sullen, and to make matters worse, she felt like a porcupine looks: severely needled.

As Nickie and Hot Hole drank on Tit's money, they told their repertoires of dirty jokes. Nickie couldn't remember very many of his, but Hot Hole told a bundle with seamen locales. Exotic backgrounds, rather niggardly described, supplied the half-ass effect of an elegant but partly furnished room.

The night droned on until someone suggested that it was time to sack out. Then the three departed. Nickie and Hot Hole walked together, Nickie on the outside, while Titania meandered back and forth on the sidewalk as though she were keeping company with herself. She was a loose thread which trailed randomly behind.

That night the sleeping positions were assigned without a word. Nickie took the bed. Hot Hole settled on the davenport. And Titania refused the chair in favour of the floor where her legs could roam. The power of authority was designed by a secret quality, virility, and the caste system was invoked with all the rigour applied by hens in a chicken yard.

In the morning Nickie ordered two eggs with no mayonnaise.

"Mayonnaise!" Titania shrieked. "I never heard worse."

"My old lady puts mayonnaise in the eggs to stretch 'em out," Nickie explained, "so we all get some. I like my eggs pure."

"I like mine hard as hell," Hot Hole put in.

"Sorry, only two eggs, and they're spoken for."

"Gimme some grits," Hot Hole reordered.

"Sorry, no grits. A boogily ate them all up last week."

"Whatcha got?"

"Ya want a slug?"

"I'm not up to fisticuffs this morning. How 'bout shredded wheat?"

13

"Put strawberries on it."

"I'm saving the strawberries."

"What for?" Hot Hole asked, clenching his fists and marching towards the small alcove which was the kitchen.

"For your shredded wheat," Tit added quickly.

"Don't fight, you guys," Nickie warned. "I'm too tired."

He rolled over on the bed and buried his face in the pillow.

Titania poured the cereal in a bowl before she cooked the eggs, so the eggs wouldn't cool while she was preparing the cereal, but she didn't serve the cereal until after she had served the eggs. Nickie got the plate with the big blooming rose on it. Hot Hole got a plain white bowl with a fluted edge. And Titania ate her toast, which she had made in her lopsided oven, without a plate. Nickie moved over to the chair to eat. Hot Hole balanced his bowl on his knee. And Titania sat on the edge of the bed and used her free hand to catch the crumbs.

They all had coffee. Coffee was a social equalizer.

After Titania had finished her toast, she lit a cigarette and inhaled the nourishment of the smoke.

"Nickie, lamb," she cooed, "would you, please, pass the ashtray?"

Nickie spoke through a mouthful of eggs: "What you think I am, your servant?"

"No, I just thought—"

"Well, I ain't. I'm nobody's slave. Besides, I'm goin' to use it – later."

"Never seen you use one yet."

"Always a first time."

"Don't you think she's actin' up pretty much for a slut? Want me to take her down a peg?" Hot Hole offered.

"I'll handle her, if there's any handlin' to do."

14

Titania snickered. Men, she thought, reasoning with their pride.

As Titania did the breakfast dishes, she sang "Melody in F" in shrill tones with smutty lyrics.

After, Nickie slept through the afternoon, and Hot Hole played solitaire. He won every time. Titania went out to get groceries.

Nickie woke up at five o'clock. He put on Tit's sport shirt, the one with the blue and white fleur de lis design. Titania told him that the pattern was the crest of the De Medicis so he wouldn't object to it on nationalistic grounds.

"What's for supper?" Hot Hole wanted to know. He had pulled in his gut as far as his fat self would permit.

"I already eaten," Nickie said.

"When?" Hot Hole asked. "I ain't had nothin' since breakfast."

"That's when I eat. How much you gotta eat?"

"I guess I ain't hungry," Hot Hole decided, then headed for the poolroom to start his day.

Titania backed a game for the other two to warm up, but Nickie put up his cue as soon as Gunner walked in.

"Hi, Gun," Nickie said.

"Nice shirt ya got," Gunner said by way of a welcome.

When Titania overheard the compliment, her chest swelled out to its normal size. She expected to be personally commended for her good taste.

"Thanks," Nickie said. "What's with you?"

"I got a little somethin' on for tonight. Want to come in?"

"What kind of somethin'?"

"A job."

They broke away from the group and strolled towards the john.

15

"What kind of job?" asked Nickie, who was particular about the jobs he took on.

"A motel. Out on the highway. If we wait late, it might go as high as three hundred."

"I'm on," Nickie said. "Count me in." Nickie knew that Gunner had good taste in stick-ups. Showing his appreciation for being cut in on the deal, Nickie asked Gunner if he wanted a little.

Gunner raised one eyebrow and looked around before he looked at Nickie and smiled.

"Hey, Hot Hole," Nickie called. "A customer."

Hot Hole giggled, then bubbled up to Gunner.

Gunner frowned, then shrugged as he ambled towards the alley exit.

Titania remained behind with Nickie. She stayed close to Nickie, just in case he wanted something. Nickie couldn't think of anything he wanted, anything which Titania could provide. He was thinking about the three hundred dollars. Three hundred dollars, split down the middle, was an investment which required a great deal of thought. It would take a lot of thinking to dispose of that much money.

When Gunner returned, he told Nickie that he had been mistaken about Hot Hole.

"Glad ya liked it," Nickie said.

Gunner and Nickie divvied up the haul after the holdup. Nickie was anxious to spend his half, but Gunner told him to wise up.

"If you're smart," he said, "you'll stick with me and don't go walk the streets so no two-bit beatman can pick ya up. Lay low 'til the look goes out of your eyes. You don't know how you act. You're always watchin' in back for some cop to come up from behind and nab you. You gotta cool down, limber up, so you can go out and act like nothin' happened, act like it happened a long time ago, so you ain't tender to it. Take a tip, stick with me. Just lay low for a month or so 'til the job is back in the books somewhere and not on the front page of the police blotter with every cheap tinhorn cop buckin' to land you like a big fish."

"Okay," Nickie said, but wondered, "how we gonna work it?"

"I know this roomin' house joint on Dauphine. Ain't no palace, but we can do better later. We just hang around there and pay our rent regular and on time, say we work nights and sleep during the day, then go to a neighbourhood joint at night. Got it?"

"Don't the cops check roomin' joints?"

"Yeah, but they don't know about this one. She don't report nothin'."

Nickie didn't have a suitcase, but he did carry some personal things, a busted razor and a tiny square of hotel soap, in a paper bag, which he hitched to his belt. After he got settled in the rooming house, he figured he could steal some shaving cream and whatever else he needed.

Gunner stood in front of the rooming house with his legs spread and his arms folded across his chest. He rapped on the door with his fist.

The landlady opened the door and stood solidly on the two stumps which were her legs.

"Whatcha want?" she asked, blocking the doorway with her bulk.

"We're lookin' for a room, ma'am," Gunner told her.

"Can you pay in advance?"

"Yeah."

Her gaze passed over Gunner and reported to her brain: black hair, nice build, stubborn chin, twisted smile, no,

17

shifty smile, but kinda nice manner for a construction worker. Then she shot a glance at Nickie.

"He doesn't look like he can pay in advance!"

"Yeah, he can," Gunner answered for him, "if we like it."

"Well, I just happen to have a real nice room."

As they started up the stairs, Nickie smelled tomato sauce in the air. He looked into the kitchen and saw two plates which were piled high with steaming spaghetti. She didn't need all that food, he told himself. Maybe she'd invite him down for a feed. The landlady huffed and puffed up the stairs.

"Always like my pay in advance," she said. "Policy around here. If you're a longtime guest and I like steadies, I make an exception once in a while, but that don't apply to you yet. No monkey business in the rooms. I clean once a week if my rheumatism ain't bad. The bath's at the end of the hall. I don't like queers, and don't fill the tub over the red watermark. My husband didn't paint it just to pretty up the tub. I got two other guests. I live on the ground floor – with my husband. There's a wrestler in 2-B and a boxer in 2-C. You can have 2-A, right by the stairs. Where you work?"

"At night."

"Then you ain't in construction?"

"Naw, never said we was. We work in a bar back of town.".

"Yeah? Well, remember the rules 'cause I ain't repeatin' them, and if you break the littlest one, out you go with no kick back, understand?"

"Yeah."

When they reached the first landing, she stopped to catch her breath. "You go up and look around. I don't go to the next flight 'less I have to."

The door of the room was ajar. Gunner pushed it open

18

with his foot and looked in. There was a big brass bed which was retouched with white paint, or a white bed which was retouched with brass paint. He didn't know which. There was a dresser with a cracked mirror and a rocking chair. The white plaster walls bulged in places, but, all in all, he figured the room would hold up for another month, so he said, "We'll take it."

"I ain't told you how much yet," she reminded him.

"How much?"

"I'll give you a special price. Ten dollars."

"That's what I pay for a single. We'll pay eight for two – since we're quiet guys."

"Eight-fifty."

"Can't go no higher than eight."

"Gotta include the water and lights," she explained.

"Eight cold."

Nickie, who hadn't said a word or seen the room yet, said, "I don't like it."

"Eight," she agreed. "But you gotta realize that's a special price, so I gotta have it in advance right along. I'm takin' a loss – just 'cause you're quiet guys."

Gunner handed her eight dollars, which she grabbed and stuffed down the neck of her dress.

Her parting words were : "I'm sure you'll be very happy here, if you mind the rules. Shut the door when you're in the bathroom, and call my husband when the toilet clogs." Gunner slammed the door. The door banged shut but opened again, inching its way back into the room as if gasping for air.

Then Nickie shut the door. When it creeped back into the room, he lifted it up and fastened a loop through a hole in a metal bar which was provided for a padlock, if the roomers had a padlock.

"This sweat box will do," Gunner said, yawning. "It ain't permanent."

"I don't like it," Nickie said uneasily, but he threw his paper sack on top of the dresser.

Gunner didn't answer because he didn't hear. He had flopped on the bed and had fallen asleep.

As Nickie joined him, he felt a warmth which was not accounted for by the room or by Gunner, but, as he conked out, he clamped his fist over the source of radiation, the wad of bills in his pocket.

The next morning Gunner bought two po' boy sandwiches and a couple of soft drinks for their breakfast.

When Nickie saw them, he said, "This is eatin' high on the hog, man. Ain't never had a po' boy for breakfast."

"A lot of things you ain't never had you'll get if you stick with me."

"Some team, man, Nickie and Gunner," Nickie said proudly.

"Gunner and Nickie," Gunner corrected. "You ain't been brought up right."

"Man, we'll travel," Nickie said, changing the subject. He didn't care whose name was first in the title of the corporation. As long as that corporation continued to bring in as much money as he had in his pocket at this minute, he was first, regardless.

"This is just the beginning," Gunner assured him. "I got big plans. Big plans. And we got plenty of time to make them stick."

They had plenty of time. Time fell in that room as slowly as water drips from a leaky faucet. Each moment was filled with the same amount of vacuous silence. Long ago they had exhausted their plans, which had been discussed down to the last detail, memorized, and rehearsed to perfection.

After they had outslept themselves, Gunner sat in the rocker and rocked himself to a standstill.

Later, Nickie propped open the door in order to watch the other two roomers as they went up and down the stairs. Nickie decided that the dark one must be the boxer because he left in the morning with a pair of gloves, lacings tied together, dangling around his neck, and sometimes he carried a paper sack with some purple silk sticking out the top. The blond's stocky frame was overloaded with muscle like a wrestler.

When the boxer headed down the stairs one morning, Nickie commented dryly, "He's goin' to the gym."

And when the wrestler walked past the door with a blanket over his shoulder, wearing only his shorts, Gunner said, just as dryly, "He's headin' for the patio and the afternoon sun." The Gunner reminded Nickie that the wrestler may have the patio sun, but soon they would have the real stuff on the wide open beaches of Miami.

"Yeah," Nickie sighed, but, as Gunner continued to remind him, his "yeah" ran uphill until it became a full-fledged question. Nickie was convinced that anything in the present was better than the best in the future, but he didn't tell Gunner that nothing was worth waiting for.

When Gunner stood up and walked around the room, Nickie grabbed the rocker. As he rocked, he counted the rocks until he did the impossible: he fell asleep.

Gunner rapped the wall with his fist. There was a resounding smack, but Nickie didn't blink. He opened his eyes and wondered if the days were longer than the nights or the nights were longer than the days. They seemed about even. All too long. But he never resolved the wonder, for, if he had, he wouldn't have had anything to think about the next day.

The boxer passed by the door with his hair in a sweaty tangle.

"He's back from the gym," Nickie announced. "Been workin' out, probably."

He listened for the door of the boxer's room to slam. After the door slammed, he said, "He's goin' to take a shower. They probably ain't got a shower at the gym."

"What kind of gym is that?" Gunner wanted to know.

"No shower gym," Nickie explained.

"Probably some cheap tinhorn place," Gunner guessed.

"Yeah, some real cheap tinhorn place."

"Yeah, some real goddamn cheap tinhorn place."

"Yeah, some real mammy-lovin' goddamn cheap tinhorn place."

They expanded the thought with adjectives in order to postpone the arrival of that menace, silence.

"What you mean, a shower?" Gunner asked. He had poked around in the discussion and had seized upon any discrepancy in order to prolong the conversation. "How's he gonna shower in this hole?"

"I meant a bath."

"All right, a bath. Why didn't you say so in the first place?"

"I was thinkin' 'bout the showers we're gonna take in Miami."

"Yeah, real tile they got," Gunner reminded Nickie as the picture of Miami softened his voice. "Pretty colours."

Nickie said nothing. His mind saw the boxer dropping his shorts and tugging his sweat shirt over his head.

"He's puttin' on that maroon bathrobe," Nickie said.

"Yeah, I seen him in it, too," Gunner said.

One door slammed, then another. The sound of water.

"I wonder if he uses over the red line?"

"How's she gonna know if he does or not unless she goes in there with him?"

"Maybe she does."

"I wouldn't doubt it."

Nickie choked on a phony laugh.

He heard two streams of water.

"Now he's runnin' the cold," he said.

"Where you been P It's all cold. He's takin' a leak." Their voices dropped into silence as if they had fallen into a deep pit in the centre of the room. They listened to the water as it gurgled down the drain, but neither mentioned it, for they knew what the other would say. Statement and response, response and statement, question and answer, answer and question, it didn't matter which came first or who said it. They were all the same.

A door slammed, then another.

"He's goin' to sit on his gallery and soak up the sun. How's come he got a gallery with his room?"

"Yeah, how come?"

"'Cause he puts out to that slut, that's how come."

"Yeah," Nickie said. "He puts out. I bet he don't even pay rent."

Nickie heard the heavy, stiff-legged thumping of foot-steps on the stairs as though pillars were walking away from the temple. Long pauses were interrupted by heavy breathing.

"She's on the landing," Nickie narrated.

More footsteps, more pauses.

When the landlady passed by his door without looking in, he rolled over on the bed and buried his head. Through the pillow he said, "She's on her way to collect his rent."

A smile grazed Gunner's face, but disappointment, dis-content or impatience deflected the smile so that there was no trace of it on his face but the small scar which parted his lips. He switched his concentration to his knife and started to clean his fingernails. A tear in the window shade let in a beam of light, and, as the fight struck the six-inch blade, the blade reflected the beam into Nickie's eyes. Nickie blinked.

"Shut the door," Gunner ordered. "I'm tired of listenin' to 'em." There was no trace of the smile in his voice, either. The smile had ricocheted off the discontent which had been firmly fixed on his face.

Nickie slipped off the bed and slammed the door. Then he slammed it again. The third time he held the door with his foot while he fastened the latch. After securing the latch, he flopped on the bed and began to dream, but Gunner started in with a story, so Nickie saved his dream. He had already spent most of his dreams, and dreams were hard to come by since the demand was so much greater than the supply, so he saved his dream gladly.

"Man, when I was up at State, I used to get it any time I wanted," Gunner began. "We used to soap a guy up in the shower and have him done 'fore the guard came to let us out.

"Sometimes the guard was on top. Then he would see that the guy got two desserts for supper, whether he wanted them or not, but most guys wanted them, and from then on we all knew that he would be easy pickin'. What you think of that?"

Rat bastard, Nickie thought.

"Well, what you think of it?"

Rat bastard, Nickie thought.

"Once, when I was in parish," Gunner began again, "they toss this kid in a cell with me and this big clammy brute, whose face was all cut up somethin' awful. This goof tried to heist a plane, but when the cops started chasing him, he got so excited he ran right smack into a moving propeller. Well, I had a knife sealed up behind a loose piece of plaster in the cell wall. I didn't want to miss with the kid 'cause I'm kinda partial to cherries, and this kid didn't know nothin', so I use my knife on him and tell that mangy dog, that cut-up homely bastard, to keep an eye out for the guard. Like I knew, I had a little trouble with the kid, but he didn't want to get cut up 'cause he only had six months to do, and I was just stoppin' over on my way to State, so I didn't care if I got more time or not. So, just as I start to ease in, this beam of light hits me in the face, and the guard sees what I'm up to. The guard don't take the kid, but real tough-like he orders me out of the cell and down to the dispensary. When I pass that big moron, I spit on him. That jerk! He was watchin' me and the kid instead of keepin' an eye out for that guard.

"It's a funny thing about some of them guards. You'd think he'd go for the kid, but, no, he hustled me down to the dispensary and started in before he turned on the light."

"Did ya get two desserts?" Nickie wanted to know.

"What you think?"

"Yeah, what were they?"

"Bread puddin'."

"They never gave nothin' in reform. They just said, 'You're lucky you're livin'.'"

"Did they get you?" Gunner asked.

"Nah, none tried."

"Well, that night when I got back to my cell," Gunner said, going on with his story, eager to end it, "that brute goof says to me, 'Thanks, pal.' He says it real big-like. Then I knew he was goofy for real. I didn't do nothin' for him but spit on him. 'Thanks for what?' I say. And he says, 'For warmin' up the kid.'"

25

As Gunner talked, he flicked the dirt from under his fingernails with the knife. Nickie thought of the knife instead of the story. He wondered how far in it would go if it were driven into his chest up to the hilt. Six inches, he decided. The thought shrank his insides, but his outsides were calm and unaffected, frozen in place.

The commotion, the giggles and gasps which escaped from the boxer's room ran down the hall into Nickie's room. As he listened to the noise in the distance, he rolled over on his stomach, and an urgent desire to dream pressed in upon him.

Gunner rocked faster.

"You're a funny guy," Gunner told him.

"What you mean?" Nickie asked, grateful for anything which would crowd out the noisy reality in the distance.

"Always on that bed. You don't sleep on it or use it for nothin', but you're always on it."

"You want me to sit on the floor?"

"You want a fist?"

"Naw, why?"

"Keep smartin' off, and you'll get one."

"I ain't smartin' off," Nickie said. "What you so touchy about?"

"Nothin'. Just keep wisin' off, and you're going to get it."

"Aw."

"You heard me!"

Nickie checked to see if he could spot the source of the irritation. He could. Gunner had his legs spread. A taut crease in his pants extended down one leg to his knee. He squirmed in the rocker.

Nickie smiled weakly.

"Strip," Gunner ordered.

"I was just kiddin'," Nickie confessed.

"I'm not. I think you never had it before."

"I don't like it," Nickie added hurriedly.

"How you know if you never?"

"I just know. I don't need to find out."

"You're talkin' gas. What's a matter, you selfish? Can't ya help a guy out?"

"Get some free rent off the landlady," Nickie suggested.

"I couldn't make a dent in that hog fat."

Nickie laughed in spurts. He put stops on his laughter, but the laughs gushed over the stops. Then he held his breath, but that, too, was an ineffective dam.

"I don't want to," Nickie whined.

"You don't, and I'll give ya a cut the length of your front." Gunner slashed the air with his knife to demonstrate. "I'm slippin'. Sleepin' with a virg and didn't know it. I told ya I was partial to fresh meat."

"Aw, come on," Nickie coaxed, "let's have a dart game with your knife. See who can stick it in the door the most times."

"You still achin' for a cut?"

Nickie sat up on the bed, threw his legs over the side, and fumbled with the buttons on his shirt.

After, Nickie sat on the bed. His nonchalance was restricted to his exterior, and only there in a shrug.

"I told ya I didn't like it," he said.

"Ya never do the first time," Gunner explained. "Did I ever tell ya about my first time?"

"Naw, I don't wanna hear." Nickie didn't want to hear anything. He wanted a calm reality which would set an example for his chaotic insides.

"Well," Gunner began, ignoring Nickie's request, "I was in junior high, and this creep of an English teacher calls me in after class and tells me I'm gonna flunk. I told him

I didn't care. 'So what?' I says. He gives me a spiel about how I can keep the red mark off my record, if I want, 'cause I act older than I am. Get that! Then he gets up from his desk, and I see somethin' I ain't never seen before: a hard. He tells me he can fix things up if I let him. How you like that? He didn't even know how to say prick. So, he takes me in the cloakroom, and I fix up my English grade. Next year it was current events."

Gunner spent more and more time away from the room. He patronized the local grocery and picked out some crackers and cheese in the mornings, and in the evenings he brought up quarts of beer.

The retired life became more attractive to Nickie. Drunk, the nights went faster. The beer lubricated his mind, and the many conquests which would be his with money lay, in full view, on the periphery of his mind, and they advanced towards the front of his mind when they were set in motion by the catalyst which was beer.

One night, after Gunner had polished off his quart of beer and had pushed aside a half-empty jar of cheese, pineapple-pimento it was, he started talking about the wrestler.

"You know that wrassler?"

"Yeah," Nickie said dryly, "is he?"

"He is. Like a three-dollar bill."

"How you know?" Nickie asked, again dryly. He wasn't interested in the blond polack bastard, whose folds of skin, around his midriff and at the back of his neck, reminded Nickie of a rhinoceros. Nickie wanted to keep his reality in motion in order to discourage thought, so he encouraged Gunner to talk.

"That wrassler! He loves it."

"What 'bout the boxer?" Nickie asked. He asked in a

disinterested tone, but he gave his interest away by stuttering on the –er, prolonging it as if he were reluctant to let go.

"The boxer, too. Let me tell you how I found out. That's why I struck up with the wrassler, only went one time, just so I could find out 'bout the boxer. I had the wrassler goin', beggin' me to hurry, when I asks him, 'I bet you been in that boxer 'cross the hall.' I buttered him up first, conned him good by askin', 'God, what you got in there?' And that's how I found out. 'Yeah,' he says, 'I been there, when he ain't payin' his rent.'"

While Gunner was out on errands, Nickie hung around the upstairs hallway, usually around noon, when the boxer returned from the gym. When the wrestler went down for his sun, Nickie had his feet out of the way. The wrestler didn't speak. Nickie didn't speak. The boxer didn't speak either, until –

"Man, you must got it easy," he said, passing his hand through his hair in a gesture of wonder, dumb wonder. The hand dispelled a visible odour of sweat.

"I work nights," Nickie told him as casually as he could.

"Me, too," the boxer said, proudly. "Sometimes five seconds, sometimes three rounds. Depends. Nice racket, huh?"

"Yeah," Nickie said, not looking up, but he did look across, and he saw the black hair on the boxer's legs, that hair which curled out of his sweat socks.

Distracted by a commotion, the boxer turned his head and looked down the stairwell. Nickie fixed his gaze on the boxer's profile and saw the boxer's eyebrow as the unruly hair of a hairy ellipse.

"That slut," the boxer said, smiling half-assedly. "She's tryin' to talk her old man into a nap."

The hot rays of the boxer's smile melted Nickie's armour of calm. Nickie drove the point of his stare into a rosebud in

29

the carpet in order to regroup his forces against the boxer's smile, but, when the boxer put his foot on the step, Nickie's forces were routed by the perfect ninety-degree angle which the bent leg formed. As the boxer leaned forward, the vice behind his knee closed. It was a powerful fulcrum, and the weight of his thigh, or the scream of his thigh, echoed in Nickie's gut, liquefying his viscera. Something was burning, for he smelled the odour of heated rubber.

Nickie looked into the boxer's eyes in an act of formal surrender. He saw only doors in the boxer's head which were swung wide with welcome and had gone soft with hope.

The boxer smelled his armpits.

"I gotta take a bath," he said. "If you ain't doin' nothin', why don't you stop by the room? We can jaw. That is, if you ain't doin' nothin'."

He looked away when he said it, and Nickie looked away when he answered it.

"Maybe I might," Nickie said.

"Go in and flop. I'll be done in a minute."

Nickie watched the boxer as he disappeared down the hall. His heavy shoulders moved in opposition to the sway of his hips. Nickie thought, when he walked, he waddled. As the image of the boxer filtered through Nickie's brain, it turned feminine. His mind had deceived him into believing that the walk was something other than that which was clearly visible. The extensive movement of the boxer's hips from side to side and other minor things, if seized upon, could build a case for femininity around the boxer's walk, but the interpretation of evidence was only a vaporous thought in Nickie's head, which was made dense by his own desire.

Desire was stifled. An inkling of want did stir within him, but it could not be labelled desire. He mistook the feeling for friendship since he knew the sensation would never rise to the pitch of desire, but he suspected that it would sustain its low level warmth over a long period of time.

"He's a dumb, good-looking dope," Nickie said as he grabbed for that point which lies outside the self, which few can reach and where fewer still can remain for long. Then he fell back into the shell of self. He fell gently, willingly, not breaking the shell. He slid, and now he spoke from the other side of his mouth. "But he's got something. I wish to hell I knew what it was."

Half of Nickie walked into the boxer's room and sat down in the proverbial rocker with which every room was furnished. Half of Nickie waited for the other half.

The other half of Nickie entered the room, dripping water. His body was too big for an ordinary bath towel, and dampness had blackened his maroon bathrobe in spots.

The boxer didn't speak, but his animal's body spoke for him. He stepped back from the dresser and shadow boxed with his image in the mirror. His left jab and right cross forced his bathrobe into a rhythmic dance.

Nickie stared at various objects in the room, but none of them detained his gaze.

The boxer took off his robe and threw it on the bed with positive gestures. He grabbed a towel and rubbed his back briskly, rhumba-style. Then he bent over the bed and fumbled with the tassel on his robe. He arranged it coyly, obscenely.

Nickie thought. He's killin' time so he won't have to get dressed. Everything about him said yes. Now!

Nickie leaped from the rocker and charged. He was about to apply a hug when the quick-footed boxer side-stepped, and Nickie landed face down on the bed. With the same fleet movement the boxer fell on top of Nickie and pinned him to the bed. The boxer was a silent, dead weight for some time. That time ended.

Nickie was numb. He felt as if he had stacked a deck of cards only to discover, after he had looked at his hand, that the gods had intervened and had reshuffled the deck on the sly.

"Do ya like it?" the boxer asked.

And, strangely enough, Nickie did.

Their happiness clamoured. They were aware of nothing but the sharp focus, the pin-pointed desire which throbbed in their loins.

The boxer promised the world. He said he had a bid for some exhibition bouts around the country. That meant easy dough, but he didn't want to go alone. Did Nickie want to go with him?

He did. The boxer's shadow loomed over Nickie's body and gave a shape to his feelings, a direction to his

The strains of happiness, now as minutely orchestrated as a symphony, forced their reality to recede to a point where both exclaimed, "I've been away." The clamour was the sound of trumpets, interspersed with lyric violins, quivering high notes without a trace of dissonance, until a bassoon rose above the ecstatic clamour.

"I thought so!" shrieked the bassoon, rasped the landlady. "Been here a week and queered every guy on the place." She swung her broom wildly. "I knew you were queer the minute I saw ya. Ya never said nothin', just snuck around and did your dirty work."

"Get out of here 'fore I punch ya silly," the boxer yelled.

"You're the ones gettin' out. If you and that bathrobe ain't out of here by nightfall, I'm callin' the cops."

"Don't worry!"

"That goes for Lady Godiva there, too."

The landlady slammed the door. The boxer resumed, and in no time at all he reached the climax of the symphony by spouting a galaxy of stars.

After Nickie shimmied down the gallery pole, the boxer tossed him a beat-up suitcase. A suitcase and everything, Nickie thought. Everything was three pairs of shoes: tennis shoes and canvas shoes and moccasins for dress up. He couldn't go wrong with a deal like that, so he didn't mind leaving the rooming house. The place was nothing but a trap, anyway, but when he sneaked under the kitchen window and smelled the steam from a pot of seething spaghetti, he wished he had wormed his way on the good side of the landlady, whatever side that was, and had been invited down for a feed.

I suppose what became of Gunner is of little interest, or the ensuing events which terminated his stay at the rooming house, but the events took place that same afternoon, later. Gunner spoke about them at the club, still later, and even the distance of time, memory, did not lessen the immediacy of the horror.

When Gunner returned to the room and discovered that Nickie had left with the boxer (the landlady was far from silent on the subject or from restraining herself from making insinuations in general about her roomers), Gunner sat in the rocker and slashed the cheesecloth curtains with his knife.

The wrestler was no less enraged. Whether it was the disappearance of the boxer, the possible threat of inheriting the free rent privilege, the abundance of Italians on the premises which ruffled his nationalistic pride, the presence desire, or the feeling of having been wronged by Gunner which prompted the wrestler's rage, I suppose we shall never know, but we do know that he was motivated quite beyond the minimum requirements for drastic acts.

Anyway, he marched towards Gunner's room and shoved the door open with a determined fist. The door swung open and closed with a force which equalled the wrestler's determination, so he shoved it again. So fierce was the second blow that the doorknob stuck in the wall and left the room permanently exposed.

"What's the idea, Polack?" Gunner asked.

"You ain't been in to pay up," the wrestler growled. He presented the first reason which pressed to the foreground of his mind.

"What ya mean, Polack?"

"You owe me a piece of ass."

"That ain't a nice way to talk now, is it?" Gunner's words curled out of his smile. "You ain't been brought up right, Polack."

"Dare it, Dago," the wrestler ordered.

Gunner rocked slower and flashed his knife.

"I ain't afraid of your knife, Dago. I'll take it and cut off your balls. It's an old Polish pastime."

"You're talkin' kinda big for a Polack, ain't ya, Polack?"

The wrestler lunged as Gunner sprang to his feet and readied his knife. The wrestler faked with his fist and kicked Gunner's hand with his foot. The knife flew out of Gunner's hand and stuck in the ceiling. Then the wrestler tore off Gunner's shirt. When Gunner resisted, the wrestler planted bruises on his face and arms until the last blow knocked Gunner into the corner.

After Nickie ditched Hot Hole, Hot Hole dumped Titania. Hot Hole ended his apprenticeship as a whore by returning to the sea, but he didn't end his servility, for he only changed masters, from Nickie to the sea, that hard, cruel, watery master.

Titania's grief was frivolous from having been abandoned. She employed her grief in order to extract a little sympathy from her few abiding friends. Her friends gave her little sympathy, but they did provide her amply with I-told-you-sos. Her only recourse was to try her wings alone. She flapped them in the public square. She became so bold in her manoeuvres that people suspected that she operated with a licence which was stamped with the seal of City Hall. She was as familiar a sight in the public square as the statue, that man in Civil War dress who was blotched white with pigeon accuracy and was decorated with blue-maroon smears which didn't attest to his valour under fire but did prove that a mulberry bush was stationed nearby.

Titania felt an affinity with the bronze man which I can't explain, or which I don't care to explain, but which she can. "We're both the shit-on hero," she confided.

Titania sat on a bench in the park, and, from a distance, she surveyed the nigger mammies who were tending white kids and the lazy lovers of guiltless leisure who were walking their primped pups or were feeding oatmeal flakes to the scrawny pigeons. She knew nothing of the apartment houses which flanked the square but that which she could see from the outside: the staid fronts.

When there was nothing better to do, she watched the randomly moving crowd of respectables as the narrow slats of the bench corrugated her bottom, but, at other times, when the scene was peopled with interest, she watched hair, shaggy lengths which impaired hearing, and arms which were constricted by a jumble of sweaters, shirts and coats in all colours, sizes and weaves, different sizes on the same body and worn regardless of the weather, for the shoulders, arms and backs were the only closets, racks and hangers of the owners.

She restricted her gaze to one knight of the highway, the one who rose from his bench and walked slowly, carefully, towards a drinking fountain which emitted a pathetic trickle of water. He moved imperceptibly in a gradual forward movement which replaced air molecules with body. He leaned over the fountain and took a long drink. While drinking, he fumbled with the handle and tried to increase the flow of water without success. Then he stepped to one side and removed his soiled and sundry garments down to his t-shirt. He looked at them as if they were responsible for his failure to produce more water from the spout. After he had scorned them sufficiently, he bent over the fountain as if he were about to take another drink and splashed his face with water. He swore unconvincingly. Then he repeated the act with his hands. After several rinsings, he threw his hands up in the air in a gesture of final dismay, kicked the base of the fountain, and shook his head. He put his clothes back on and returned to his seat on the bench with a jaunty little step at a lighthearted pace.

Titania was not moved by the sociology of the affair. Sympathy was only skin deep, she knew, and pathos had shallow roots. Too bad he wasn't good-looking, she thought.

Then Destiny walked onto the scene and into the park. Surely Destiny was aware of his casual grace, that lazy rhythm in his walk which hinted at quiet desire, that shuffle which reorientated proverbs and jumbled their meanings. Though maybe it was the look in his eyes which Titania read as desire. It was a look of anxiety over the general state of things, his state of things, but his black hair couldn't be improved, for it was reminiscent of the black which was found only in fabulous nights, Italian black. She banished his frown by kissing the wrinkles out of his forehead with her mind, and there was a tear in his shirt which proved he had taste, enough taste to restrict the growth of his hair to the appetizing parts of the body, the head, the arms, the legs, the chest, the groin, for the wound in his shirt had been inflicted across the back of his shoulders. The bagginess of his trousers couldn't conceal the fullness of his thighs.

If he would only grace my face with interest, dedicate a smile to me, Titania thought. Christ, why did he have to have a dimple in his chin which gave off light! Angular and forceful the chin was, pinpointed with whiskers whose strength would have made Samson cringe.

He was his own myth, a miracle in flesh. His shirt, open at the neck, sported the colours of stained glass windows. Titania hoped that he was unique, the rarest of the rare, a practicing deity. He seemed kind, gentle, good-looking, and Italian. Not much of a godhead, perhaps, but many religions have flourished on less.

"I must be dizzy with the heat," Titania told Destiny, "to think that gods mix with mortals."

"Huh," Destiny drawled in a bass lyric. Titania thought his voice held a certain anthropomorphic charm. "I don't get you."

"No," Titania giggled, "but I may get you."

"I don't go that route,' he said, smiling painfully.

"No, of course not, none of us do, but one good turn deserves another, and if you turn just the right way, I might turn over a little cash to you."

"I'm back on my luck," admitted the down and out deity.

"Natch. But, of course, it would only be a loan," Titania

assured him. "I wouldn't expect you to pay me back until you got good and ready." She giggled, dipping her words into a vat of whimsy.

"Talk plain."

"I want to help you out, financially, if you'll help me out, sexually." She tripped over the last word, stumbled and fell. She pronounced the word silently with her lips as if she were touching a sore. "O, I can be discreet when I want," said that girl.

"If I didn't need the dough," Destiny considered aloud.

"I know how it is," she assured him, applying understanding as if it were a thick goo.

"I gotta go some place after."

"Naturally," Titania said. She bad no intention of erecting dams to impede the flow of destiny.

On her way to her apartment she became dizzy with the heat, but this time the heat was generated by a source other than the sun.

Her happiness made her garrulous.

"If there's anything I hate, it's pimples," she said, for she despised any likeness of herself. "I can't stand a blotchy butt. You don't look like you've got—"

"I ain't."

"You're sure?"

"Yeah."

"Some of them lie," she reminded him. "But come to think of it, most of them lie."

In her apartment, without asking his name, Titania said, "You may use the bathroom, Black."

When Black returned, he watched Titania stuff a five-dollar bill in an empty pack of cigarettes and place the pack in an accessible place on the coffee table, an old trunk which had been camouflaged with free-flowing green denim.

"Whatcha doin'?" Black asked as he dropped his pants and unveiled his legs.

"Just being discreet," Titania answered. She was not disappointed with the view.

"Ain't ya got more?"

"It just so happens that I'm fresh out."

"Make it snappy then."

The sight of the black, wiry mesh on his legs accelerated the proceedings, and the afternoon light enabled her to witness the operation.

"Quite the lady," she said as the filigree on his chest reminded her of lace, black lace.

"You took your time," he said with words which were intoned downward.

"Don't look," she screamed, then disappeared into the bathroom. While she washed, she carried on a one-way conversation with Black, who was still in the other room. "Everything must have a precise order with me. Even this. I don't know what that order is half the time, but it must be. You can only follow one order," and she went on and on until she had finished washing. She felt as if she had to speak in terms which would reach Black, which would travel through walls and round corners, so she spoke in generalities.

When the buzzer sounded, Tit thought a sharp knife had sliced the episode in half.

The buzzer was Sovastapole Harry, sometimes incorrectly pronounced Sevastopol. He was a frustrated Russian.

For bait he wore a bemused smile which hypnotized angels and persuaded them to surrender their wings. When the angels were hit by his smile, the wingless creatures dropped from heaven with a thud. He called his friends "his ponies," and he rode them more often than might be suspected from the fierceness of his mount. Needless to say, Sovastapole qualified. He was the sire in desire. After he had become soggy in the middle and had gone out of vogue, he grew a beard of kinky brown mesh, but it did little good, for he still appealed only to Titania, but he was satisfied with that arrangement, for Titania's money appealed to him. With her money he bought vodka and took it to the public square on off nights to drug winos. After nine o'clock in the evening the trembling of the bushes could be attributed to Sovastapole getting his.

"Hi," Sovastapole said as he burst through the door of Tit's apartment.

"You could at least have the decency to knock," Tit scolded.

"What's the matter? Did I bust somethin' up?"

"No, but almost."

Black had slipped on his shorts, and Titania had fluttered into a robe.

Sovast looked at Black and started. "Looks all right," he appraised, gouged his groin, walked over and picked up Black's clothes, examined them with a sniff, then said, "Give him an extra two so I can ride." He dove for Black. "And while you're at it, go chill the wine."

Tit obeyed. She knew that Black needed too many things for her to pick up his option. She would never be able to support him, but she knew that Black would go on to the great things. Even without technique he would be able to attract really rich clients. The thought saddened her, but she sighed and told herself that she was resigned to the inevitable.

After Black hurried into his clothes, he stomped over to the coffee table, and with his all too gentle fist he swooped down on the empty pack of cigarettes, empty only of cigarettes, and stormed out, muttering something about cheap bastards.

Titania saw Black frequently after that afternoon, but he was always at the club. When she recognized him at the bar, she thought that he had gotten better looking, but after a closer look she decided that he was only getting better haircuts.

Her prediction had come true. His slick gabardine suit with razor-sharp pleats, his face without a trace of stubble, and the strong, sweet scent of rose oil in his hair: these things erased all traces of his past. The only hint of his former life was the sullen expression on his face which tilted his features downward, also his gaze, things which wouldn't wash off, things which resisted even the strongest detergent.

After becoming accustomed to the new Black, the girls at the club had christened him King, Titania thought she would try her luck. She sidled up to him at the bar.

"Quite the lady," she said in a reminiscing sort of tone.

He gave no sign.

"I knew it when," she went on.

He moved down the bar.

"O, it's just too, too," Titania scoffed, supressing a tear.

During periods of trial which mostly reeked of ennui, when mourning had cast its stifling veil over Titania, she paraded her grief and forsook her lovers. She resorted to the companionship of her friends. Then, and only then, did she have anything to do with her friends.

On just such a night, when the gloom within emulated the pitch of night, she strolled into the club. Through the smoky, grey dawn of the interior, she sensed possibilities. Some ship had deposited its most precious cargo at the bar, the full length of the bar, had lined it up side by side. It was a most impressive sight, that sight of restless apples, apples bursting their white skins. Each apple was supported by two limbs which were sheathed in birch bark which flared out at the base just like bell-bottom trousers.

"O, goodie," Tit screamed, "it's open season on seafood."

Then she hung her head but not because she was in mourning. The events of the afternoon had flashed across her mind.

"Your mouth watering, too?" Burnished Rose asked.

"No," Tit said, "for a minute my mind had exceeded all human capabilities of the flesh." It was an expedient phrase.

"Mine runs wild on me, too," Rose confessed, then added, "But condolences, darling."

"On what?"

"Your demise, of course."

"How could you? I've told no one."

"That doesn't stop me. Your death occurs at regular intervals, and it's way past due."

"True," Tit admitted. "I'm in mourning for myself, but it was a quick, almost painless death. He slipped away in the night."

"The best way, I always say," Rose said, then tried to brush the dusty flakes of age out of her hair. She had a nasty habit of sitting in a booth and combing her hair to amuse herself, but no matter how much she combed, the dandruff of antiquity remained.

"Have you seen Hog Fat?" she asked.

Titania hadn't seen Sir Denis. "But I haven't reconnoitered yet," she explained.

"Well, I'm supposed to meet the tided one here."

"She's probably cruising on Decatur," Titania guessed.

"No, not that one," Rose said. "She has spunk. I want

42

you to know that I've never seen her on Decatur before three in the morning."

"You should know."

"Jealous?" Rose spit.

"Of what? Denis! Really, Rose, you're impossible. Why, the way you carry on with your own sex is positively incestuous."

"O, I don't know."

"Sir Denis and Louise, those sluts! Why, there's nothing complementary about them."

"The trouble with Denis is that she's too fat," Rose admitted freely. "Nobody listens to her." Rose shrugged, for she didn't know what she was talking about. She only knew that she wanted to talk about something else.

"Nobody wants to hear what she has to say, wants to buy what she has to sell," Titania said. "She's fat and artistic, and that's all. I can't think of two more loathsome characteristics."

"Now, tell me," Rose said, having hit upon that something else, "was last night really the ball that was predicted?"

"A real palace function. You should have come."

"I know," Rose lamented, "I wanted to, but I couldn't get away. Louise threw a fit."

Titania reviewed the evening: "Gunner stole a car for the occasion. Brestalysis filched a tie, and Gorman beat up a queer and heisted his wig. The masquerade is always the gayest of the gay. Of course, I was the gay, widowed one."

"But you summoned your resources and forced a smile?"

"Natch, I couldn't let mourning rule the evening, could I? After all, it's only once a year."

"Big of you, I'd say. One mustn't let little personal grievances interfere with the gaiety of the group. I wish I'd thought about that last night when Louise insisted on having her way."

"If you're going to talk sociology, I'm leaving."

"So must I," Rose sighed. "Fate is a crooked stick up my navel. I'm going to toss Louise to the lions. She's been so neutral lately. Just out of spite. The situation has become impossible."

"Give her back to the group," Titania suggested.

"Precisely."

"That one stinkin' night, was that the night I left you but not alone?"

"Exactly," Rose sighed again, "you remember that blond Ares?"

Titania remembered Rose quivering in a state of expectancy. No matter how many times she was screwed, the old slut always looked forward to the next time, that divine moment when she thought she would be converted into flame.

Why the seaman picked Rose out of the club, Titania didn't know until Rose told her. "He said he knew there would be a lot of talk with me, but he guessed I had good squeeze."

Rose took the least little thing as a compliment and paraded it around the club after. Titania suspected that her age had something to do with it, but, if Rose hadn't acted that way, Titania never would have known what had happened when Rose took the seaman up to her apartment, that domain which was ever in want of a master.

The shabby white lace curtains in Rose's apartment wished for a hem. The old antique sofa longed to be reupholstered, and the stiff tapestry, which was sewed on the back, needed the itch taken out of it.

Rose placed her prize on the sofa, which was the best piece of furniture in the room. She felt her prize, stroked it, mussed it, fussed over it in general as if she had won an Oscar for a great performance in the movies and had restrained herself from showing her gratitude in public, so she was now making up for it in private.

Lightly, with her fingers, she flicked the buttons on his shirt, a broadcloth job in blue stripes, which resembled a rain-streaked sky. She kept after the buttons until she revealed the bushy terrain of his chest. She felt as if she had lifted a piece of sky from over a field of brush. With two bold thrusts she freed his belt. Then she coaxed his zipper to descend.

"I hate hair on the back," she said randomly, but she had flipped his collar away from his neck to make sure that her remark wouldn't offend. "It seems so out of place, needless extravagance. But I love a thick trail from the navel down. That hints at prosperity."

The seaman reached out and grabbed her neck in the crook of his sweaty arm and pulled her towards him.

Noticing his swollen biceps, she was forced to add, "But I have always been wild about overstuffed furniture."

Suddenly, Rose stood up and walked to the window. She wanted to savour the anticipation. She pulled the torn lace to one side and stared out as if she were checking on someone who might be standing across the street. The windows were in French doors, so anyone who stood across the street could see in.

"I saw a shadow hiding behind the statue, pressed up against it, and I thought it was you on a vicarious kick," Rose told Titania. "But it wasn't. Later, I found out it could have been none other than—"

"Louise?" Tit asked.

"Yes, that slut. That's how she found out."

"I don't know why I do this," Rose lamented, having passed back into her story. "O, they give lots of reasons at the club, but none of them fit me. I'd give the world to know the reason why, but then, I guess I've already given the world."

She walked over and flipped off the light, then darted onto the bed in one kangaroo-like leap. So rapid was her decision and her leap that she left her doubt standing in place by the light switch.

"Give me a little," the seaman growled.

"O, crucify me, you gentle beast."

Later, she pleaded, "Get greedy!"

The next morning was not unlike other mornings when the night before had been a smash. It was liquid, lazy, and reverial. Her limbs floated about on the pillow as though they had been carried out to sea by some delicious under-tow. Her hair tossed lazily, and her responsibilities, as well as her doubts, floundered elsewhere. They hadn't caught up with her yet. Her legs drifted back and forth over the sea of sheets effortlessly. They were seaweed, caught in the tide. It was an aftermotion which she was unable to stem by will power alone.

Right then and there she decided not to visit the club that evening. She would wait until the next night. Make them think it lasted two days.

She walked to the windows and pushed the curtains out of the French doors to flap in the breeze. She was hanging out flags.

She turned to the bed in her best holiday mood. She was going to dream. She rarely dreamed any more, for there was never a powerful enough stimulus in her reality to conjure up a new image. She dreamed only old dreams which were worn through the middle and frayed at the edges. The muscles in her dreams had already swollen to gargantuan heights, and beauty had surpassed itself, so to improve upon that she would have to invent monsters which she couldn't contain in her head. The task before her seemed extremely difficult, but the idea to attempt it appealed to her.

But her dreams were exhausted, and she couldn't debate with herself because she no longer asked herself questions, so she restored to perfecting her colour theory of life.

Rose became colours out of black. The black period was the usual accidents of life: suicides, chronic ailments, guilts which had filtered down through the generations, and revenge which was instilled at birth or shortly thereafter.

With the past too painful to recall, Rose devised a method of freeing herself from pain. She shed her memories. That was her blue period. The method, of course, she admitted all too freely, was to surrender her identity. She christened herself Rose, Burnished Rose, to be exact, and, as time advanced, she became a thin line. The only difference between Rose and her friends was one of age.

Titania recalled the time when Rose became ecstatic because she had copped a young one who was only forty-eight.

During her blue period life became easy, elemental, and amoebic. The greens and yellows followed the blue period and mounted to reds, at which time the colours started to whirl. She was in this whirling stage now, and she could only guess the outcome. What with despair and desperation (the difference between the two is that despair is low and desperation is high – desperation has wings) poured into the crucible of life with jealousy and envy and set into torrential motion by the swift passage of time, a catalyst to be feared, the colours blended, and the result was a single, blinding flash of light, all white.

Even though a blinding flash of light was the logical conclusion of Rose, in the past she had been denied so many things that there was no reason to believe that she would not be deprived of her own destiny.

The friend of Rose, Sir Denis, waddled up in all of the middle-aged tonnage of her green and yellow period. Sir Denis was somewhat of a slob and so fat that not even her lovers would go swimming with her.

At first the colours were muddy. They had to be purified, become more of themselves, before one could advance to the next colour. Sir Denis was obviously somewhere in her green and yellow phase, for jealousy, envy, spite, and words dipped in bile were her trademark. She had not yet reduced herself to the finely etched line of age, but she had reduced herself to two rather loathsome (to Titania) traits, which were an outsized body and a trace of an artistic bent.

Rose had tally-hoed, and Tit had wished her a *buena siesta* before Sir Denis placed her bulk in the booth.

"Have you heard the worst?" Sir Denis asked, always concerned with the loves and misfortunes of others since she had so few lovers of her own and such a galaxy of misfortunes, more than her share, even for a fat one. "Well, the latest is," she began, "that Dolly Mae called up. You probably know her as Sweet Piece, and she was all in a dither, in a positive state. Some construction worker had violated her and then left her hung up."

"What an awful thing to do," Titania sympathized.

"Yes, the poor thing," Denis agreed. "She says that from now on she's hanging out only where they're putting up new buildings."

"Some people have all the luck."

"True. I'm the fat, neglected one myself," Sir Denis informed.

"What about Daniel?" Tit reminded her.

Daniel worked in a record shop, so Denis got all her

records at discount. It was a glorious affair. Each new disc was a product of their love. They spoke of their record collection as their family, their children of music. When Brahms was on, Denis mused in a motherly way, "My favourite child, so happy and well-behaved." But one day the affair blew up, so when Tit asked, "How are you and Daniel and things?" the titled one cried in falsetto, "O, boohoo, I don't get my children at discount any more."

With one foot firmly entrenched in her blue period and the other foot inching its way into her green phase, Titania etched her words in emerald, "You're inconsolably large, Denis. Why don't you share your wealth?"

"I try to," Denis said, responding in pure yellow. "See that lovable face, that sloping front, those bundlely arms, and those all too short legs for that teapot which is his body?" Her eyes wandered down the bar until they spotted this *pièce de résistance*. "I bet he's furry as a bear," Denis guessed. "A teddy bear," she added.

"A koala bear," Tit trumped.

"He still looks like a teddy to me," Denis insisted, "and you know what little boys do with teddy bears."

"No, what?" Tit bid.

"Go to bed with them!"

Bengal the Greaser didn't carry the high ethical standard which Nickie Machete did. Bengal didn't care whom he robbed. He rolled queers, called them "his girls," sponged off them even when he didn't have to, and whenever possible he instituted a harem. When it was to his advantage, financial or otherwise, he consented to be done by them.

Bengal didn't meet Titania by accident. He met her by plan. Tit never had a lot of money, and, goodness knows, she never flashed it around unless it was absolutely necessary to impress somebody, but she did have enough to keep her going, cheques from home and little gratuities from other sources, so she was not classed as a pauper's pauper. Knowing this, Bengal figured that she must have enough to keep him going, too. So, he hung around.

Surely Titania saw him in the poolroom on many occasions, but she gave no signs. During brief encounters, when they bumped accidentally, Bengal applied a hasty pressure.

"Pardon me," Titania said with genuine disgust.

"You're welcome," Bengal said, heaping his words with nonchalance.

Titania's indifference to Bengal could probably be attributed to the fact that Bengal lacked eye appeal. He was too off centre Mediterranean for the first rank of Titania's taste, as we already know, but, too, he had an ass like a Chicago gangster, one of those straight, flat- back affairs which made it difficult to tell where his back left off and his ass began. But, since Bengal hadn't received a definite no, he hung around.

"Really," she said, "you should watch where you're going." ^

Titania frowned upon him the next time they brushed.

"I know where I'm going," Bengal quipped. He had laid enough queers to know how to turn any bit of conversation, no matter how irrelevant, into the direct path of his intentions.

Titania neglected to heap reprimand upon reprimand, so Bengal hung around.

When they bumped again, Titania said, "Pardon me," genuinely.

"That's okay, baby, think nothin' of it," Bengal said grandly. He stuck his fist in his pocket and extended his forefinger.

Titania noticed his eyes, how they verged on the unusual but not the unique. They were drowned in stupidity. "Get lost," she told him.

But his cleverness was soon exhausted. He hadn't laid that many queers. And when Titania refused to feed him the straight lines for his wisecracks, he had to improvise.

But Bengal hung around even without Tit's remarks, for she bought beers which unwittingly encouraged him.

The next morning, as surely as if he had said hello, he welcomed Titania.

Titania pulled out a cigarette and lit it. She hollowed her cheeks and dragged deeply on the butt, and, as she walked away, she flaunted her bottom in a tease.

Bengal dived for her, but stopped short of the doorway which led into the bar. He had rolled so many of the barroom's customers that the management had banished him from the premises in order to protect their business.

Once, when they collided, Bengal locked his knees around Tit's leg and rubbed passionately as if he were transplanting desire.

The following day all he said was, "Unhhh!"

Tit didn't think, the primitive's primitive. She thought, Satan's Satan.

And so that was how Bengal courted Titania, all but the proposal, which follows:

Late one evening Titania left the hall, desolate and alone, except for a little change which she had on her. Later, Bengal confessed that he was attracted by the little change which she always had on her. On that night when Titania slipped into the night, she took a short cut down an alley. The short cut didn't save steps, but it did pass a peg house, which was why she rerouted her course.

Bengal was hot on her heels until he saw that his

advantage lay in taking a real short cut which enabled him to meet her half-way up Gin Alley. He waited, then lunged on the approaching shadow like a lonely caged bear, caged for several springs.

After, since Bengal was entirely without scruples and employed flattery with abandon, he fed her a compliment. "I knew you had good ass," he said.

When Titania propped herself against a building, Bengal hung his arm around her shoulders. His arm hung limply. Titania thought that his act, providing shelter with an expansive chest, had exhibited a hidden grave which was surely divine.

"I know the feeling," Bengal said as his mind lingered on the recent activity. "When I was in reform – they called it 'House of Correction under Divine Supervision' – doin' six months, I was put on a work detail out in a field with twelve other guys. I was the youngest, so they tied me to a tree and screwed me, all twelve of the sons of bitches. When the guard found me that night, before he united me, he helped himself."

"O?" Titania asked, unmoved. She felt that she had done her part by letting him retain his faith in his lonely principle, so recruiting sympathy from her was asking too much. For, even to arrive at that low pitch of desire, she had to rent her passion.

Bengal stood up and fished in his pocket. He pulled out a ring which he had heisted from a queer. The setting was something less than rhinestone. The queer had no doubt filched it from a dime store tray, and if Bengal had had the ethics of a Machete, he would have eliminated the middle man and would have clipped it from the tray himself, but now the ring lay in Titania's palm where Bengal had thrown it in an easy, underhand toss.

"Like it?" he asked.

Titania fingered the ring uncertainly, then bounced it on her palm a couple of times as if she were trying to guess its weight.

"Like it? " he asked again.

"Where did you get it?" Tit asked suspiciously.

"Around. Some jewellery store on Canal."

"It's lovely," she said, slipping it on her finger, the ring finger of her left hand. "I'm flattered."

"Don't need to be that." Bengal thought she had said "flattened."

"But if you want to go whole hog—"

"It's lovely," Titania repeated.

"Then we're hitched."

"O, no, I couldn't. I couldn't accept a ring right off." She took the ring off and handed it back to him. "Without a ceremony or anything?"

Bengal scratched his head in thought. He was considering the expense of a wedding. Then he considered the loopholes.

"We elope," he said.

"Well, in that case," Titania said, looking around for some assurance. She stared at the moon. The moon tilted its big, fat face on Titania alone and returned her stare. "As long as the moon approves," she said, "I guess it's all right."

On the way to Tit's apartment Bengal swaggered, for he thought that Titania expected him to; and Tit glided, for at this rate she was sure to have a date for the annual masquerade which was coming up.

When the newness had worn off of their marriage, on the third day, Titania settled down to domesticity.

"First," she told Bengal, "that name will have to go. The

53

Greaser doesn't befit your new-found station in life, your newly acquired dignity as the husband of Apollo."

"You don't talk sense," Bengal drawled. He scratched the back of his head as if throwing the switch to the rusty machinery of his brain. Titania soon learned that this act always preceded thought and told her that Bengal was now thinking.

"I can't think of none other," he said, slipping his head in his hands to rest it after the exhaustive labour.

"I know," Tit said, "First Husband, that's it. From now on you're First Husband. Firstie, for short."

Bengal scratched his head again.

"I don't think so much of the Husband." he said, "but I kinda take to that First part."

Firstie had a way of being vile. Titania knew that from the course which her courtship had taken, but now she considered it a delicious vileness as if he were throwing back the numerous sheets on the bed of his personality and were revealing the bare him.

Not long after that Titania noticed a dry film on each and every object in the room. Had she looked closely, she probably would have discovered that the film was dust, but it was not dust which had generated the rose glow in the grey draperies.

"I must get the tenuous melancholy out of the apartment," she told Firstie one morning. "It's passé. I think I'll convert to beige. I'll make the walls a sandpile shade, the drapes Sahara white, and I'll slipcover the couch in a ruddy, continental shade."

"I'll clip some cactus from the park," Firstie volunteered.

"Perfect. But what about the rug? I've run out of shades of sand."

Bengal scratched his head before he came up with, "Wet sand."

54

"Doll, resourceful you! That just goes to show that I married the right Mars."

"What's with all the money?" Bengal asked.

"O, we'll save. Snipe out a drink here and a cigarette there."

"Ya want too much."

"Don't be glum," Titania said. "I just wanted to clean out the sadness, that's all."

But there were deeper regrets and bickerings, too. One day Titania wanted her anniversary celebrated. Her three-week one. She wanted some tangible object like the ring which had marked her elopement in space. She needed something to touch in order to know that her love was real and reciprocated. After all, her anniversary was only once a week, and Firstie stole more often than that.

"I want a present," she told Firstie as she dusted an unadorned dresser.

"What for?"

"For my anniversary. Our anniversary," she amended.

"Analversity of what?" Maybe Firstie stumbled over words, but he never fell. He straightened out his tongue and went right on. "Ain't a year yet."

"Maybe a day is a year to me or maybe a week is a year or maybe a month."

"Cut that crap. What you want?"

"A present. A surprise."

"You're a little early, ain't ya? You know I don't do the department stores 'til Thursday."

"O, I don't want something you just go out and clip. That's too easy. I want something special, something you make with your own hands, no matter how simple, how formless."

"I don't do that. You think I'm common?"

"Go on, make something with your own hands," Titania urged, almost teasing.

Firstie scratched his head before he obliged. He gave her a bruise.

But Firstie knew how to reinstate himself in Titania's affections as quickly as he thought ways up of falling into disfavour. One way was to play a tune on the buzzer when he returned to the apartment. He waited for Titania to answer the buzz and let him in, even though he had a key to the door. After she buzzed him back, he played a tune on the buzzer, just so she would know that she had a certain caller, a very special one. In this way she had time to prepare for his entrance. She prepared by assuming a flagrantly indecent position.

When he entered, Titania sighed, "O, so it's you. I was expecting someone else."

"Who?" Firstie blurted.

"Ares, at least, or Jupiter in the form of a bull."

"I'll bull ya," he offered.

"Happy me," she said, verbalizing the modifier.

One morning Firstie woke up and punched Titania with his leg. Then he said, "Good morning, Tit."

"Good morning, Firstie," Tit replied.

Then he said, "Good morning, Firstie."

"What's that for?" Tit asked him, unable to suppress the astonishment in her voice.

"O, I don't know," he said casually, "I haven't seen myself since last night, that is, not so as to speak to."

At night, when First Husband refused to come to bed, Titania lay on her side and itched.

"Aw, come to bed," she whined, faking her impatience.

"I can't," Firstie said as he sat on the davenport with his head in his hand. "I'm thinkin'."

"What about?" Tit wanted to know.

"Sometimes I get lonely and gotta think. It don't do no good to have people around, not even you, Tit. I just gotta sit and think out my loneliness."

Firstie returned to mumbling to himself. Talking, when he didn't care if others heard him or not, was thinking to Firstie.

"Think in bed," Tit told him. "I'm cold."

"I'm not like you, Tit. I can't sleep and think at the same time."

"Pooh-brain!" she called him lovingly. "Come to bed, you goof!" She kidded him and called him names because he had confided his innermost secret to her when he said "I don't think so hot," and this had endeared him to her and had made him altogether lovable.

She walked over and sat down on the couch. Gently, she shook the loneliness out of his head. She was a mother who had rectified the grievance of a floundering child. She had set things right by a slight, almost effortless gesture. But, when Firstie came to bed, Titania was the child. She snuggled up against the trunk of a massive oak and pulled one of its branches around her.

The life which had generated the rose glow in the grey draperies was interrupted as starkly as it had begun. A spectre from the past intervened. The spectre took the shape, form, face, body and limb of Hot Hole. He had returned from the sea, from a trip to the Far East, with a fat wallet.

It was Thursday. Firstie had gone to a department store to pick up an egg beater. He had worked the location often, so he was sure he could pull the job off alone. The clerk had refused to come near him ever since the first time. She had thought him crude and had said so. She had threatened to report him to her superiors, but her threat had been too hysterical to faze him.

When Hot Hole pressed the buzzer downstairs to

announce his arrival, he played a tune on it, a simple melody which had worked up to his fingertips.

When Titania heard the tune, she thought that it was the triumphant return of her bonded Ares. The egg beater had fallen, so she assumed the position to welcome her victorious hero home from the battle, but when she looked up between her legs and saw Hot Hole, she was shocked into silence. The blood in her head didn't know whether to run up into her neck or down into her brain, but it tried to do both before she recovered her balance.

"Knew who was comin', huh?" Hot Hole barked. "I'm hot out of China."

He waved a bottle of scotch and told her to crack open the ice.

"Seamen do all right by themselves," she suggested in an attempt to erect a barricade.

"Too salty," he complained, then tipped the bottle and drank. "I never did forget you, Tit." He laughed, spread his legs, then squirmed on the couch as if he were digging a hole in the sand. "I had it good before I left. Never should have went."

"I've changed," Tit blurted to waylay his advance. It was the only defence which occurred to her.

But Hot Hole talked and drank and ignored her.

"O, I've had plenty all right, but most do it just to help a guy out. No zip. I thought of you right from the time we passed through the canal."

"I've changed," she said again, still unable to think of anything which might impress him. She showed him her ring, but he ignored it as if he were unable to see beyond the bottle which made regular trips to his lips.

"Changed," he said finally, "what you mean, changed? You like dogs?"

Disgust turned the corners of her mouth down.

Hot Hole placed the bottle on the floor by the bed, then said, "This is the way I dreamed it, Tit. All the way from the canal to New Orleans. A bottle in one hand, a hug in the other."

Titania threw up her hands and headed for the door.

"Where ya goin'?" he asked, stepping in her way.

"I'm getting out of here but fast." She tried to step around him. "You don't listen to reason."

"The only reason I listen to is the one for my being here. Get them clothes off 'fore I rape ya."

Titania stood firm, so it wasn't the threat which laid her prone on the bed. It was the right to the jaw. Hot Hole knocked her out, dragged her over the bed, and undressed her.

His overheated body ignited nothing in the cool, unconscious body of Titania, but Hot Hole proceeded to materialize his dream until Firstie returned from his raid on the department store.

Firstie didn't buzz before he came up. The job was too routine to excite him, so he used his key, but when he looked in the window and caught Titania in an infidelity, he dropped the egg beater out of his shirt and rushed in.

"This your girl?" Hot Hole asked.

Firstie nodded, dumbfounded.

Hot Hole reached down and picked up the bottle. He drained off a gulp.

Bengal flopped in a chair and scratched his head hard. He scratched it again, harder this time, as if he were shifting his brain into high gear.

"You want a little?" Hot Hole asked. "You want a drink? Help yourself," Hot Hole offered. "It's better when you're drunk, but not too drunk. Go on, take a swig," Hot Hole insisted as he watched Firstie twist the neck of the bottle back and forth with the palms of his hands.

"It's you, Mac, who's gettin' the swig," Firstie yelled as he brought the bottle down on top of Hot Hole's head.

Hot Hole rolled onto the floor.

Firstie ran and got a wet rag, which he placed on Tit's face. He didn't look at the mound of bleeding flesh until Titania had regained consciousness. When Tit awoke and saw the blood spurting from the gash in Hot Hole's head, she shrieked her relief.

"Mother, my favourite colour!" Then, as she realized the seriousness of the act, her voice deepened. "God, First, what didja do?"

"I gave it to him," Firstie said. "I had to when he said he knocked you out."

"He looks dead," Tit said.

"We gotta blow. Get a bag, quick!"

Tit ran into the bathroom and packed a shaving kit with her razor, cream, toothbrush and paste. Then she reached for the mercurochrome, just in case she discovered some wounds which she had overlooked in her haste. She tried to stuff the red bottle into the bag, but she couldn't get the bottle in and the zipper closed at the same time. Then she shrieked, "O, my God, I must be out of my mind. The vaseline!" She threw the red bottle on the floor and replaced it with a tube of vaseline which squashed nicely into the empty space at the top of the bag.

While Tit was packing, Firstie was going through Hot Hole's wallet. He found two hundred dollars in bills. "Must be some racket," he told Tit as they ht out of the apartment. "Two hundred bucks for paddlin' a boat!"

They spent the night in a small hotel on the edge of town. It was a night where the stars dipped low in the sky, so low that they applied a dusty salve to Titania's wound, and she was healed. Her wound was only a bruise on the jaw, and, after all, a bruise had been the present which Firstie had given her on their third anniversary. She was soothed by the thought of her anniversary and she mentioned it to Firstie, but Firstie was not. His bruise was in his mind, and, like interior bleeding, he couldn't get to it from the outside, nor could the stars.

"Tit, I ain't never knocked off a guy."

"We don't know if he's dead yet. You hit him on top of the head."

"So what?"

"You could've just knocked him out. There was too much blood to see how deep the wound was."

"You think so?"

"Sure," Tit said with wobbly conviction. "Don't you feel it?"

"I don't feel nothin'. What you think about that guy who gave us this room?"

"I don't know."

"You think he levelled with us?"

"I guess so."

"He said he didn't care about us not havin' bags, but he looked square to me. They don't mind so much downtown. They get bums there all the time, but I don't know out here."

"He looked on the up and up to me."

"Yeah, them up-and-ups are the first to rat, just to get their kicks."

"Don't worry."

"My guts are all jammed up like I never felt before."

"Go calm," Tit told him, as she tried to go calm herself. "What didja think when you hit him?"

"Nothin'."

"When you saw the blood?"

"Nothin'."

"Didn't you feel anything?"

"Not much."

"What?"

"Somethin' far off, cuttin' into me, like a floor sinkin' fast."

"I don't get it."

"He was cuttin' me out, out of air, understand that?" Firstie punched his neck as if he were unkinking an artery.

Titania swallowed her next question.

"That puff ball and his fat words. He griped me. I had to do it, Tit."

"I know you did, First."

"Do you, Tit?"

"Yes," she stammered, but she stammered so badly that maybe she only said sounds and thought yes.

Firstie almost smiled. The corners of his mouth twitched upwards.

They huddled together in the darkness.

When Titania strolled into the club, she turned her anxiety to good advantage by letting it propel her lightly through the air as if she were an advancing cloud of mist and no more.

As soon as Rose and Denis saw the cloud on the horizon, they crowded it into their booth and began to interrogate it slyly.

"What's with you?" Denis asked the cloud.

"O, nothin'," Tit replied.

"You thirstin' after?" Rose asked, not suspecting that it might be a rain cloud.

"Not really," Tit admitted, "but if you're buying

"Have a beer on me," Rose offered graciously.

"All right, I will. Thanks – as long as you're treating, but bribes will get you nowhere."

"Why, I don't know what you mean. I try to be nice in this joint, and everyone accuses me of slimy motives."

"Knock it off, Rose. You're past your bloom," Denis put in, trying to abort an argument which would alienate Titania. Denis suspected that there might be some juicy bits of gossip in the offing, and she didn't want to be rationed just because Titania's feelings were hurt.

"Haven't seen you around lately, Tit," Rose said, pointing the conversation at Tit. Denis smiled her approval.

"Haven't been around," Tit admitted.

"Well, when you haven't been around and we haven't seen you around, that can mean only one thing," Rose pointed out.

"What thing?"

"Something must have kept you away."

"I've been observing the bourgeois. You know, what Denis does when no one is having her."

"How were they?"

"The bourgeois?" Tit asked back.

"No, the police, Hot Hole, Bengal, and things! " Rose blurted, exposing the issue, but Titania was not ruffled.

"I don't know what you're talking about."

"It's just like her to keep something really big to herself," Denis said.

"So true," Rose agreed. She reached across the table and took a swig of the beer which she had bought for Titania. "Remember," she said, "that's one beer you owe me."

From now on Denis knew Rose would be a drag, so she disengaged herself from Rose, untwined her legs even, and attacked from a different angle.

63

"Really, Titania, I think you're becoming lovelier with every passing year."

"Flattery will only get you in bed with me," Tit warned.

"Come clean!" Denis said, speaking on a level of frankness which was new to her. Her voice dropped an octave into her God-given register. "We know Bengal's in the clink for rolling Hot Hole. In case you didn't know, he made the papers and the police blotter in the same day."

"And we know," Rose added, "you were traipsing around with that Greaser for the last aeon or two. It was disgusting. He's no catch. Why, any one of us, even Denis, could have had him for the price of a beer."

"Then why didn't you?" Tit asked.

"No one wanted him."

"Well, then, what's the stink?"

"Maybe we were wrong."

"So unlike you to admit it."

"I'm busting to know all about it," Denis confessed. "The papers were so vague."

"You're both making too much of it."

Rose boiled, and in her anger she consumed the heat of next year's passion. "Where's the ring?" she fired at Titania at point-blank range. "We know you married the thug."

Titania was silent.

"Be a slut, see if we care," Denis huffed, and Titania bridged the silence with a smile.

"A slut, hell," Rose corrected. "She's a prick teaser from way back."

Titania gathered the insults into her silence.

"I'll never tell her another thing," Denis promised, excluding Titania with her fat back, but Titania was unaffected by the snub.

"We'll just have to change our policy around here," Rose decided. "Some whores have to be shown their place."

Titania gazed around the bar. She couldn't imagine what she had ever seen in the place. Anxiety of the most acute kind had prompted her to read meaning into every object, even Denis. The meaning was a levity which soothed her, but it did not exist in the object itself.

Titania didn't tell the girls anything about the affairs of the last few days. She didn't tell them that Hot Hole ratted to the police because he had been fleeced of his pay. She didn't tell them that the hotel clerk was square, got suspicious, and reported Firstie to the police. She hoped the clerk had gotten his kicks out of it. Nor did she say anything about how Firstie met Hot Hole accidentally at the station where Hot Hole identified him as the one who had stolen his wallet. Nothing was said about where or how he had done it. The usual procedure was assumed: in a john, in an alley, in a hotel room. Firstie let it go at that. In fact, he preferred it that way, for Titania's name wasn't mentioned. Tit wasn't sure that she was glad about being out of the room getting groceries when the police converged on Bengal. All these things Rose and Denis were dying to know, but Titania spoke about none of them. She kept them to herself as exclusive memories.

Before Firstie had been sent up to Angola, Tit visited him in the jail. She brought him cookies which had been baked in her lopsided oven. The cookies took the form of drips, but after she explained about her poor cooking facilities, Firstie told her that the shape didn't hurt the taste none.

They didn't speak of the past which had been cruelly and abruptly severed by circumstances. They spoke of the future, their future, which meant that they said nothing. The silence was decorated with stares. They exchanged longing gazes which, they felt, had a better chance of winning reality if they didn't talk about them.

As Titania left the jail, she felt a tug which pulled her in the opposite direction. She felt that she was slipping down a greasy slide instead of advancing up one. She knew that slime can only move forward in slime, and this thought prompted a shiver, a queer feeling that she might not ever arrive at her yellow period in a pure state. At best, she felt that the period would only mount to chartreuse.

She dismantled the barrier of silence which she had erected between Rose and Denis and herself.

"Denis," she said, not unkindly, "you don't look your usual fat healthy self."

"I haven't been getting much lately, Tit," Denis explained. She thought that she might as well try sympathy to open up Titania. She had failed with everything else. But then she changed her mind and decided to heap pity upon Rose. "That may be," Denis admitted, "but, Rose, you look positively on the wane. You know, you're not the bud you once were. You're losing your sepals."

"I died again last week," Rose said. "Besides, I haven't been at all well lately, and you, Tit, aren't helping matters much."

"I suppose you'll insist on roses at your wake," Denis suggested.

"Who said anything about dying?"

"O, the gods consult you before they do anything?" Denis scoffed. She was getting a big kick out of pummelling Rose with death threats.

"Of course," Rose said, joining the game, "they wouldn't think of doing anything without consulting me first. After all, they wouldn't want to do anything rash!"

"Now that you mention it, Denis," Tit said, injecting a serious note, "you do look a trifle pale, Rose."

"Paler," Denis corrected.

"Have you seen a doctor lately?"

"No crap, Rose." Denis feigned concern.

"You're absolutely right, Denis.

Denis slid over towards Rose, but Rose slid out of the booth and headed for the bar. She turned around and threw her words on the table, face up. "When I want to be picked on, I'll hire vultures."

"Poor Rose," Denis sighed, "she never did have good taste. She doesn't even know that this is the season for worms."

Rose spoke softly to the person next to her at the bar, and the person replied, "Your motor's missin', honey. You're only hittin' on one cylinder."

"O, boohoo," booed Rose, "they're all too fast for me. I can't run them down any more."

"I'm the lone and longing one," Denis told Tit.

"What about Daniel?" Trying to be helpful, Tit reminded her of Daniel. She knew that Daniel and things had blown up, but on the spur of the moment she couldn't think of a more recent love.

"O, him," Denis scoffed.

Immersed in memories instead of dreams, Titania left Denis sitting alone in the booth to contemplate her misery.

Titania walked randomly past buildings and trees. She noticed a banana tree which hung over a patio wall. The leaves were riddled by an irate wind. She pictured the tree submitting to the wind as long as the wind asserted its will, but after the wind had passed, the tree snapped back to its upright position. Admirable, she thought. Too bad people were not endowed with the flexibility of plants.

Tit wandered into the public square and took up a position on a park bench. A familiar body approached. The body wore only a t-shirt, levis, and a frown. Filthy dirty and reduced to the barest appeal, Tit thought, just to conceal its true state of depravity. The body had discarded its rags, overcoat and sweaters so that Tit would think that it was prosperous and had a place to hang them other than on its shoulders.

"Where ya been?" Tit asked.

"Around," Nickie answered.

"A guy?" Tit asked. ,

"A guy," Nick replied.

"What happened?"

"We fell out."

And Titania didn't ask any more questions, for she knew that most wonderful phenomenon, a guy, and she knew his way of just happening by and falling away as if he were drifting in and out with the tide.

Titania didn't offer to share her apartment with Nickie, and, surprisingly enough, Nickie didn't ask her to. He didn't mention it or even hint at it. He spoke to Titania when he saw her in the public square, and that was all. He seemed content to sit on the park bench and talk, and, as talk wore on, or rather, as small talk wore out, he told Titania all that had happened to him since he had left her and had gone off with Gunner.

If you would like to recall what happened to him, you may. Now is the time to do it. But if your mind is rumpled with chaos, too jumbled to see a direct line into the past over the hillocks of more recent disasters, you may re-read those chapters. That is, if you feel the need for a reprise. Most musical comedies have one. Of course, the chapters include those feelings which Nickie felt but was unable to express at that time or, for that matter, at any other time, too, but when Titania asked him what his feelings were or prompted him as to what they might have been, Nickie responded quickly.

"Yeah, somethin' like that," he said.

Nickie's silences were no longer blank, filled with a vast accumulation of nothing, but exactly what they were filled with, Titania wasn't quite sure. "He's growing up," she mused. "It happens to the worst."

A windowless bar, whose doorway was blocked by a screen, a place whose interior was *always* corroded with deep shadow, day and night, was Sparafucile's Bar and Grill. Early, before the fall, Titania entered innocently . . .

At Sparafucile's on Saturday night there was a crowd around an old duck, and she absorbed the attention which was being lavished upon her as though she deserved it. She carved elaborate circles in the air with a hook of a finger. What flesh there was on her body was smooth, soft, and white. She looked like a plucked duck, and the fluency of her gestures enhanced the worn aura which had enveloped her. She appeared to be rubbed weary.

A young thing approached and imparted a question which he relayed with his eyebrows.

"O, you!" the old duck poohed, "you're just doing that." She manufactured a blush, chorded, then blessed the young thing on the head with two taps of her fingers. "I'm holding court now," she said, pumping regret into her words. "Maybe later."

Turning back to the group, she garnished it with a smile and intimated that she was in the possession of some secret. "I just can't recall when I've been so popular," she said, then, unwittingly, revealed the secret of her popularity. "Of course, there's a surprise in store for the privileged few."

"You always throw the uniquest parties, Rose," someone reminded the old duck. "The just too, too."

But Rose, the old duck, didn't answer. She focused her

69

attention on a disturbance down the bar. She marched over to attend it.

"Blubber! Bee-Butt! This is no time to quibble. Now tell The Burnished what it's all about."

"Well, Rose," Blubber began, "we were just arguing over the colour of copper under blue light."

Rose fingered Blubber's earrings, which were copper.

"I said that the sheen was simple Paleozoic, but Bee-Butt insisted that it was only Cro-Magnon."

"I did not," Bee-Butt corrected. "I said *wholly* Cro-Magnon."

"Don't fuss, you two," Rose said. "Copper is only copper. Besides, you're both wrong. I have already made out my guest list."

Rose returned to the spotlight, or rather, carried it with her back to her bar stool.

"Here comes Mars the Second," someone blared.

"She walks like an athlete," was one murmur among many which were unsolicited from the group.

"How's that?" Rose wanted to know. "All athletes don't walk alike. The gangly walk of a basketball player is both modified and enhanced by the start and stop of a tennis player. The powerful, graceful stance of a baseball player is discriminating when compared with the thundering lumber of a football player, especially a guard, whose shoulder padding accentuates the hyperbole already imposed by Nature."

"So there !" someone yelled.

"So how does Mars walk?" someone else still wanted to know.

The one whom Rose had assaulted, whose little shape had shrunk to a still smaller size, said meekly, "She walks like an athlete." Then, a brilliant idea occurred to her, and she boomed, "A sumptuous composite, like virility was everything, fully developed muscles which are not without being fully realized, too."

Rose unravelled an imaginary guest list, sought a name halfway down, found it, then scratched it out mercilessly with a determined finger. "Take your composites elsewhere," she ordered.

Mars the Second dallied with Bee-Butt, who whispered something into her ear, something which propelled the godly one to the foot of Rose's throne. She shuffled her feet as if she were wiping them on the royal carpet. A natural golden lock, amid the peroxide mass of her hair, genuflected on her forehead.

"What you doin' tonight, Rosie-posie?" she drawled infectiously.

"Sorry," Rose lamented in a tone of sincere regret, which surpassed the serious tone of the question. "Not available, but I'll try to squeeze you in next week – early."

"Can't wait," Mars said, then addressed the periphery of the group. "I'm thirsty."

A couple of wallets fluttered, and their owners broke away from the group and re-formed around Mars.

A voice behind Titania said, "You're staring." It belonged to Sir Denis, but before Tit could reply, she flew at Rose.

"I thought you said it wasn't drag," she bellowed. "Here you clank jewellery while I'm caught respectable. It isn't fair."

"It's not," Rose said. "I permitted myself this one extravagance just for the effect. Besides, the cutest sailor sold it to me at half price." Rose gathered up the collar of her shirt modestly, then batted her eyelashes at Denis. "You don't see me in flounces, do you?" She turned to her nearest attendant and whispered, "I don't see why I have to explain to that thing, just because she's my best friend."

Denis backed away, then ushered Tit into the centre of the group as if she were playing the ace of trump.

"And what have we here?" Rose asked, shuffling her shoulders, wiggling into her best manner. "Pleased, I'm sure." She extended a limp hand, but when Tit refused to take it, she completed the circle of motion with a wild arc, smoothing out the awkwardness by counting noses. "Well, here we are," she said. "I guess there's nothing to do but adjourn to the party."

"O, you," corrected a body as lithe as flame, "you're just saying that. You know your party is always the splash of the season."

As they pushed out the door with Rose making attentive noises, Tit hung back. Something was missing. She was about to ask Denis if there were any more guests when she changed her mind and phrased the question humorously in order to conceal her disappointment.

"Is this all? Sort of one-sided, isn't it?"

"O, you mean the men. Rose never has men at these functions. The competition is too stiff. She'd lose out the minute the wine expired. But her parties are rather nice, a brief respite from the frantic emotional impedimenta of our daily lives."

Denis cast a wry eye in Tit's direction and explained her backward glances with, "Miss Timidity, herself." Rose raised a knowing eyebrow, swung back into the group, and disappeared in a flurry of giggles.

"It's the little things you do at yours which make them so exquisite," Minerva told Rose.

Rose maintained her silence, not about to contradict her. "I work hard to create a mood," she explained, finally, when she sensed that the conversation was about to take a turn.

"Like last year," Minnie recalled. "Who would think of decorating a Christmas tree with phallic symbols?"

"How exotic!" someone claimed.

"You mean erotic," someone else corrected.

"I meant exotic. When I mean erotic, I'll say it."

Tit swayed, tipsy with laughter. They were the curve of her progress. She harboured the potential to be like them, but, as yet, she was undeveloped. Still, their image was at the top of Tit's ladder.

"I'm trying for something different this year," Rose admitted. "Actually, I suppose you'd call it a religious theme."

"Rose's religious party!" Minerva scoffed.

"Well, actually, Minnie, it is. But that's all you'll get out of me. Not a stitch more. You don't think I'd squeal on my own party, do you?"

Laughter burst from the group and primed Tit's enthusiasm. But, by chance, when she looked, she saw a tall lean man with rust-coloured hair and freckles.

Denis, having tried but failed to interlace her arm with Tit's and having seen her stare at the stranger loping along in back of them, said, "O, him! He just comes for the wine. All you'll ever get out of him is 'I prefer muscatel!'"

Rose veered to Tit's side and pointed a remark at her.

"We really must get together soon and have a little chat. I'm sure we'll find we have lots in common. Maybe later tonight but before she could finish, she was yanked back into the mainstream of the group by an arm which she had neglected to disengage before veering.

Denis warned Tit not to pay any attention to her, for she was always going for broke.

Rose ran on ahead as the group ascended the stairs in pairs. She waited at the top of the stairwell. The door of her apartment was swung wide, and her eyes were glazed with excitement. She slipped through the door and flipped a switch which revealed the apartment in a cranberry light.

"It 'riches flesh tones," she explained slyly, but no one listened, for her words were drowned in the shouts which went up as soon as the *pièce de résistance* came into view.

"Rose, no!" someone squealed, then rushed to the foot of the altar, waved her arms frantically, ecstatically, and bowed in front of the Kwin-yin which was installed on the dresser.

The other guests genuflected nimbly as they passed in front of the supernatural image.

The flowing lines of the statue ironed out Tit's gaze and calmed her sight. Such a liquid appearance defied the nature of the material from which it was carved, which was wood with a flat paint finish. Her dead white skin was perfectly toned with the dull grey and maroon of her garb which, even though ample, covered her body scantily. She stood on a rock which was undercut to a precarious degree, but her expression belied her danger. Her facial expression was serene but puzzling. There was no doubt about the genuineness of her godliness, for her left hand was raised in a benedictory fashion, and the last joint of her index finger was crooked, enabling her to touch her middle finger in a graceful but mortally impossible way.

Rose stood to one side, quite content to share the spotlight with her Kwin-yin. She absorbed the compliments, the simple pleasure, and the surprise of her guests. She had done it again.

"Didn't I tell you? Didn't I tell you?" Minerva bubbled. "The little things!"

"Where did you—?"

"The shop," Rose said flatly. "It's borrowed. I told Mr. Jeffries, 'It'll give the *prie-dieu* a rest. That poor prayer box has been supporting this Kwin for ages.'" Rose fussed with the silk scarf which protected the dresser from the weight of the idol or, perhaps, shielded the dresser from the idol's superior smile.

"I prefer the emotional approach to the evening. If I can't feel, I ain't happy." Stressing the crude word gave Rose's ears a chance to feel the phrase.

"So," Denis cautioned, "keep it sensual, girls."

A flurry of giggles signified the approval of the group.

Rose stationed herself near the idol-less end of the dresser where the wine, casked in bottles and glasses, waited stoically for her administration. "Chianti, white, sherry, and muscat," Rose announced. "Orange wine for Denis. Just in case she's still working on that boogily novel, and a little Dr. Pepper for myself."

"Rose! You're not drinking at your own party? Why, I won't stand for it. I'd rather—"

"Don't be so generous with my wine," Rose quipped. "I'll have a bit later on. After I hostess."

Rose served the lean, red-headed man who had said "I prefer muscatel." Then, having poured the first round of drinks, she poured another drink for the lean man who still preferred muscatel.

Rose overlooked a comment from someone who said that it wasn't much of a party if it didn't have sauterne. Her happiness tempered the remark and rendered it harmless. But when Minnie asked her about a rival's party last week, Rose said, "O, dull, darling, dull. Fabulously dull. Everybody there had had everybody else."

Rose glanced in Tit's direction, then passed on to Sir Denis, who was sitting comfortably smug on the love seat beside her. The red-head was slumped on the floor on the other side of Tit. He looked blearily content. Rose passed her gaze over the bleary one and mumbled something about how he would never move now that he was drinking from the bottle. "Really, 'Scat," she scolded, "you could move a bit now. There's nothing so special about that spot."

But 'Scat acted like a baby acts with a different kind of bottle.

"It's not like you, Denis, to miss out on a discussion of poetry," Rose said.

"O, where?" Denis asked.

"Across the room."

"Who's in it?"

"O, lots, back over there."

"Well, let's start one of our own," Denis suggested. "I go for the pure abstractionist kind myself. I'm almost completely sold on the stuff."

Rose looked bored, and the bottle hadn't left 'Scat's lips. Denis looked at her empty glass, shrugged, then squirmed, but no amount of yearning refilled her glass.

"There's more on the dresser," Rose said helpfully.

"Do be a dear and oblige," Denis said, holding out her glass.

But Rose was busy. She was sniffing her Dr. Pepper, inhaling the aroma.

"Come, Denis, the party's not as formal as all that. Help yourself."

"O, hell, I might as well," Denis said. "I'm not getting anywhere here."

As Denis rose, Rose slipped into the seat and smiled triumphantly at Tit.

"Now we can have that little chat I promised you. Or, if I didn't actually promise you one, I meant to. I thought maybe tea later in the week, cocktails before dinner, or a light lunch, but everyone seems perfectly satisfied, so why not now?"

Tit looked away, to the 'Scat side of her, but he was still occupied with his bottle, so she looked back at Rose, who said, loading her words with disdain, "He prefers muscatel."

"I simply fritter the days," Rose said. "But the nights are glamorous, though. Lush and deserving. Never could wear yellow. Black is my colour."

"I like music," Tit said, finally, resentfully, having tired of her drivel.

"O?"

"Jazz," Tit qualified.

"With me it was Wagner," Rose began, stopped to take a deep breath, then flitted from opera to opera, from subject to subject, as if she were sublimating her desire for flight. She gestured wildly like a frantic spider who was spinning an invisible web. Her tongue was also at work, spinning a web of sound. Her hands filled in where her words fell short, and on the many trips that her hands took about her face, from side to side, across Tit, even threatening to disrupt 'Scat's concentration on his bottle, the Dr. Pepper tipped and swished but failed to evince the effervescence which should have been there.

After 'Scat rolled his empty bottle across the floor, he eyed Rose's bottle as it circled, plunged, and retreated in front of his eyes. He sniffed briefly at the bottle when it was thrust under his nose.

A rumble of discontent was fomenting across the room when first one said, "The sherry's gone," and then another lamented, "So's the chianti."

The next time Rose thrust her bottle, 'Scat inhaled deeply. In the time that it takes an impulse to travel to the brain to be converted into a sudden realization, 'Scat's face was expressionless, but shortly after that he stood up and shouted, "You stink!" He turned to the group and announced, "She's drinking sherry brandy!"

He stomped out of the room, and his indignation sparked the group. A parade formed, and passed through the door, fulminating.

Rose tried to head off the stampede, but as her explanations and apologies grew stronger and longer, the line of guests grew shorter. When Tit followed at the end of the line, she appealed to her. "But I haven't shown the Kwin in her best light yet. You should see her by candlelight."

But nothing reversed the incensed line.

From the top of the stairs Rose yelled at the top of her voice. The sound echoed and re-echoed down the stairwell as if it were being confirmed by a group. "After all, it was *my* party!"

The Agony of the Apocalypse

As Sir Denis passed by Tit's apartment, it started to rain, so Denis dropped in for tea. The rain was a spring torrent which drenched all the brave or, more likely, desperate souls who ventured out into it.

Sir Denis curled on the divan. Her apple-bottomed butt was a crimson moon, a full moon, which showed through her rain-soaked trousers. Denis wanted to shed her clothes. "To let them dry," she said, but Tit assured her that that was not necessary, so Denis posed like a well-fed foetus. She had to prepare for love-making in advance since her desire had to fight its way through so many layers of fat.

"What's the stew over at Janice's?" Tit asked, taking charge of the conversation and directing it away from both present in order to neutralize it. "I passed by Janice's the other day, and there was an ambulance, police, and everything out front. I didn't go in 'cause I thought she had gotten hard up and started to put out free. Frankly, with that crowd, I suspected a gang bang."

"No, nothing quite so social," Denis said, then added carelessly, "Just a suicide, you know."

"O, that," Tit said, just as carelessly.

"You remember when Serioso popped his cork over

Minerva? He was wild on her," Denis said, but Tit couldn't remember as long as the conversation was pointed away from her. "Well, he had a positive fetish on that girl, on Minerva, of all people. Why, she thinks fidelity only applies to the transmission of sound, and, here, Serioso thought of no one else. He used to walk the streets 'til dawn, waiting for Minnie to come home. He wouldn't look at another soul. I know. He refused me time and again. Then, one night he caught Minerva in the john with a travelling salesman. Minnie had feigned dysentery for weeks, just to discourage Serio, so he was out of his mind when he finally found her. He beat up the salesman and spit on Minnie. Then he went back to her apartment, and you know how Minnie prides herself on her all-pink apartment. Well, all that red just didn't go. It was the wrong shade entirely. Poor Minnie was sick. She had just bought one of those pink, bloated pigeons, the expensive kind with sex, and—"

"What did she do?"

"What could she do? She moved. What a mess!"

"Poor Serio," Tit grieved. "He never got through his black period."

"The other night I had this seaman going Denis was into another story to keep her desire fired up, or to fire up Titania. "I was racked with abandon. You know how I usually seek out the higher values in mankind? Well, this one was just too cuddly. He inspired a poem which I composed on the spot. Shall I grace you?"

"Please do," Titania said, but she meant, "Please ramble on until the rain stops."

"You must realize that my poems never sound quite as good as they do when the inspiration is present."

"Get on with it," Tit ordered.

"Well, I think I shall call it *Sea Sky*.

80

"O, New Awluns sky,
So light, so high,
I can only call you
A New Awluns blue.
So lofty, so serene,
You wear your storm clouds well,
As well as I've ever seen.
But don't say no.
Let Pride expire.
May your lightning strike me
As I desire.
Can't you realize the view
That I am lonely, too,
As lonely as lonely you?"

After Denis had finished reciting the poem, she lowered her gaze to the floor.

The silence was immense.

"Well?" she asked, breaking the silence gently. She appreciated silence, but she considered it a rather low-level, mute form of praise.

"Well?" Titania slipped the word into the second silence.

"What did you think of it?"

"It's just too beautiful. I'd rather not talk about it."

"I suppose you'd say it's a kind of a sonnet. Of course the seaman didn't get it. He said he didn't know about those things."

"Utterly crass of him to admit it."

"He didn't know that he was the sky. The storm clouds were his furrowed brow, and he didn't get it about the lightning at all. Such a waste. He didn't even say thank you. He just walked down the bar as if he hadn't heard. But, then, the herd never does respond to anything genuine, and he was a moth-eaten buffalo if I ever saw one."

"You should have tried another approach."

"He didn't give me a chance," Denis whined. "He simply didn't appreciate art. That is the only explanation."

"I wouldn't say that," Tit said as she watched Sir Denis' shape provide an explanation of its own.

Sir Denis huffed.

"I know one," Tit said, after she looked out the window and saw freshly spattered rain on the pane.

"A poem? I didn't know you indulged."

"No, a story about a little boy I used to know."

"A love?" Denis asked eagerly.

"No, a relative, you might say. Distant."

"O," Denis said, disappointed.

"I shall call him 'Loveless.'"

"Loveless Schwartz?"

"No! No never, no never. No!"

"What was his name?"

"Let's leave it at Loveless."

"O, cloaked in a clandestine coat. Wait a minute, Tit. I want to get that down. Cloaked in a clandestine coat. I think you have unwittingly supplied me with an idea for my next poem."

"You're welcome."

Denis took out a pencil and scribbled on her cuff "Cloaked in a clandestine coat." Then she put the lead to her lips and mused, "Coated in a clandestine cloak. O, well, I'll work it out later."

"Loveless was a little boy," Titania began, "and like most little boys he was in need of love, a pat, or just a kind word before he went to bed, but on this night his mother was pacing the floor, biting her nails, while Loveless used any excuse he could think of to brush up against her, but she only pushed him away. He didn't know why he was being kept up late unless it was going to thunder again, for whenever his mother was alone and it thundered, she interrupted what he was doing, even sleep, and took him into the cloakroom, which was dark and windowless, and they huddled there until the racket had subsided. And now, as he schemed for his nightly hug, he wished it would thunder, but all he heard was a sound in the garage. His mother rushed into the kitchen, slammed the dining-room door, and barred Loveless from the scene, but he placed his ear next to the crack of light at the bottom of the door, and he heard his father, in a gravelly voice, say that he had lost. The cards had been against him. The word 'lost' evoked a torrent of words from his mother. She spoke of how they couldn't afford gambling, not working, carousing, and she didn't know what she was going to do. His father mumbled something about how he'd quit, if only he could hit it once. His mother went on about drinking until she had run the gamut of words, and then, even more forceful than anything which had come before, she screamed, '*I* have to put Loveless to bed!'

"The next morning Loveless ate his cereal extra special slow when he should have been getting ready for Sunday School. He used any excuse which his little mind could muster so that he wouldn't have to leave his mother, the distributor of pats. When that didn't work, his discontent flowered. He resorted to the violence of a five-year-old, but his mother pulled him into the car with a force which was six times five, and Loveless was on his way. He pouted, but the pouts didn't deter the car. They didn't even slow it down, so he ranted and cried, begged and promised, promised all sorts of impossible things, to hang up his clothes, put away his toys, clean out his bureau drawers, and even wash: all to no avail. He struck with his tiny fists. She slapped his face, but he didn't mind the sting because she had driven past the church. He had won. Maybe now he would get that long overdue hug. But the hug did not materialize. She turned the corner and headed the car in the direction of the creek bridge at the edge of town. 'If you don't go to Sunday School, I'm going to drive off that bridge and kill us both.' She trembled as she spat the words. Death appeared to Loveless as two black bodies, afloat and speckled with yellow. He didn't know what death was, but the sound of kill, the way the word fell with a rush of air, impressed him that it was more important than the other words. He knew that 'over the bridge' meant to float, and the blackness of the bodies was only his interior despair which had surfaced."

"Did she drive off the bridge?" Denis asked, impatiently.

"No," Titania said, sadly. "Loveless lost and went to Sunday School, but all he did was to sit in a little stick chair and kick the one in front of him in little jabs. And from then on he was as cold and as mute as a boulder.

"The simple mishmash of living could have drowned the incident in a miasma of joys, and we would have heard nothing more from it. Soft rain can wash a dirty building if there is enough soft, gentle, joyous rain."

"Wait! I must get that down," Sir Denis said, pulling out her pencil. After she had written on her cuff, the other cuff, she said, "Fertile day this."

"Ready?" Tit asked.

"Cast off, as the teddy bear seamen say."

"Well, the smallest germ, even the most innocuous one, can create serious damage if placed in a wound which is already infected, so Loveless turned to his father, who seemed less ruthless. But Loveless' love light was not strong enough to penetrate his father's shell, which was calcified with worry over lack of money, so he took his cue from his mother's actions. He stole her dresses and put them on, not forgetting to don a squeaky voice. When his father came into the living-room, Loveless began to dance. His whirls were crude but intense, and they became increasingly violent until it was obvious that he was trying to disengage his shadow. But his father asked, 'What have we here?' And his mother answered, 'He's young.' When his father didn't offer to cuddle with him on the davenport after supper, as his father did with his mother, which was the act which had inspired the dance, his skirts flew higher. His breath grew shorter. And his leaps took on more conviction until he fell exhausted in a heap, a little heap, alone.

"He didn't realize that he was using the wrong approach. He thought that he wasn't working hard enough at the right approach, the dress and the dance. So, his whirls grew still more intense until he was seven, which was the year of another cloudburst."

"You knew him well," Denis said.

"It's not surprising," Tit admitted.

"Is there a chapter three?"

"Yes. Loveless had a brother whom I shall call 'Kissable.'"

"Kissable? O clever, clever."

"Loveless and Kissable were fishing off the stern of their father's boat. The stern hung over a deep body of slimy, green water, and there was a tussle. Loveless had something which Kissable wanted, though for the life of me I can't imagine what it was. More likely, it was Kissable who had something which Loveless wanted. Perhaps, it was a mouldy doughball, the last one in the sack, and both of their hooks were unbaited. It matters not, for what was important was that they fought, but only briefly, for Kissable, who was older and stronger, pushed Loveless into the bay, and Loveless sank until he had passed the green and had entered the deep, black bottom. In his terror he opened his eyes, and, empty and alone, he saw the blackness. Then he bobbed to the surface, and his father fished him out of the water.

"Loveless jerked his small body with sobs. Kissable curled away from him, laughing, 'You're all wet.' His father said, 'You're all right, 'Less. Nothing's hurt,' and he returned to the fisherman with whom he had been talking. Loveless stood stiffly in his wet clothes, so the dampness wouldn't touch him, a dampness which was the chill of despair, but he couldn't make himself that small. He waited patiently, silently, and alone. He wanted to be hugged.

"And now, whenever he closes his eyes, he can see the blackness, the cold, underwater gloom which he saw on that day."

Titania told the story with a pathos, mingled with a mockery, which she could feel only for herself.

"The germ was a big boy now, and so was Loveless. He was twelve. Puberty came with a bang, and death showed itself in gore when his father decided to take a powder, gunpowder. The shot still rings in Loveless' ears, a seashell calling, but at the time it must have echoed around the world. The shot taught Loveless that death was a virtue, a glowing reward forever withheld from the undeserving. And so, Loveless was orphaned, orphaned by idea, his own."

Titania closed her lips tightly, as if she had slammed the covers of a book.

Sir Denis said, "I like the way it ends on a note of death. That makes it cosmic."

"Too bad it wasn't the death of Loveless."

"O, no, you've missed the point. That would make it soggy."

"O, well," Tit sighed. "The rain has stopped, eased up anyway, enough so we can go out."

At Titania looked at Sir Denis' shape, she saw a mass which was contained in an outline. She felt no malice towards Denis. She was blank, not limp from the story, and remarkably free of all feeling, as if she had eliminated an approaching menace.

"But tell me," Denis asked, "what became of Loveless?"

"Who?"

"Loveless, that's who. You know, the character in your story."

"Sorry," Tit apologized and drifted towards the door. "I don't know any Loveless."

"You must. You even said that he was a relative of yours. Distant."

"Must be too distant," Titania said. "I never heard of him before in my life."

Alone, Titania gathered her memories around her as a picnic table plays host to a family reunion: she was the centre of things, but she didn't say much. Tit's family of memories was large. She had many distant relatives, one of whom was Thomas. Thomas was the closest yet at the same time the most distant relative. One day when Thomas . . .

In junior high, while playing right field, Thomas caught the last out in the seventh inning. His team-mates held their collective breath while he manoeuvred clumsily for position. The necessity to catch the ball suddenly loomed larger than any casual observer might suspect. The act swelled in his mind and pushed beyond the immediate limits of the scene until he felt that catching the ball demonstrated his personal power, and the act became totally significant.

When he realized that his glove had caught the ball, a

warmness radiated from some interior source. The feeling spread until the light of the universe was poor competition for his private source of heat, his interior sun.

"So this is what it's like," he told himself as he trotted off the field. For the first time in his life Thomas felt what Robert must feel all the time, and when Robert shook his head in amazement, a passive act so very unlike him, Thomas realized that he had incited wonder in a male.

When Thomas came to bat in the next inning, Robert's wonder improved. It expanded or contracted, Thomas didn't know which. Thomas was that unfamiliar with his ability to incite wonder in others. He hit a little looper over the second baseman's head, and the ball rolled to the fence before the centrefielder caught up with it.

Suddenly, he heard Robert yell, "Go, go, go."

His happiness ran wild, and his imagination kept pace with it. He thought he deserved black hair in a heavy buff, which he had seen on bodies which were overloaded with muscle. Black hair would speed him to third, but the next three batters struck out, and he didn't feel confident enough to do the impossible: steal third.

In the next inning his proud light failed. He overtaxed the new feeling when the first fly ball which was hit high enough and long enough to reach him in right field was also hit hard enough to slip through his fingers. With a suddenness as great as the weight of the plummeting ball, his right to black hair was revoked, for Robert looked at him with a disgust which would have been unbearable if he hadn't been playing third base. The distance softened the scorn and enabled him to squirm out from under Robert's gaze.

Thomas wondered where his wonder went. He knew that he no longer retained that sunburst of pride, for that good, hot feeling had vanished and had been replaced with a cold, dark hollowness which cried out to be filled. Now his capacity to absorb the wonder which others incited was unbounded.

He looked to Robert. He was Robert, the one whose disgust had infiltrated his skin.

In the locker room, after the game, Robert returned from the shower. He had washed off everything but his smile, an accountable grin. Thomas was still tugging frantically at his jockstrap although there was nothing snug about the way it fitted. A timid soul, recently overpowered by disillusionment, can have considerable difficulty getting the lecherous thing off. Removing it can necessitate assuming vulgar positions quite without volition. Such was the case when Robert stood over Thomas and shook the water out of his hair with a ferocity of a cocker spaniel after a reluctant bath.

Robert's smile broadened to capture while Thomas waddled into a corner as fast as his binding jockstrap would permit.

Robert followed, pushed Thomas' head down with a sprawling hand, and inserted his finger in Thomas' bottom.

His strength prevented Thomas from resisting. Surprise caught in his throat and stifled speech. He remained in this mute and helpless position, wishing that the rows of lockers which jutted out from the walls hadn't isolated them in an enclosure.

"You want somethin' bigger?" Robert asked.

His inability to respond became significant to Robert, for he added, "I knew you never hit that two-bagger. You couldn't. I must of hit it myself."

Thomas didn't answer.

If anyone approached Thomas as He was getting dressed, Robert managed to intervene, to intercept them. And if anyone spoke to Thomas, Robert answered in a verbal thrust which forced him to retreat.

When Thomas asked him why he acted that way, he gave him a smile which curled down at the edges.

"I ain't got a mother," he said with a finality he seemed to think explained everything. "She took off when she caught – she died," he said. "My old man's got a toca place up on the through way. You wanna see it?"

"Sure."

"Come on, then, what you waitin' for?"

Thomas caught up with Robert, but not for long. He was not much taller, but his strides were superior.

"'Course it's just the front of a house," he admitted, slowing his pace. "He had it did over. We gotta live in back."

"You live in a restaurant?" Thomas asked with surprise.

"Yeah," he said uneasily.

"Gee!"

He resumed his pace as if Thomas' enthusiasm had accelerated his pride and had enabled him to overtake his regret.

When they approached the house, Robert pointed to a large, neon sign which flashed Mexican food in the front yard. "That sign cost five hundred," he said, "and it costs a lot more in two colours."

Thomas liked the gaudy red neon, and, as he read the word Mexican, it scraped across his mind. Had there been soft blue neon, too, he would have thought that the sign was a symbol of Robert and himself, but, as the sign stood, it symbolized only Robert.

Inside the restaurant Robert led him down a narrow hall. They passed a kitchen, then a room with a double bed. At the end of the hall they turned into a small room which contained a narrow cot, squeezed along the long wall. Robert's cot, he thought. The room was unaccountably held in shadow until he realized: no windows. A scrap of raw leather curtained the top half of an orange crate. On top of the crate was an old revolver which was speckled with rust – not a rust of neglect but a rust of age.

Thomas picked up the gun. It felt heavier than a toy.

"My old man gave it to me," Robert said. "I polish it on Saturdays."

"Nice," Thomas said, not knowing what to say since he was unfamiliar with guns. He ran his fingers lightly over the barrel to conceal his embarrassment.

Robert grabbed the gun, jerked open the chamber, and stuck his finger into the barrel. "Gotta keep it wet," he said, showing some grease on his finger. "Oil kills rust. Guess it'll hold 'til Saturday."

He sprawled in a chair, which was an orange crate with the top half of two sides removed.

Thomas sat directly opposite him on the cot. His stare took in the frayed cuffs of Robert's levis, the flare of his pants as they tapered to his knees, the cloth which gripped his knees, and the material around his thighs which seemed to appear lighter as it stretched tighter across his hips.

Robert tapped his foot with an insolence which ran up the inside of his leg, up through his body, and escaped through his smile, which was broad but not broad enough for the amount of insolence. His eyes rallied to accommodate the overflow. He was relaxed, yet his body exuded an urgency which tensed Thomas' senses.

Thomas didn't know how he looked, but his look must have prompted Robert's remark.

"Why you always call me Robert?" He wanted to know. "My name's Bob. Only teachers call me Robert."

"Okay, Bob," Thomas said, testing the sound. He felt, he felt, he didn't know how he felt. An emotion bounced out of his throat and carried the sound with it, so it fell from his tongue in a heap, in a small blob of affection.

"You ever play?" Robert asked.

"Play what?"

"O, fool around."

"Yeah, sometimes."

"Yeah? Well, I'll play witcha."

He got up and stood in front of Thomas. Before Thomas could move, he stepped inside the arc of his legs. He didn't know what kind of a game Robert had in mind, but his breath caught, and the desire to swallow became urgent but impossible. He choked to derail a weird sensation which was rising from somewhere in his middle. He looked up at Robert's face and saw droplets of water forming on his forehead and at the corners of his mouth and eyes.

"Go on," Robert urged. "I'll play witcha."

Thomas didn't know what to do, but he was doing it. His shirt, his arms, his shoulders, his legs. Robert lay motionless while his skin absorbed Thomas' touch. Thomas experienced a miracle in feeling: he saw a mirage, then touched it. At that moment when Thomas' desire caught up with his shame, he did what he wanted to do more than anything else in the world: he touched him.

From the first sunburst of pride on the ball field, through the crate of shame which resulted from that explosion, and on to his first attempt to fill that deep pit is the part of his life which Thomas calls Sunny California.

If it wasn't Bob who said, "If it ain't red, then I don't care what colour it is," it should have been, for his body was dry, smooth, and shiny; rough, hard, and moist – like cool red silk and hot black leather.

His image insinuated itself under Thomas' skin, and pitifully feeble brain cells tried to seal off the contaminated area in an effective cyst, but white corpuscles curled and died, gave themselves up for pus, in a desperate attempt to overpower the wash of Robert's brilliant hues : the blues in his smile, the ochre in his walk, the cadmium in his disposition, the sienna in his lies, and the raw umber in his intentions. Even his hair which was black was gaudy.

Thomas needed an antidote to counteract this chronic infection of colour. He decided to flood his brainy canvas with more of the same colour but from different palettes. He needed a jazz theme for background music, some music which would wail his discontent, scream melancholy off key, in order to be in tune with himself.

When he stepped off the train in New Orleans, he expected to see high blues and yellow-greens intermingle and become strangely compatible, but he was disappointed. At first, he didn't see anything. He heard a train grind its wheels. The sound distressed him. Dissonance was not a foreign element in his make-up, but it represented chaos, and chaos was indecision. He had made his decision, so his future was based on a strange pattern of harmony which had divorced the earlier chaos from his life. Dissonance spoke to others. He had outgrown chaos.

He ignored the piercing cries of conductors, all sharp and murky sounds, and he snubbed the random bustling of the crowd. He smoked a cigarette leisurely in the waiting room while he waited for the lines to disperse in front of the baggage counter.

On the street, a t-shirt, inflated with flesh which was in turn inflated with muscle, dispelled all doubts which he might have had concerning the appropriateness of the location.

A hand thrust a folder in front of his face, and a voice asked, "Tour? Tour the Quarter. See the sights. Sightseeing here."

Just as Thomas saw that the arm which held the brochure was gabardined in a fatal shade of blue, the guide heaped his voice with innuendo.

"Sightseeing?" he insinuated. "See the sights *here!*"

But, in ascribing boldness to him, Thomas also supplied the reason for rejecting his pitch. He didn't want boldness per se, he discovered at that moment. He wanted a boldness which was tempered with something. Maybe it was the suddenness of his attack which prompted Thomas's refusal. Maybe Thomas was deliberately misreading his intentions, but, even though he had inferred a special meaning from the guide's words, it wasn't Thomas who put that wistful look in his eyes, wistful of conflagrations. Thomas had only tampered with the guide's voice, and, after he thought about it, maybe he hadn't even done that.

Thomas had no difficulty getting a room in a small hotel.

He said, "A room with a bath," and the clerk said, "How long?"

He said, "Overnight," and the clerk said, "Two dollars. Pay in advance."

He said, "Fine," and handed him the money. The clerk said, "Head of the stairs," and handed Thomas the key.

When Thomas opened the door of his room, an eternal evening light prevailed. He saw some linoleum and oilcloth in a profuse rose pattern. It looked as though it had been designed by a caged and distraught Renoir who had gone mad here. On the other side of a partition which cut into the square of his room he tested the bathroom. The toilet coughed. The faucets leaked cold water, and the bathtub was stained in dirty greys, green and yellows. The grey was dirt. The green was long-accumulated lime, and it was anybody's guess what the yellow was. Later, the red neon from the street fused with the blue plastic curtains, and a gentle mauve light pervaded the room. As he lay down on the creeping spread, he decided that, if nothing else was satisfactory, at least the light was just about right.

A vague sense of disquiet refused to let his body relax. He brought up the image of the sightseeing guide whom he had seen earlier on the street corner. As he reconstructed the scene in his mind, he still wore that deadly shade of blue which dared to emulate the sky, and, if his hair wasn't black, it was darkest brown. The yearning still lingered in his eyes. He decided that it was a look of gentle helplessness, but perhaps now it was more pronounced. The words on sightseeing were gone. The exact meaning of the words had baffled him, so he banished them with silence. He replaced his blurred intentions with a smile, a bold one, so that there was no mistaking his inference, and he fell asleep, seeing his face crossed, double-crossed, with a gentle helplessness and a bold smile, thinking that he was capable of all things.

Bedrooms are private, obscene, and sad. He flopped down on the bed and surrendered to sad memories.

Mother had called him out of his bedroom while he was listening to his records on his portable phonograph.

Through an overlay of surface noise came news of a Harlem house party when she yelled "Dinner!" with an urgency which forewarned him to be prompt, but when he walked into the kitchen, she was still putting the last touches to the evening meal.

Her condiment cupboard was rainbowed with little bottles of artificial colour, which she used regardless of the occasion, so the breakfast grapefruit was served green, a slimly lime green. The sections resembled bloated, gangrened grub worms.

He sulked at the kitchen table while he watched her doctor up the apple sauce. It was to be red.

"I thought dinner was ready," he said.

"It'll only take a minute," she sang merrily as she poured in the deep red liquid. It paled as though cringing at the thought of mingling with mushy apples.

"Why did you call?"

"You don't have to tell me what you were doing in your room. I heard you."

"So what? I wasn't going to."

"You were listening to that fat ole negress sing those awful songs. I can't, simply can't, understand why you insist on staying in your room and listening to that inferior music when there is the console in the living room and all those nice records."

"I told you why. I'll be more than glad to sit in the living room if—"

"You know I can't stand that music downstairs."

"So I don't sit in the living room."

"Your music isn't even pretty. It's sordid, and I can't understand what you see in it."

"I don't expect you to," he fired back, then added weakly, "It's colourful, for one thing."

"I fail to see the attraction."

"It's reee ... al!" he shouted, stretching the word as if reaching for something.

She plopped the dish of apple sauce in front of him, and he had to swallow her view of life. In the excitement of the argument she had beaten the apple sauce to a shimmering pink.

*

"You went straight to your room last night after supper, and I had to sit down here all evening, all by myself," she reproached him.

"I sat up there, too, all evening, all by myself."

"But I wanted to talk to you – in a quiet way, of course. What did you do up there all that time?"

"Don't you know?"

"I know, but I'm not going to say it. It gets you so upset whenever I try to reason with you. The minute I try to impress you, you flare up, so I'm not going to say a word."

"What did you want to talk to me about?"

"Nothing."

"I thought so."

"It was nothing only because of your values. You would think it silly, but it was very important to me. Sometimes I wonder where you get your ideas."

"Not from you, that's a cinch."

"I would rather discuss something which won't upset you, but I don't know what that is."

"Try music."

"The least likely, but I will try anything. I know things are difficult for you. They're difficult for me, too. We don't have the balance that other families have, but you don't seem to realize that I try. I can't pound a father out of the wall for you."

"I know! I know it wasn't your fault, but – but what did you want to discuss with me a minute ago?"

"Nothing."

"Go on, tell me. I'll listen."

"I don't want to upset you now that you're talking in a civil manner."

"I said I'd listen."

"You won't laugh?"

"I won't laugh."

"Well, it was just that I've worked out a new shade for the vanilla pudding."

He didn't laugh.

She went on excitedly, "An exquisite vermilion!"

He stomped out of the room.

It seemed like hours that he sat motionless in his room, and it was. After the shot they placed him in a chair and folded his hands in his lap. He didn't move to the bed where he could have bedded his grief in comfort because all thoughts of comfort had exploded with the gunpowder. The shot had come from his father's bedroom. He didn't remember the circumstances because he never knew them, but he did recall the sound of the shot, an ear-piercing finality, and his mother's scream which erupted in the living room as though it had been part of the rifle's recoil. So, whenever he heard a loud noise, suddenly and with a shattering impact, he always thought, "Like Father."

The scene was an emotional blot. He had not yet learned to deal with big emotions, so the emotional fallout, like an atomic blast, had encompassed too large an area for him to ascertain the total impact of the episode.

He sat in his room, fixed by outside hands. He was reluctant to attempt feeling.

Ever since, he lumped this emotional blot under die general feeling of sadness which he associated with bedrooms.

"Are you still upset?" Mother asked as he walked into the living room.

"Right. Tread lightly," he warned.

"But what was so upsetting about last night? I saw no reason for you to stomp out of the kitchen before you even sat down to dinner."

"I was trying to understand."

"Understand what?"

"Why the macaroni had to be green !"

"You didn't let me explain. The macaroni was a golden yellow before you came home. Just slightly deeper than cheese. I did it to please you. How did I know that your extravagant tastes in music didn't coincide with your tastes in colour?"

She rushed her words together as if she were bridging a gap, as if the spaces between the words were traps which she would fall into and lose sight of him if she stopped talking, as if her slightest hesitation would catapult him elsewhere.

"When you came home," she continued, "you slammed the door. The jar knocked over my bottle of blue. I had it all fixed yellow, and if I do say so myself, it was the best shade I've evolved yet. Dinner was on time and everything – until the blue spilled. It was your fault the macaroni was green. And such a horrible shade, too. I could tell by the slam that you were already difficult, so, when you stomped out, I didn't try to explain."

She looked at the floor and spoke to it softly.

"I felt death," she shuddered. "Now I know what it feels like to die. It's that feeling I get every time you walk out of the room before I've finished what I had to say."

"Where did you go?" she asked, lifting her gaze and raising her voice.

"Out!"

"Did you get any supper?"

"I went to the first bar I came to and drank until I puked."

She flinched. "You didn't come to my room and say good night. You went straight to your room, and – and I heard the music."

"I guess I had it on too loud. There was something in my ears. No matter how far up I turned the volume, it sounded muffled."

"Maybe if *you* stopped drinking *you* could hear better, and *I* wouldn't have to scour your wastebasket every morning."

"I thought I got it all out."

"It stains. I thought you said you were sick in a bar. I'm really more thankful that you confine such activity to your room."

"Then both you and the town should be happy, for I retched in both places."

"But I thought you said

"I brought a pint home and started in all over again. It's better with my music."

"Just what are you trying to do? If you don't care about yourself, think of me!"

"I'm trying to wash the rainbow out of my stomach, and, if I can't do it with beer, then I'll scrape it clean by retching."

He stomped out of the room, and this time he didn't stop. He left her, the room, the house, the town, and the state, and he made her feeling of dying chronic.

When Thomas woke up in the hotel, he felt tired. He had spent the night blindly fighting his way through an exhaustive labour with no hint of a conclusion. He turned in his room key gratefully, glad to be rid of it, as he blamed his sleeplessness on the condition of the room. When he laid the key on the desk, the clerk looked up long enough to scrape it in.

"Hope your stay with us has been pleasant," he said with his eyes on their way back to the ledger.

Thomas walked to the corner and bought a newspaper to read the apartment ads over breakfast. He looked around and saw a black and white hamburger joint. The windows were slashed with signs which read ORANGE JUICE SQUEEZED TO ORDER.

He thought, Breakfast.

Inside, the brief length of the room was partitioned with a low counter and eight stools. He took the stool by the window. The place was cleaner than he had expected, cleaner than was typical, and ordered with a thoroughness which came with pride.

A fry cook stepped up in front of him and asked, "What can I do for you?" He stressed the oos.

"Orange juice, toast, and coffee," he told him.

"Guy's got good taste," he told his buddy in white. "He knows good orange juice when he sees it. Squeezed to order, ours is." He packed his words with nuances, so the word squeezed took flight and attached itself to any number of acts.

His buddy smiled meaningfully, reducing the number of acts to one

Thomas opened the paper to the ad section and scanned the listings of furnished apartments. He found one section which was devoted to French Quarter apartments, and, when his gaze dropped from French Quarter apartments to one-room jobs with kitchen facilities, he was in his element. There were three possibilities, and all three were listed under one broker's name. He jotted down the name and address of the firm and figured that he had a good jump on the business of the day.

The fry cook returned with orange juice and conversation.

"You really ought to try this," he said, waving his free hand in back of him carelessly.

"What?"

"Why, the apple pie, of course!" He pointed to the shelf in back of him and giggled. His emotions appeared to originate from just under the surface somewhere. Nothing as fragile as feelings could penetrate the deep fat of his body. It was a miracle that his voice was not more distorted than it was. His voice sounded pinched as though it had to fight its way out of his neck.

The toast arrived with a flourish. A huge arc placed it in front of Thomas. He was a court chef presenting his prize pudding.

"O, fiddle-lee-dee," the court chef exclaimed. "I forgot to inquire if you wanted it buttered or just any old way."

When he saw that it was buttered, Thomas said, "Buttered is fine."

"I thought so! I can spot the refined type a mile off. There's a hesitation in the eyes."

Thomas paid his check, obeyed the sign above the cash register which admonished no tipping please, and departed. Outside, he let his thoughts surface. He did his best, he thought, but his best wasn't good enough. But he couldn't laugh because he had handled the situation badly. He hadn't known the proper replies to parry the fry cook's verbal thrusts.

In the real estate office the broker matched his tone of voice, which was soft. The broker asked if Thomas knew his way around the Quarter, and he mumbled something which was meant to be a yes. He handed him the keys to the apartments as if he had mumbled a confident one.

After tracking down the first apartment with the help of a tourist map, he decided that the broker was so much of a shark that he didn't bother to shark. The first apartment was too colourful to be considered. He decided on the second apartment. It was a slave quarters, one long room, which was converted at one end with kitchen and bath. The room was furnished sparsely, but he had a fondness for spaciousness in small areas.

After accepting the second apartment, he settled with the broker and wired home for more money. Then he took a cab to the train station and arranged to have his luggage delivered. When the baggage arrived, he deposited it, unopened, in one corner of the room, looked around once, and decided to eat out.

He returned to the hamburger joint to celebrate a busy day. He also returned because the fry cook had been the only person who had treated him in other than a business manner. When he walked in, the fry cook beamed a welcome.

"Well, well, well," he welled, "the return of the swallow."

Thomas blushed white. He wanted to accept his conversation on the top level and reject it on the level of innuendo. He wanted to sidetrack his intentions without alienating him. His remarks swung wildly from total rejection to total acceptance, so he uttered none of them.

He grabbed a sponge and wiped off the counter in front of Thomas.

A lady reminded him that she had come in first.

He looked at her blissfully, then polished more crumbs. She left.

Thomas tried to decide how he might put together a dinner from the wall menu since the only meat was hamburger and vegetables were non-existent.

"See anything ya like?" the fry cook asked coyly.

"Yeah," Thomas said sarcastically, "the cash register."

Thomas was sorry he said it after he eyed the cash register and saw a non-uniformed man standing in front of it.

He was checking the sales receipts against the cash in the drawer. He wanted to explain that it was the money in the drawer which had appealed to him.

The man swung round and gave him a brief stare in query.

He answered by looking away. Finally, Thomas stared at his back which appeared to be giving off fine emanations of excitement. He thought, He's projecting more than back. As Thomas tried to eat the hamburgers, his throat was blocked by swelling excitement.

After the manager finished counting the receipts, he hesitated. He fumbled nervously with his fingers, but it was a fake nervousness, for fingers which were that sturdy with muscle were not the quaking kind. When there was no apparent, or even obscure, reason for hanging around, he left for the back room. The ropes of

Thomas' stare snapped when he disappeared around the corner, and his body was free of tension.

Thomas looked at the fry cook. He looked hopelessly inanimate. He had no intention of probing for a mysterious attraction which gave no evidence of existing.

Thomas left the restaurant, feeling strangely triumphant. He had looked over a tray of jewels and had settled upon the row of diamonds which had appealed to him. He had also spotted the diamond which had outshone the rest.

Thomas returned to the hamburger shop often in the hope of finding a way to break the web of silence. As long as the manager was there, he stayed. To stall for the right moment, he stuffed himself with hamburgers which were mostly wads of dough, then washed them down with umpteen cups of coffee, cup after cup, until he had to leave in search of a rest room.

Once, the manager came out of the back room in uniform. He busied himself as a counterman. His shirt was unbuttoned down the front. The wide V was restrained by starch until he leaned over to sponge off the counter in front of Thomas. Then the V buckled, and the fleshy expanse of his chest was revealed to Thomas alone, as if in secret, almost discreetly.

Thomas responded by asserting his timidity.

Another time he propped himself against the waist- high milk box. He did it casually, with lassitude. He languished there, but his arms, folded across his chest, composed an attitude of compactness. He appeared as a concrete block, formidable and terrifying. The block was formidable, and the casualness with which he had interlaced his arms, a casualness which Thomas had inferred as a willingness, was terrifying.

Thomas would have assumed a similar stance if the calm hadn't deserted his body.

When the manager rearranged his arms, akimbo now, they dripped with muscle. The new pose reassured Thomas after he construed the spaces between the manager's arms and body as holes in armour, but the stance was not reassuring enough for Thomas to assert anything more than silent admiration.

One day the manager was nowhere to be seen. Thomas thought he would wait for him. He ordered coffee and drank it slowly, painfully so. The fry cook was obviously in command, and there was a new counterman, who looked more like the fry cook than the former one had, which meant that he was all belly and bottom and eiderdown flesh. The new man approached as if he were propelled by giggles.

"The orange juice here is squeezed to order," he said with a straight face which he rippled with a smile.

"So what?"

The man retreated to the fry cook. The fry cook draped a fat arm around his shoulders and consoled him with a loud whisper.

"O, that! Social-climbin' sis there. With her it don't rate unless it's managerial."

"Waste of good time, eh?"

"An executive lover!"

And Thomas left, feeling superior.

Thomas had to dismantle the wall of silence which he had built up between the manager and himself. He had to learn to shade his words in order to talk with the fry cook without having him presume that he was talking to him. He wanted to talk through him.

Once, on his way to the shop, Thomas saw a familiar figure enter a bar. He followed to investigate, but he couldn't place the bulge until he heard it comment to the bartender:

"I'm not really a fry cook, you know. I just do that for the money. I'm thinking of giving it up."

"Why?"

"It's a drag, and it doesn't really pay, but the experience is good. I'm an artist, you know. Novels, poems, stuff like that. I'm thinking about writing a mood piece on the indelicate life, but it's not worth it. One simply has to crucify himself socially to get material."

"You got a lot there to crucify," the bartender told him.

The fry cook smiled insincerely, then motioned for another beer. The bartender put a fresh one in front of him, and the fry cook sighed, determined to make his point.

"I expect this mood piece to go over big in New York."

"They moody there?"

"Terribly." When the fry cook spoke, he didn't raise his voice, but he did speak distinctly. He enunciated around the bartender's head.

"My mother was a Hessian princess, you know."

"No, I didn't know," the bartender said.

"I know it shows on me. I can't help it. But, unfortunately, when she married a commoner, she lost her claim to royalty, among other things. Of course my uncle is in the Luxembourg line. He promised me the tide of a count."

"Just promised, huh? Nothin' but near misses. Why don't you take him up on it?"

The fry cook's voice stumbled, but only for emphasis. "I would, I would, only I hate to give up my American citizenship."

The bartender shook his head and walked down the bar, automatically including Thomas in the conversation.

"The girls call me 'Sir Denis,'" the fry cook inserted after he had succeeded in making himself the vertex of everyone's stares. "To compensate for my great loss," he explained.

"I thought you said Hessian," Thomas reminded him.

"I did, but baron doesn't appeal to me. It makes me feel strangely self-conscious."

Then, sensing that sides were being taken and that he was without an ally, he quickly reversed himself. He leaned forward to join forces with the opposition. His bulk on the slant was menacing.

"I gotta meet a guy," Thomas lied and retreated through the door, but not before he heard him cry, "Christ! What does he want?"

All Thomas had to do was to follow the dominant line of his past, recognize the way in which it pointed, then submit to it, which was hardly attack; but still, he was the perpetra-tor of the conflagration. He held the match which would set off the blaze, even though the forest had been seething for years, had been smouldering below the friction line, below the first intensity of flame.

The time was now.

Standing across the street in the ghoulish light of neon, he waited for the manager to drive up in his car. He pulled up to the curb alongside the hamburger shop, then stepped out of his nifty Studebaker, nifty in colour and line, but the motor rattled like an injustice. The colours of his sport shirt were the trappings of a peacock, royal environs, which fell just short of spangles. He braced his body against the cream background, which was his Studebaker. He was using his car as a girl uses her sweater.

He waited matter-of-factly. He stood there without attempting to justify his right to that spot.

Thomas waited nervously. An inertia had set in and had paralyzed his body.

The lull seemed interminable. Two camps had declared war, but neither camp had worked itself up to the frenzy of attack.

He started to walk down the street into an area of light-less stores, but when he turned around and saw that only Thomas' gaze was following him, he returned to the glitter of his own shop.

Thomas looked away to regroup his forces in an effective defense since attack was impossible for him. His paralysis seemed invincible. He saw the manager in the background like a general. In the foreground was the general's envoy, Sir Denis, about to cross the street, a tank advancing to spearhead the attack.

Thomas shifted from foot to foot, waiting for the

stoplight to change. Impaled by his own inertia, he couldn't think of a reason which would justify his presence. He tried to imagine what Denis would say, but none of his suppositions made sense. His innuendoes took on innuendoes until he could no longer follow the meaning of his words back along the path from which they had come.

"I saw you standing over here," Denis began in a dull monotone, "looking in the window there." He pointed vaguely to a travel bureau window which was strewn with brochures of Havana, Mexico, and Cuba.

Thomas stared at the window to confirm his supposition. He was about to reassure him when he said, "I got a friend who is throwing a party up at his place Saturday night. His name's Rose. You're invited, if you care to."

Thomas thought he had heard him incorrectly. He was too busy rearranging his words in order to extract their exact meaning. He thought, He will be there. The manager is at the bottom of this. The idea banged crazily in his head until he finally distinguished it from other equally bombastic thoughts.

He didn't know how much time elapsed before he said "Yes," but after he said it, he realized that that was all he had to say.

"Rose works in an antique shop, steady," Denis went on. "He's quite prosperous but impoverished for friends." He waited for Thomas' reaction. When he didn't react, he continued, "We're meeting at Sparafucile's before we ascend. Know where that is?"

He told him, then departed abruptly. From across the street he yelled, "It's not drag!"

Thomas ran to a bar and drank whisky on beer and beer on whisky. He was not drinking to escape from the despair of the past or to prepare for the impinging future. He drank to dilute the elation which had broken out of control in the present. The rampant surge of happiness, if left in its present state, would have charred him on the spot.

After the party Thomas saw Rose often, at Sparafucile's, the hamburger shop, the pool hall, and other places, but he never spoke of his party or its outcome. There was no trace of additional malice in his voice, but he never referred to it or even hinted at it. It seemed as though both of them had agreed, a priori, that it simply hadn't existed. But for Thomas the party was the beginning of a fluency, a mingling, the dissipation of his reluctance, and that alone made the party unforgettable.

To be cruel, one day, Denis confronted Rose with, "Who've you been sleeping with lately?"

"Moonlight," Rose countered, conceding nothing. "It rushes in my window all eager and nude white, only to spill upon the cold, hard floor." Rose sighed, then smiled painfully, but Titania felt that somewhere along the line, between his words and his actions, he had answered Sir Denis' question.

"I'm going to quit," Denis told Titania from behind the counter of the hamburger shop. "Why should I put in eight hours a day doing something which doesn't contribute to my art?"

"It contributes to your wallet, doesn't it?"

"One can't just keep himself," Denis contended. "I have to keep my talent, too, don't I?"

"It's the same thing," Titania told him, craning his neck to see into the back room. "What's one without the other?"

"I suppose if I fed my talent and my body I would be even more overweight than I already am."

"Where's the manager?" Tit asked abruptly with a mild interest which surprised him.

"Done gone," Denis said. "Florida. Opening up a new franchise."

Tit's interest was replaced with disappointment, but she retained both the mildness and the surprise.

"There's something about Massillon that I just can't stand," Denis admitted after Massillon's show of indifference had convinced him that they weren't meant for each other. "Something about the way he stands. Have you noticed?" Denis phrased his question as a purely rhetorical query by a purely disinterested spectator.

"It's his levis," Rose suggested. "He subjects them to a pressure from within which is simply maddening."

"You mean, like he was poured into them?" Denis explained, putting words into Rose's mouth.

"No," Rose said flatly, then gagged, spit out the phrase, and supplied his own. "Like he was born in them."

The ease and fluency of the days which followed is difficult to describe. A levity infused everything and snapped the tension which had been the dominant part of objects around Titania. The basic condition of her existence had not changed, had not become less hectic, but an overlay of calm had been imposed upon that condition and had made her existence serenely hectic.

Don't ask Tit how she got into the apartment! She doesn't know. It seemed to be assumed. The banter of their conversation at Sparafucile's had been meaningless, not even banter, but a sludge of moments filled with unimportant details which proved interesting only in what they failed to reveal about the two participants, which was everything.

111

Titania felt that taking him up to her apartment, letting him come, was a concession of such magnitude that it incriminated her to an advanced degree, for it placed her in space, gave a shape to air. In the span of one evening she was tossed back centuries until the hours levelled off in some preliterate age when man was not man but was only hulking shadow.

"It's you that gets it," he said, finally, after he had discarded the uncertainty in his voice and the hesitation had gone out of his gestures.

Titania was standing at the bar in Sparafucile's with Rose and Denis when they disappeared from sight as if banished by a royal order. Then she noticed the soft gaze in conflict with the body, which was replete with tension. Resplendent. Titania's confusion was tantamount. There was something subvocal about the gaze, eyes with innuendo, yet the eyes were anything but quiet. She was mesmerized by the rhythm of the wrinkles in the levis. Seduced by a clumsy grace.

To account for the intense expression on his face, Tit put words into his mouth. "Only with your help, you know, can I complete his murder," she made him say.

Obscene words interlocked, fought, and subdued the milder, the less willing. A nettle of nerves exploded, blowing the tangle out. But after it was over, only their sweat intermingled.

He walked to the refrigerator, checked, found it unstocked, then kicked the door shut.

"I'm goin' for a beer," he said and left.

'Scat was the only one who ever spoke about Rose's religious party, and he only spoke about it once. That was one night in Sparafucile's when his jumbo wine glass was dry.

"I don't believe all that crap about them Chinese ladies!"

he said in a tone of voice which was too convincing, too positive.

"What crap?" asked Titania.

"All that stuff about white-faced statues lookin' at you like they didn't care if you done somethin' wrong or not."

Titania bought him a drink.

"I don't like a selfish guy," he told Titania, taking a tiny sip of wine. "I don't need much myself. I can get along without a car, suits, even a house. Guess you'd say I ain't demanding. Not that sort." He sipped from his glass to prove his point. "My one big fault is, well, you know my big fault." He turned on a sheepish grin. "It's drink. But I think I got off pretty lucky with only one fault. Some folks have two or three. I don't even like to take money from friends. God knows I could use some, but I ain't got the heart to ask. Just a way I am." He lifted his glass, shrugged, then downed his drink. "I do that," he said, shrugging again, "so strangers know I can take it or leave it."

A tired feeling crept up Titania's legs and closed her eyes. She pressed fifty cents into 'Scat's hand.

'Scat brightened, shuffled his shoulders as if to order his enthusiasm, and assured her as he was going out the door, "I'll pay you back. You don't have to worry about that. First chance I get."

'Scat told Titania what it felt to wake up in the morning and, before he knew it, find himself in front of a plate of food.

"It's enough to turn a guy's stomach just lookin' at those chunks of egg and hard bacon strips. I don't let it happen when I can help it, but sometimes I get forgetful, and then I get downright disgusted. There's a pit in my stomach which starts gnawin' like crazy. I don't know what it means, what it's cryin' for, but then almost like an accident I take a little sweet wine, and the gnaw goes away. I can tell by the purr which sets up in my system. Things start lookin' up right away. It steadies me, that's what it does."

He misread Tit's silence for understanding.

"I bet you never knew I was married once, now, did ya ?"

"No, I didn't," Tit said, wondering why he would think that she would know since he had never mentioned it. "What happened?"

". . . divorce."

"What was the trouble?"

"Oh, I don't know . . ." His words trailed off into a void which was sobriety.

He followed her in a succession of eyes and smiles, faces edged in black and bodies in animal splendour, which was sensuous power less conscience. In his usual manner he carried his hands in fists as though they were knots on the ends of well-moulded clubs, and the girders in his neck, thick, substantial were essential to the bulwark of his chin. The faltering eyes and the high-voltage smiles were not denied. The size of Titania's response varied in direct proportion to the size of his muscles: the slimmer, the dimmer. A smile shorted until he plugged it into his stare. Then the voltage was turned up, and the evening sizzled in static, in a lush confusion which gave a name to the evening. The evenings were measured by the length and the breadth of the smiles. Smiles didn't come in depths that season.

Titania was getting undressed when he came up to her apartment. It was five o'clock in the morning. She had just thrown her shirt at a chair when he walked in and said, "Hi." He said it as if he meant it.

"Hi," Tit said as if it were the farthest thing from her mind.

"What's a matter?" He came back at her. "I crap out?"

"What makes you think that?" she asked back.

"You act teed-off," he said carefully.

"Why shouldn't I be? You're the last thing I expected to see. You only come when you feel like it."

He slanted his gaze at the floor, but he stumbled forward, moving in on the oblique. His actions were riddled with hesitation and thrust, conscious withdrawal and cautious advance, as if he were unsure of himself on the outside but positive of himself on the inside. It could mean only one thing.

"Yeah," he admitted, "and I feel like it now. Let's go to bed."

"No finesse, that's you," Titania told him crossly. "Sometimes it's better not to blurt out your intentions. Don't be so obvious. Just let things take their own course."

To be irksome, Denis said, "Seen you with 'Scat an awful lot lately."

"Yeah," Titania admitted, then turned and ordered a beer.

"Is it serious?" he wanted to know.

"I feel sorry for the son of a bitch but not *that* sorry!"

Some say that orgasm held down the second spot in her hierarchy of delights because of the intense physical sensations which were involved. The urgency which preceded and the huge release which accompanied the climax carried away the tensions which had accumulated in the pursuits of living. Those people are naive. If thrills were so important to her, then how could anything as intangible as victory with words, as intermediary as words, words being only a means to get at conditions, qualities, feelings, objects, and

115

acts, possibly hold down the top position. If physical release was so important, nothing would supersede it.

The obvious lie fascinates. Titania is prone to absurdity. Orgasm is the most obvious lie yet devised to thwart man. It can so thoroughly convince him of something which is unreal when he believes that the power of his excitement lies somewhere other than in his own physical apparatus. That point where two become one implies a union when he says, "We got it good." Titania seeks the conditions of love in man, in men, because they hold the possible, all the gaudy delights of the opposite. *He* fills her with wonder, which is a large part of terror. *He* exudes a mystery which is the spirit of desire. Titania's desire lies in the folds of over-whelming flesh. Bristling, this flesh is, with a hair texture, bright and stiff, which is a radical departure from her own, so radical a departure as to be the opposite of her soft, drab locks. Of course there is a discrepancy here which is too obvious to overlook, but it is as insignificant as it is obvious, though it leaves her in a state of wonder, of loud-spoken confusion. The impossibility of woman also fosters anxiety. Her mood is identical with his own, except for a few minor physical details which are as easily overcome as the discrepancy in men, thanks to the power of concentration in the mind; therefore, the act of cohabitation with her would be as gross a perversion as has ever been perpetrated by man, so Titania is confounded either way.

The humour was total, spread over everything in a brittle salve which reduced everything to ludicrousness. Desperation deprived humour of its role in diversion and made it wear the gown of necessity. The world was cast in a single mould and rendered harmless with one weapon. One stroke of humour capsized the world.

To say that he was without wit was as fallacious as to say that he never cried. He never cried, but on those occasions which deserved tears his adrenal glands dripped ; his way of crying. He possessed a silent wit which was imparted by his eyebrows. A stretched eyebrow after a remark indicated that he knew that the remark was funny. It was a powerful way of acknowledging humour. At times his retort was a frown, and, at other times, when the joke was on him, he quipped with his fists.

After Titania's facetious thought about his unappealling use of euphemism, she was furious. Some deeper tendon in the situation had been exposed and irritated, and her reflex was rage.

"Get out!" Titania screamed.

'Scat retreated to the far corner of the room and stood with his face to the wall as though he had blown there by the sudden fury of her rage. He stirred. He approached from the opposite end of the continuum. He became humorous.

"You through?" he asked softly. "Wipe good after that one."

He turned around slowly and inserted a grin into the silence to test the tension.

"Wise up!" he ordered. The test must have been negative. "Straighten up and fly right! "

"Why?"

"Why?" he echoed.

"Yes, why?"

"I know why," he whined. "You never want to get tired of that."

"Why?"

"Always why. I don't know why. Why you always gotta know why for? It's the top, that's why."

Thomas heard a soundless crash. It came from somewhere

in the back of her mind. It was as though an elaborate theorem had collapsed.

"You tee me off, too," he whined, building his house with soft bricks. "But I pass it by. What's a matter? Why not me? I know it's there. I just can't reach it. Ain't I clean or somethin'?"

"A point!"

"I'm always clean!" he shouted, routing all doubt.

He rarely was. On nights when they decided to go out after it was too late to bathe, he showered in Titania's shaving lotion.

"I stink like a whore," he said, after he had doused himself under the arms with the lotion.

"What did you stink like before?" Tit asked him.

He threw the bottle at her.

Tit knew she would never get rid of 'Scat, five o'clock in the morning or no, so she started to get dressed.

'Scat didn't interfere.

"We goin' out?" he asked. He asked with the lilt of victory in his voice. Or, if not victory, then with the promise of victory, for he had secured the better part of a compromise. He knew he was irresistible, but he also knew that it took time for the chemistry of his charm to take effect. Sometimes his charm had to seep in.

While she was dressing, 'Scat was showering in her lotion.

Titania jerked on a tie, and 'Scat waited impatiently.

"You never could tie a tie," he said with friendly reproach. He walked over and straightened Tit in front of him. He unknotted her tie and adjusted the ends to equal lengths, sawing her neck gently. He flipped a knot in it and pinched the bottom of the knot. Then he fussed and fumbled with it unnecessarily, clumsily.

When he raised his arms to attend to the tie, Titania got a whiff of lotion and sweat in equal parts. The odour was a fetid sweetness or a sweet fetidity, she didn't know which, but it was a sweet-fetid odour which implied intimacy. A warmness suffused her body. The warmness was not inspired by the submissive role which Titania had played in the tie drama. It was not from the dependence which she felt, for by this time she could easily identify that feeling, the feeling of being done to or done for. That feeling was a dull thud, a throbbing awareness which promised to mount and become more intense but never did. This feeling was entirely different. It was a gentle warmness with a limitless intensity which was generated by the affection which he had displayed in performing the act. A tie loving.

Titania stepped back and examined her body briefly in order to spot the possible cause which made it react so violently to such an unpretentious act. She glanced at her feet, her legs, her hands, her fingers. There was nothing unusual there. Nothing was out of place until she looked at her fingers again. She choked in horror. Her index finger was held aloft in a position of readiness, on the alert for instant contact with someone, anyone.

Titania dropped her arm to her side to control her alarm. She let it fall loosely, so her forefinger could fall in line with the other fingers on that hand. Then she busied her other hand with a cigarette while she glanced slyly at the disturbing forefinger. She watched that finger deliberately defy a command from her brain. She took the finger and forced it to mingle with the others, but it remained obstinately aloft. Not to seem anxious, she ignored it. She took a cigarette and held it in the hand with the rebellious finger. As she placed the cigarette between her fingers, she realized that that forefinger was prevented from joining the other fingers by the way in which she held the cigarette. She smoked a lot, too. It was a conditional response from smoking. Nothing more.

But she was not convinced. She watched the finger in public: in a bar, on the street, in a restaurant, in the pool hall, and, in private, in a john. There was no change. That finger stuck out prominently as it would have if it had been splinted.

She walked, but it wasn't until she passed a bar which emitted a trickle of light and a flood of sound that the idea of the river occurred to her. The juke box blasted a lament. Distraught saxes and pungently struck piano keys were laid over a drumbeat which thumped loudly and steadily. On the last line of the lyric the drum beat faster until it was silenced by a cymbal crash. The voice was Fats Domino, and, like the lyric, the voice was plaintive but not exceptionally sad. "Goin' to the river. Gonna jump overboard and drown," he wailed through his nose.

The next thing she knew she was standing on the levy, looking up at a wry moon which spotlighted the area. She looked down at the water. The spring tide was churning its own discontent in a riled brown. The river was restlessly ordering the sediment of a continent. She tried to see under the surface of the water, but couldn't. Not even a foot. Underneath, down under, it was calm, warm, inviting, a temperate climate which was unrelieved but for the hot flashes of affection, she told herself. But tonight's river gave no indication of that state. She thought that she just couldn't see far enough, but the river churned on tirelessly. She waited for the angry waters to subside. When she looked at the surface of the water for the last time, she still couldn't see through it. It was clouded with a swirling clay colour which was not about to give way to a middling, restful green. The moon passed behind a cloud. The current was constant, unchanged, but now the water was revealed in a dim light, a light which wasn't distorted by glare.

"It's muddy on the other side, too," the moon seemed to say, reading her mind, as it peeped out from behind the cloud and graced the area in a half-light. The neutral light made the scene more attractive, but –

"It still looks cold," she told the moon. "Too cold for the likes of me."

As she turned and walked away from the river, she thought of the strange brightness of the moonlight. The moon had appeared as a generator, a source of light. The light had seemed too bright to be reflected. Then, she thought of him, of all his gaudy appurtenances, but she no longer thought of him as a sun. She saw him as a bright moon. They were both moons, lost moons, which had strayed into the universe, off their orbits, and had taken up positions which were light distances apart, but still they reflected the same light, from the same source, the light of another, the tight of a pirate sun.

On her way back to her apartment she met 'Scat. He was looking for a place to flop for the night and/or a sponsor for a drink.

Titania sponsored him.

"You know," 'Scat said, brushing his nose with his shirt sleeve. He caught himself, apologized briefly, then pulled out a rag of a handkerchief and picked his nose. He took his time so he could do it right. "You know," he said, "I appreciate this." He held up his empty glass. "Had rotten luck tonight. It dissatisfies me when people ain't generous. You'd think they'd learn, but no, not them. All the time blamin' others, like that son of a bitch tonight who said I could stay on the wagon if I had any guts at all. Blamin' me for one fault. He don't look at hisself and see all the flaws."

"Drink up," Titania told him.

He raised his empty glass and coaxed the last drop to descend with his tongue.

Titania went home and slept. She slept late, woke up at five o'clock in the afternoon, and went to Sparafucile's.

Rose looked pale and sat next to Denis, who reminded her that her flesh-toned shirt looked lovely. It created just the right effect with her skin, a striking contrast. Titania sat next to 'Scat, who sat next to the wall. 'Scat got thirsty.

"Hey, lemme out, will ya? I want a beer."

Titania ignored him, or tried to, until he said, "Look, I got my own quarter."

"Yell," Titania told him.

"I can't catch the waitress' eye. Say, buddy, can't you snag that waitress for a poor parched patron?"

"Why me?" Tit asked irritably.

"You're closer than me."

"Not that close," she assured him.

"Aw, for chrissakes, it ain't like I was broke."

Denis was spewing words on this, that, and everything, but he didn't make his point, and Rose was keeping up with him.

"One beer!" Scat seemed in agony. "I got through," he sighed as the waitress nodded.

Only 'Scat made his point, for three sailors walked in and stood at the bar.

When Denis saw them, he said, "They look lonely and bisexual, so I ought to fit in somewhere." He excused himself and let the evening degenerate into a patriotic duty.

'Scat crawled out from under the table and swore that he would never get caught in out-of-the-way places again.

Rose and Titania were left in the booth, looking into the distance.

Rose broke the silence with, "You know what I always say, 'If I can't feel, I *ain't* happy,'" but she fixed her features in a wan expression when she said it. Her threadbare flesh was rubbed weary by the friction which was incurred in satisfying the lusts of men whose orgasms precipitated only indifference.

'Scat was walking beside her, running beside her, bumping the suitcase which she was carrying. He knocked it once too often.

"Cut it out," Titania told him crossly. "It slows me down."

"Buy me a drink, will ya, huh?"

"No!"

"Aw, come on, just one."

"No!"

"Where ya goin'?"

"'Way."

"'Way where?"

"I don't know."

"Runnin' out, huh?"

"Yeah."

"Runnin' out on me when you know I can't get a job."

"That's right."

"You miserable, selfish bastard," he called Titania, then upped his fury with a flurry of threats. "You'll go to hell, go to hell, go to hell!"

Titania looked at him with gargantuan disbelief, then parried his stare with the full-faced bluntness of her indifference.

"What makes you think I haven't been there?" she asked,

and her words were sharp enough to wound 'Scat, to slow him down, anyway, so Titania's speed left him in the distance until she saw only the corners of his mouth pointing down, and those she saw in her mind. Titania turned right, away from the river and out of the Quarter. She walked up the main drag towards the bus station. She knew that further ahead lay the green- hushed residential section, stilled by the heat of the noonday sun, and even though she knew that she would turn into the bus station before she had travelled that far, she knew that the houses were there, partitioned by air and ordered by family. Then her thoughts were interrupted by a wail, the wail of Fats Domino, but she couldn't tell where it was coming from. She knew that the voice was on a record which was coming from some juke box in some bar, but there were too many bars around here, all packed in side by side, all different shapes with the same essence, so the voice seemed to be coming from thin air – from everywhere.

"Goin' to the river. Gonna jump overboard and drown . . ."

She didn't take the advice, for she had already made a decision, her second decision. She didn't know how many decisions she would make, but this decision might well be recognized as her first, first of its kind, anyway.

The Tyranny of Moonlight

B lack hairs curled on his fist as though blunted by his bullishness. He must have overestimated the strength of his hair, for it had buckled.

Titania forced his wrists limp, then flapped his hands like paddles. Their suppleness was his essence, the emblem of his shame. When Titania noted suppleness in others, he was jealous, consumed in an envious rage; but, when he detected it in Pelvis, he was overcome with sadness.

Titania had run full circle, and, as he reviewed the course, he could find no trace of woman. She lay outside the circumference of his being. He did not know in what position she was lying. It may have been a voluptuous position, for all he knew. He couldn't recognize voluptuousness in a woman. He couldn't recognize any womanly trait but unpleasantness.

He bothered to look at her. If someone happened to tell him that she was looking at him indifferently, his reply was a look which said "I find you equally uninteresting, madame."

"You better watch that," he said, showing Titania what he meant by trying not to flap his wrists. He flapped them awkwardly in order to prove that he didn't know how to flap them properly. The reproach in his voice was mild. His gentle amusement infuriated Titania.

"Why?" he asked at top volume. He didn't inject a softness into his voice, which would have implied submission, because he wanted belligerence. If Pelvis had to be amusing, he had to oppose him. The hardness and sharpness of the word made Titania feel manly, but he could endure the hardships of a long journey into virile terrain as long as he knew that the trip would be temporary.

"Why?" Tit snapped again.

"Some big guy might come along and decide he wants something," he drawled, grinning thickly.

"I invite disaster," Titania told him flatly.

Then, when he uncrossed his legs and disclosed his hope, Titania knew that the crisis had passed. There was no need for him to pretend any longer. He responded softly, naturally. He held his arm in a goosenecked pose to illustrate his point.

Titania remembered another time when softness was involved. He thought softness instead of relaxation because the two bodily states are similar but not identical, and relaxation had nothing to do with this episode. They were wrestling playfully. Pelvis' idea of playfulness was different from Titania's. Since he did everything with a determination which kept his muscles alert, he fought. Titania played. He roared. Titania giggled. His hands worked Tit over while his body worked over Titania. He hated a heart which beat wildly from exertion like his did. His beat from excitement. To excite himself further, Titania relaxed, or rather, went soft. He let the strength ooze out of his body in order to make room for Pelvis' shadow. He felt disconnected; therefore, he was powerless to resist.

Pelvis stopped, stood up, and walked across the room. Since he exerted determination in everything he did, he departed with spirit.

"Let's go shower and have a bare-assed fight," he said, propositioning the wall.

He had said "hairy-assed," but Titania replaced hairy with bare because hairy reminded him of another incident, one which happened much later. At this later time they were watching the couples dance to the music of a juke box in the back room of a nightclub in New Orleans. The music was soft but unpleasant. Some visible emanation informed Tit that he was beyond the periphery of his being. There were women there.

He said, "This is no place for two hairy-assed men."

Titania agreed, and they returned to the bar and finished their drinks, but he had made his intentions quite clear, even though he had cloaked those intentions with pride.

Both statements were identical in essence, but the conditions surrounding those statements were different. The trappings were so different that Titania reserved hairy to mean "in public" and bare to mean "in private."

He tipped Titania's shoulder with one hand while he poked him in the stomach with the index finger of his other hand.

"Why did you do that for?" Tit asked.

"What? For."

"Always put your hands on me."

"I wanted to talk to you," he said. "I wanted you to listen."

"There's no one around. There's no need for hands."

"I wanted to make sure," he said.

"That's not the reason," Titania said. He knew the reason, and he wanted him to admit it.

127

"I seen the way you look at men," he said. "You like it."

His frankness bruised, but he was stalling with words in order to give Titania a chance to withdraw his question. When Tit didn't relent, he socked him on the arm harder than could be attributed to playfulness alone.

Titania forgave everything but the bruise when he looked at his hand and saw that his forefinger was extended. His index finger never rested, never joined the other fingers on that hand when they were relaxed, held limp, with a limp wrist, which we know was a concession in itself. His forefinger defied gravity. That finger was ready to establish contact with anyone on the shortest possible notice. It proved that his determination was always with him.

"That's why you do it," Titania said, after he explained why Pelvis always put his hands on him. "You are rejected!"

In later episodes, when the discussion arose, Titania only had to say "You're rejected," and he looked at his finger to see if it was extended; and if it was, it convinced him that his diagnosis was correct. It was. Always.

Pelvis liked to win with words. Winning with words made him feel as if he were slaying the enemy with his own sword. Even if he used the enemy's weapon clumsily, if he succeeded in using words at all well, he derived a satisfaction which was fierce. It was his supreme delight.

"Why you always look away when I talk to ya, huh, why?" He was baiting Titania with words. Titania was about to be guillotined with his own razor.

"'Cause I don't listen with my eyes," Tit told him.

"Yeah!" He agreed, but he did not sound convinced. "That ain't the reason. I seen ya case the bar. What you lookin' for?"

"Don't you know?"

"Yeah, I know. You look at 'em like they was girls."

"How's that?"

"Kinda pitiful-like.'

"How do you know?"

"'Cause I know, that's how."

"Then why did you ask?"

"Ask what?" he asked back. The discussion had been prolonged beyond his ability to sustain a single idea.

"Why did you ask what I was looking for in the first place if you already knew?" Titania measured out the words in his question. In that way he sharpened the razor before handing it to Pelvis to decapitate him.

But instead of answering his question. Pelvis opened an old wound.

"You're a tramp," he said.

"You're too beautiful," Tit told him. His insult forced Titania to admit the real reason for not looking at Pelvis when he spoke to him. "You hurt my eyes. I can't stand the glare of perfection."

What prompted the smug expression which overcame Pelvis' face after Titania told him that he was beautiful? He hadn't used words the least bit effectively; yet he was wearing that smile which he wore after he had demonstrated his supremacy with words.

The flaw. Those words which Pelvis used most frequently were the only words which rippled off his thick, well-muscled tongue. He subjected those words to his own meanings and shaved those meanings with a precision which was stark; so, in omitting the words which he used most frequently, the swear words, unfortunately his accomplishment had also been omitted, the meaning of the scene, and the beauty of the scene; for, you see, he trilled swear words.

Since the canons of good taste do not permit his supreme delight, you won't mind if he is given his second relish, which is orgasm. There is a great gap between the first and second satisfaction in the hierarchy of his delights, for nothing can quite approach the satisfaction which is gained by surviving a suicide which is perpetrated by the self. In winning with words, which is slaying the enemy with his own sword, he is responsible for the self-murder when he is not the self. Therefore, he can enjoy the act and still walk away from the scene of the crime blameless and whole.

"What you got in there that flaps?" he asked, as Titania was giving him his second relish.

Titania didn't answer. He refused to stoke his pride.

He kept after Tit. "What you screwin' your face up for? You ain't as tough as me."

His motion was easy, fluent, partly because he was well-lubricated. His gigantic hips were the other part, completed muscles.

After he said "Flip the switch, baby," he crawled to the edge of the bed and caught his breath. His wind came easily now, reft of excitement.

"You act like you don't like it," he told Titania. "All you do is 'enh.'" He gave a short, high pitched grunt.

"What do you do?"

"Kick up a storm," he said. "Didn't you notice?" He had imitated Titania with derision. His "enh" was curt, his first point, which was well made; and his second point was to inject the tone of a soprano, which was also well made.

Denis' straits had become exceedingly narrow, more than dire, and he had come to borrow money to shake his ennui. Titania said that the only thing he could borrow from him was a look at his empty wallet. So Denis took him up on it and culled his real name from an old driver's licence.

"I confess, Thomas," Denis began.

"Please!" Tit ordered. "Use my city name!"

Denis had called Tit "Thomas" to appeal to the real him, but Titania turned the corners of his mouth down in a sour expression when he heard the name.

"All right," Denis huffed. He stretched his chunky legs begrudgingly. His legs appeared to roll rather than to stretch. "If you're so touchy about a little thing like a name, I'd hate to see you when something really big comes along."

"You're big enough, thank you."

"Really, Tit, you're a menace. Your nerve ends actin' up?"

"And why shouldn't they? I've been husbandless for a good week."

Denis strained his flab in order to project a stalwart attitude, but the attitude was beyond his reach, so he tried for robustness in sound.

"Abbel-gadabble-gloot-glack! I had a musician the other night," he said with a tone which invited envy.

"A likely story," Tit jeered. "Did he play?"

"We couldn't find a piano, but he said the minute I locate one he might reconsider." His words ended on the upswing, for the possibility was not stone cold dead.

"That's more like it."

"I confess, Tit," Denis said, "I have nowhere else to go. I come to you reft of pride. I've been tossed to the Fates willy-nilly. Last night Lorna Jean flew to Pensacola with an Air Force captain."

"Then you're talking pretty big for a cast-off."

"I called you Tit, don't forget. Tit, Tit, Titania."

"Take back that other name?"

131

Denis bit the air in one big open-jawed bite, then swallowed humbly.

"All right, you may stay, but suppress your ways. The first suggestion of sex will send you packing."

"Have it your way, but my body can't be confined like yours. If I'm to get any results, I have to be demure by the acre."

"Watch it!"

Denis gazed around the room. What he saw brought a frown to the top acre of his face. "Why, this place is positively Hogarth."

"O, I don't know. It has two rooms."

"Your other *one* was bigger."

"I've never had two rooms."

"You haven't even got a front door."

"I could use the French doors there. They would serve nicely, but they don't close quite right."

"The bathroom opens into the kitchen," Denis shrieked with glee.

Tit saw his mistake in inviting Denis to his new apartment, but, since Denis had been scuttled for an Air Force captain, Tit thought that he might have acquired a little humility in the scuffle; but, no, only bitterness lay under that flesh, and there was so much flesh for so much bitterness to lay under.

"At least the bathroom isn't in the alcove," Tit said. "Like that other place."

"Maybe, but look at those steps. Whoever heard of a private stairway to a john? In truth, you ascend the throne here. And look at the view."

"You don't have to, you know."

"But the view, how original! It opens right onto the vast expanse of the landlord's kitchen. And they're Italians,"

Denis noted after he had strained his stare and made out the floating object in the kitchen.

"Who else? You expected maybe Vishnu?"

"But, really, Titania, after the other place."

"O, this one has its little advantages," Tit suggested slyly.

"Well, if it does, they aren't apparent on the surface." Denis stared at the immense cotton dress which was manoeuvring in the landlord's kitchen. "She's big, isn't she?" he asked, then: "Think of the garlic!" He wrinkled his nose as if he had.

"It still has its little advantages," Tit insisted. "You haven't met her son yet."

"Sun?" Denis asked, interested. Sun or son, he didn't care how it was spelled. They were both the same to him, the bearers of light.

"Yes," Tit drooled, "he stands on the corner Friday nights – all decked out."

"Decked out in all but ambition." Denis knew.

"Is there any other way? "

"No, I suppose not," Denis sighed, enjoying the brief drama which was transpiring in his mind.

"If he had ambition, he'd pass you by, you can bet."

"Please, you're interrupting something beautiful," Denis said.

"Then you concede my point?" Tit asked.

"I didn't say you couldn't fix it up. A sure taste and a nimble finger can work wonders, can turn a pigsty into a palace."

"I fail to see the attraction myself," Denis told Rose, referring to Titania in some obscure way.

Titania was sitting in the booth, watching the bar dreamily.

"What attraction?" Rose wanted to know. "I don't see any." He surveyed the bar again, just to make sure. "The place looks gelded to me."

"Up there. At the bar. Old Pelvis."

"He says you don't get much," Titania said in an attempt to sever the neck of the conversation before it sprouted the head of a monster.

"I don't get much! How does he know? He's a city boogily, that's all. I know all about them. I wrote a novel on the type."

"Did you ever finish it?" Tit asked.

"I encountered a stumbling block halfway through, and I couldn't spend any more time on it. Life had switched me to a maritime locale. The *San Loco* had docked, and I was knee-deep in sailors. You know how it goes."

"Tell us about your war experiences, Rose," Tit coaxed.

"Which one?" Rose asked, perking up. He acted as though he were asked to delve into a grab bag which was too vast, too assorted, to discriminate one of anything.

"Why, the first war, of course," Denis said. "That one-sided affair at Sodom. You must have had a sergeant-in-arms by that time."

"No, sorry, honey, I missed that one, worse luck. I was in Babylon at the time, spent the week-end with the cutest Philistine, but I saw it from a distance. The fireworks were lovely."

"O, hate, despise you," Denis said as he tweaked Rose's nose. "But I still fail to see the attraction. O, I can see a vague quality of forced casualness which is supposed to imply a love of mankind, good fellowship, anyway, a veneer, but his past rips the veil."

"I don't follow you," Rose said.

"I suppose I am getting a bit esoteric," Denis admitted.

"Esoteric, hell," Rose contested, "you just banished your antecedents."

Denis rolled his eyes in the direction of the bar, to the far end, where Old Pelvis resided.

Rose asked him to pardon his obtuseness.

From where Pelvis was standing at the end of the bar, he could obtain an optimum of vision, a range of vision where the vertex of the angle was greater than ninety degrees. Old Pelvis was standing at the vertex. From that position he could see a great deal to the left and also have a clear view to the right which enabled him to examine Tit's booth casually. By slightly shifting his weight from one foot to the other and looking out of the corner of his eye, he had the choicest seat in the auditorium – next to sitting in the booth itself, but sitting in the booth would not offer the advantage of a perspective, which was uninvolved scrutiny.

"Look at him!" Denis jeered.

"All he's doing is drinking a beer," Tit said. "I can't see why that should cause comment."

"Defending him, no less," Denis pounced.

"What do you mean?"

"If I jibe him without cause and you defend him without cause, well, then, we certainly are without motives this evening."

"I wasn't defending him."

"Of course not, and I wasn't jibing him. Really, Titania, I can't see how you can protect him after all he has done to you."

"All what?" Tit asked.

"You don't have to pretend you're wearing the rag for us."

"Or insinuate that your piles are smarting again," Rose inserted.

"We're your friends, dear, you know that," Denis offered

by way of encouragement, but when he saw that Titania wasn't having any encouragement, he challenged, "Why don't you go over and speak to him?"

Titania thought that the suggestion was offered in a purely unfriendly tone of voiced "I don't see why," he said.

"Why, even a casual friend you'd speak to, but to ignore a lover, why "Who threw your imagination into high gear?" Tit scoffed to drown the alarm in his voice.

"You're being much too naive about the whole thing," Denis advised. "Go speak to him."

"I certainly don't have to speak to everyone who comes in this joint, regardless of how savoury the character might be. Just because you play the slut

"O, vicious, vicious," Denis said. "If you don't talk to him, then I know there's a riff. I've been trying to tie up a few things to explain your behaviour recently, and now I have all the pieces."

Denis sat back smugly.

Titania thought, hatefully.

"Why, you've been inseparable for the past month," Denis went on, " and now you don't even speak. Coincidence travels only so far. I've suspected an affair for some time but kept my mouth shut because I couldn't for the life of me see the attraction. But two people who suddenly become indifferent after being inseparable, well, really, Tit, do I have to draw pictures?"

Titania wished that he had gone up and had spoken to Pelvis when he had had the chance. He wondered if he could still do it without admitting too much, but he decided that the advisability of the move had passed. He felt the pincers of Denis' argument, but, still, Denis was groping. He could slip out sideways if the right move came to him.

"Old Pelvis!" Tit scoffed as though the idea were preposterous, which wasn't the right move.

"Condemn thy lover," Denis said. "See where that gets you."

"It must have been a very serious break," Rose inserted, wishfully.

Denis lit up with the glow of sudden realization. "Thank you, Rose, you're a saint. Serious break indeed! I suppose, Rose, you didn't know that Titania has moved, has left her subtle elegance for a sink hole. Things are as bad as all that, eh, Tit? I wonder if Pelvis knows the new whereabouts of his paramour. I thought there must be something more attractive about that place than the landlord's son." Denis dropped his voice to a whisper. "He tried to make me think he moved just to catch a guinea pimp." His voice vaulted. "Really, Titania, I'm not as gullible as all that. Who do you think you're dealing with, Old Pelvis?" Then his voice confided to Rose, "Old Pelvis spends his money outright before he even knows if he can get in. His over-confidence is colossal, superseded only by his gall. That's probably why he gets so impossible after a while. He resents his promiscuous generosity when it doesn't pay off. He's been known to break a guy's jaw for less."

Rose nodded.

Denis poked Rose in the ribs gratefully. "A person doesn't move from a palace to a pigsty just to challenge his taste – not unless it's Titania. I don't want to de-nobleize your motives, Tit, but if you take the long way home tonight, it couldn't be to ditch Pelvis, now, could it? Just remember, I told you so."

Titania regained his silence, if not his composure, but his mood was mixed. He knew that Denis was on to things, but he also knew that Denis had a long way to go before he would have the whole truth before him. For Denis to seize upon Tit's moving as conclusive proof of a break was highly incorrect. Moving did not imply that a serious break had occurred, but Tit's moving had come about as a manifestation of the break, this time, but it was only a minor manifestation. How many times had Titania moved in the last year? No more than Rose or Denis, and Denis had been known to invent reasons for moving just to heighten his turmoil and give him something to do with his moorings. To Denis the act of moving implied more had happened than actually had, or that anything which he might imagine would be substantiated as real and true if it could be linked with the act of moving. His landlady had simply gotten sick of him that time when he insisted that a drunken sailor had demolished his room with passion. Pelvis knew where Titania was living. He had seen the sign on the gate which had said VACANCY and had even told Tit about it himself, so the location of the new apartment was not a secret. Yet, Titania would tremble noticeably, audibly, if Pelvis decided to leave the bar at the same time that Titania did.

The break loomed as the only fresh reality in Titania's life. Intense. Immense. But the break only seemed final. His mixed feelings prevented the break from solidifying. He was glad to be rid of Old Pelvis, but for the mixed feelings which confused him and refused to denounce certain aspects of the episode, if episode it was. Titania was reluctant to surrender certain feelings, but there were others, feelings strong and immediate, urgent and menacing, which favoured the continuance of the break. Perhaps it was the off-hand remark of Denis which worried Tit: that Old Pelvis might break some guy's jaw for less. Perhaps that statement came throbbingly alive because recent events had proven how correct that statement was. It had come close to being materialized right under Titania's eyes, Tit's jaw, for Titania was the "some guy."

Titania was well aware of Old Pelvis' character, including his trait of promiscuous generosity. Denis had implied that Old Pelvis was generous but that he grew sullen, bitterly, vengeful, when his generosity was not reciprocated in amount, if not in kind.

He displayed his trait of promiscuous generosity shortly after he had met Titania, the Saturday night after die official meeting. At that time he was working, which necessitated the week-end meetings, but that inconvenience was soon eliminated.

"What you say I show you how to win on the horses?" Pelvis had said, and Titania had been carried away on the musical intonations of his voice, soft, smooth, confident, sublime. His words had rippled with conviction.

Pelvis was gentle with his leisure, disrespectful of money, and strangely unsuited for his job as an electrician's helper. But he only took on big jobs, he assured Tit. He had his union card. His union card was a fortification against small jobs, a shield which protected his pride from disintegrating altogether. It sustained his pride. But Pelvis ventured into high places. When he did, he was always in back of the electrician, so his act seemed less brave to him. "That was where the money was," he chuckled, "where the electrician was." He pointed away from himself, farther out. But someday he would graduate to where the money was, he said without believing his words all the way. But Titania believed his words to the hilt, he had to believe them in order to fulfill the conception of Old Pelvis which was brewing in his mind. He could do anything an electrician could do, was the line which Pelvis uttered with confidence and believed to the hilt himself. He had learned by watching the electrician on the job. Some guys weren't noticeable on the job. What they did while they were out there on some girder, waiting to feed line, was anybody's guess. But he was noticeable. For a moment he became anybody and guessed what the others thought about while they were waiting, holding onto a girder with one hand and leaning over another girder. They thought about how they were going to plotz their old ladies that night, what position they could assume in order to receive that special jolt which would set them up the following day as though past comfort offered immunization against future drudgery, and the beer after. It was cool-tasting, the beer. It cut deep down. One beer could sign, seal and deliver a wild thirst after plotzzing.

But such thoughts were soon crowded out by other thoughts – like where they could stash the weed, so their old ladies wouldn't find it and chuck it out, thinking nothing bad of what they had done. He told about all his buddy went through to hide the weed in his own house. He had to come home and get it, smoke it away somewhere (usually in back of the garage), then return, charged, way out, ready for plotzzing. He couldn't understand what his wife had against it. She rifled him with the old story that it was dope, the next thing to it, bad for his health, evil-doing – but he told her that that was just something which she had read in some old grammar. That wasn't how she felt about it at all, for he knew for a fact that she loved him more when he was whiffed than when he wasn't. When he had a head full of weed, he nearly drove her wild crazy. He never said what it did to him.

So he had to find a safe place to stash his bundle. Whenever he stuck it in his bureau drawer, he would come home at night and dig around in his underwear, looking for it, and she would stand in the doorway, leaning against it, letting him dig, until finally she said, "What you lookin' for, honey?" or even worse, "Ya lost somethin'?" And he would have to grumble, "Aw, nothin'," and leave before he made more of a fool of himself than he already had. Then, with a rubber band, he strapped it to the back of an iodine bottle, but he only tried that once since the kids were always getting hurt during the day. Finally, he hid the blast in the icebox. She was blind in the icebox, for she never once saw it, and with all her bustling and juggling of things around in there too. All he had to do was want some spread on his food which was not on the table, and he was in. Just for convenience's sake he put it by the catsup bottle. That did away with snooping moves. But one night he came home and looked in the icebox, and it wasn't there. He was sure she had found it. The game was up. He didn't know where he could hide it now. But he had to be certain. He ploughed around in the icebox on the catsup shelf until she asked him, "What you lookin' for, honey?" And he said, "Nothin'!" Then he spied it pushed back at the far end of the shelf, and he regretted his rashness. When he groped, he dislodged it before he had his hands on it, and it fell to the mayonnaise shelf, two shelves below. "If you'll just tell me what you're lookin' for, maybe I can help you. The jam's on the catsup shelf," she said. "Yeah, I know," he said, and, as his fingers gripped the small package, his wife's fingers ran up his spine. He sighed a delicious sigh which brought an understanding smile to his wife's lips. She ran her fingers up his spine again. This time, he grunted. His hand came out of the box, gripping what looked like only the jar of mayonnaise. "Well, if you'd of asked," she scolded, "I could of told you that the mayonnaise was on the bottom shelf." He didn't answer. He marched to the table, holding the

141

mayonnaise on high, then stopped short when he looked at his plate and saw only grits, but somehow he didn't mind topping his grits with mayonnaise this evening.

Before Pelvis laughed, he waited for Tit's reaction to the story, but when Tit didn't react, he held back his laugh and said, "Them guys do it. I don't. I only know what they tell me. Never married myself," he admitted as though that explained why he never had to go so far out for his kicks.

Tit inhaled a mild sense of undisclosed fact in the air. Only time and travel seemed to intervene and prevent the whole deep inhalation of fact.

Professional gambling didn't appeal to Titania, so he wondered why he had agreed to go to the racetrack. Perhaps he lavished his gambling sense on other things, like dissipating the urge before he got to the track, for at the moment he was willing to gamble on Old Pelvis before he put up his money. Tit explored the scene to discover what prompted the feeling.

Old Pelvis walked jauntily. Reason enough right there to risk a couple of chips of feeling. But he walked unassumingly, too, as though sated in all things. He was too short to lumber, stocky in a nice way, a washed way. Those men with compact muscles sweat more because they had to confine more into a smaller space, their whole being, so they needed to bathe more frequently, but perhaps a body squashed had nothing to do with Titania's feelings. It was the confinement of energy which had made him appear cramped. Those bodies which were heavily laden with muscle, heavily laden thighs in particular, when confined with muscles slack, gave an unabashed air of strength, of reserved power, and bodily cleanliness added an affront to that state. The scent of his shaving lotion curled up from his jaw, imparting the odour of a delectable sauce, but it

142

was a scent which he claimed for his own, manufactured throughout his body. As yet, his alcoholic breath did not obtrude and combine with the odour to make too heady a smell, a mixture of evil, as of scent decayed, over-ripe with complaint.

But Titania felt that there was an undeniable attraction. If it was not apparent on the surface, it was felt indirectly in some vague, mysterious way. It was this vague feeling, which, when aroused, made him conscious of the necessity to prolong the relationship in order to preserve the feeling, for, when the feeling was being experienced, it was unnecessary to look elsewhere to provoke the same feeling.

Old Pelvis stopped beside a car, a two-toned brown job with modern lines which were strangely incompatible with the rundown condition of the upholstery and the mottled overlay of mud which added several intermediate shades of beige which were not flattering. He kneeled at the back bumper and looked under the car. He reached under the bumper and jiggled something.

"Gonna lose my exhaust pipe," he said. "I tied it up with this wire, but I gotta get another wire to tie up the other end."

Titania said, "Uh-huh."

The upholstery smelled of dust, and the summer evening augmented the feeling of closeness in the air.

When Pelvis started the car, the motor turned over once, flopped over without a hitch, and he smiled. Titania sighed his relief.

Finally, Pelvis said, "It's a Nash! "

"Isn't that the car with the—?"

"Yup," Pelvis said. "Why I went Nash. I usually go first class, though."

He smiled impurely, but his face was unable to sustain

the indecent expression. His features diluted the expression until it contained only a mildness which leaned in that direction. His jokes, no matter how crude, were always of anal intensity. He could never be offensively genital, Titania thought uncomfortably, for a timid smile was trying to form on his lips, but he suppressed it even though the feeling of liquid warmth which accompanied the smile was irrepressible.

"You'd be surprised how it comes in handy every so often." Pelvis said, referring to his car. He was mouthing platitudes which held original innuendoes. "Like when I got stuck in Mamou one night. I like to go out in the back country and go to dances on week-ends," he explained. "You'd be surprised how much fun you can have out there, and the food, man, the food is good even if you can't tell what you're eatin' for the gravy."

Titania was there, was experiencing such a night in his mind, but it was a flimsy experience, mostly filled with the exchange of proprieties. They were cussedly polite to each other until the climax of the evening which was an earthy aspect of reality, but experience was on the side of both parties, so what clumsiness there was could be attributed to deliberate tactics of coquetry.

"Where's this track we're going to?"

Pelvis chuckled, then made a box with his free hand. "Don't be—" he said, completing his thought by inscribing the sign of a box in the air. "No track's open at this hour. They run them in the daytime."

"Then where are we going?"

"If we wanna go to the track, we'll have to start out in the afternoon, around one o'clock, if we wanna hit the window 'fore the first race."

"Then where—?"

144

"I thought you might like to take in a different bar or somethin'. They got carhops out here."

Titania found swallowing a thing of the past, but he was not too uncomfortable as long as he kept his fear silent.

"Drinking under the stars," Tit said, soothingly, as a slogan.

"I brought along a pint," Pelvis said, slapping his hip pocket. "Thought we might go a couple before – if I'd known I was goin' to hang one on, I'd of scratched around for more."

Rippling his wallet in a gesture of bravado, Tit disclosed a few bills. He was ashamed of the move after he had made it. Bad form, he thought. When Pelvis intoned his look with hurt, Tit couldn't shelve his wallet quickly enough.

Pelvis pulled his car into the gravelled parking lot. Neon winked shamelessly in the sky. Pelvis pulled to the back of the lot. He twisted the wheel with a short, snappy gesture which skidded the car to a stop as though he were punctuating the long ride with an exclamation point. He blinked his lights from dim to bright several times. A white-uniformed carhop came and bid them an exceedingly polite good evening.

"I just want gin'erale," Pelvis said.

After Titania ordered Seven Up, he suspected the shuffling feet which rattled the gravel was the sound of the carhop's contempt.

They waited.

Tit exploded the silence with, "The night is sultry."

"Yeah," Pelvis agreed, then lit a cigarette.

Tit waited for he knew not exactly what, but whatever it was, it was not forthcoming. In the distance he heard a pure, clear, tinkling sound as though wind were ringing good china. It was an expensive sound which comes only with the best of its kind. The sound was too deep and not reedy enough to be wind.

"What's that?" Tit asked.

"What?" Pelvis asked back, eagerly, glad to shed his silence.

"That sound." Tit listened carefully, placing his ear against the air in the direction of the sound, but the sound did not repeat. He heard a deathless void of silence.

Pelvis strained to listen and, after a brief glimpse of that void, said, "I don't know."

"I didn't hear it that time," Tit said.

"O," Pelvis said. "Well, here it is." He motioned to the carhop who was fastening a tray onto the door.

"I got it," Tit said, groping for his wallet, but Pelvis just chuckled and handed the man a quarter.

"A bucket of ice goes good on a *sultry* night," Pelvis said.

He poured more than a shot into his glass, then asked Tit how much he wanted.

"Lots," Tit said.

Pelvis poured a heap into Tit's glass. Then Tit heard the sound in the distance again. This time it reminded him of some universal metal striking glassware in clear, precise tones.

"There it goes again," Tit said softly, hushed by his own awe.

Pelvis stepped out of the car and walked over to the fence. He paced meditatively, attentively, softly, on guard. The purity of the sound punctured his alcoholic haze. "That's a nightingale," he said, almost disappointed.

"Nightingale?" Tit asked. "I thought they only had them in China."

"Naw, lots of 'em round here. That's the mating call."

How could anything so uninnocent sound so pure, Tit

146

wondered. Then he listened again. "Must be the male," he said. He could only associate such a pure lilt with the male.

"Yeah, always."

The deep, clear sound in the distance overrode the flat, cheap sound of ice clunking their glassware.

"God, listen to him," Pelvis said. He measured the width of his hand by placing it carefully in the space between the edge of the tray and the window brace before he slammed it down with a flump. The sound of the nightingale struck the night in perfect chimes. "Must be all balls, that bird," Pelvis said.

For Titania the sound peeled away a surface sham and revealed an irresistible essence.

He wasn't sure about the rest of the evening. He didn't know if Old Pelvis was in tune with the night, or whether the nightingale had made such an impression on him that he was unable to discern between mood and motive in the evening. Anyway, Pelvis let down. He had been drained of some fluid which had keyed the evening at the pitch of strain. He spoke randomly of his job, of the track, of his favourite drinks. He bragged about how resourceful he was with his leisure. After he made sure that Titania would meet him next Saturday for the races, he let Tit out in front of his apartment . . .

"There's Tit, hopelessly snared," Denis piped, as he watched Tit's vague, dreamy expression betray his thoughts.

"Wake up, wake up, sweet princess of the sigh," Rose beckoned, then warned, "your prince is stalking the bar."

"Cloyed with dreams," Denis cooed. "I don't need the proof of the moment, but, see for yourself, Rose, he is no longer resisting analysis. Shall we try the Rorschach with beer blots or just give him a fleeting couch session? The couch is really more to the point."

147

"I have always preferred the couch to the mess," Rose admitted. "You get a steadier picture."

Titania let them ramble on. He felt secure in his impure silence, impure because he was entertaining thoughts which failed to crystallize, and secure because he was thinking of Old Pelvis.

Old Pelvis pivoted at the bar, swung his gaze in an imperfect arc in Tit's direction. His stare was unmistakable and belied the casualness of the swing, but he did not get through to Tit, so he swung back to the bar. He nudged his way in to set down his glass, but his gestures were brusque and rough, nothing suggestive. He made sure that he didn't infer with his movements, for his sights were set on a single partridge, and none of the hens in his immediate vicinity would do.

"When one surrenders so easily," Denis warned, "one has to be careful. The other one does."

"Why, you've got her with the goods," Rose said. "How can she deny it now?"

Rose and Denis were scheming to expose Titania in as lurid a relationship with Pelvis as they could frame from the evidence, but Rose was too positive of his conjectures and Denis was uncertain of his facts; so, by not combatting them, their doubts could mature. It was better to let them pull each other off the track than for Titania to lead them astray.

Titania's thoughts drifted away from the conversation and clustered around the first Saturday that he went to the races with Old Pelvis. He wore a bright red and blue sport shirt to encourage a brashness which he didn't feel. "Something to ward off the sun," he rationalized, but the gaudy shirt only challenged it. His meekness set up a contrast with the colours of the shirt until his clothes reflected not a siren in good taste but a shy one in bad taste.

Pelvis drove out by the lake and parked in front of a large, white building. Inside, Titania was content to remain at the bar, for it was cast in a familiar gloom. He felt relieved but for the fact that there wasn't as much as a smell of a horse, let alone the sight of a racetrack.

Pelvis moved in at the bar and ordered a whisky. "What you want?" he asked Titania.

Tit shrugged, then ordered a whisky sour.

"You can't drink that all day," Pelvis said. "That sweetness hits me right where I throw up."

Tit ordered whisky and water, which he had wanted anyway.

"That's more like it. Let's start with bourbon."

"Where are the races?" Tit asked.

"I'll take you there in a minute. Thought you wanted to tank up a bit. Awful bother to keep comin' back." Tit yawned.

"'Course we can always drop back to refuel. It's on the other side of that wall there."

Tit's enthusiasm went into a slump. He wished he could get excited over entering a bookie joint and wagering a little money on a horse, but there was nothing in the act which suggested adventure to him.

Pelvis ordered another drink, then started up a conversation with a man in sunglasses who was stationed down the bar. But the man picked up his drink and walked into the other room, through the unmarked door, so Pelvis turned back to Titania and said, "Some drink in there."

Titania was busy interlacing the water rings made by the bottom of his glass when he set it down.

Pelvis arched his back, placed his weight square on the balls of his feet, then finished his drink. "I need another one," he said, "but come on."

They entered the inner sanctum, sanctum because the room was bare but for the blackboard along one wall, a wire cage in the corner which represented the confession box, and chairs scattered around the room, as though a mass meeting of small coteries was being held or subcommittees were caucusing. A stubby blonde was drenched in fur. A man with his shirt sleeves rolled up looked like a postal clerk. Another man in a t-shirt had a pencil stuck behind his ear at a rake angle. It was the angle which detained Titania's gaze and threatened to explode his ennui. His gaze traced the contours of the man's body from the outline of his clothes. The lines were identical, so the man passed the test for boldness. Titania hired him for a job in a mental cigarette ad, outfitted in a swim suit. Tit captioned the ad: Smooth and Gentle, Body and Flavour. All You'll Ever Want in a Cigarette. The model was very accommodating, for he lit a cigarette with a masculine flourish, but he exhaled the first puff of smoke automatically, without displaying any conspicuous relish, so Tit fired him. The man must have sensed his dismissal, for he strolled into the cage and waited on a woman who was impatient for service. When the man suggested something, she raised her voice to make her wishes more exact. The man said "Okay" and tried to soft-pedal her voice. She stared at the ledger until the man had finished writing on it. After she had approved of what he had written, she returned to her chair in front of the blackboard, shuffling some tickets in her hand. Titania thought, She didn't even notice that he was good-looking.

Then Pelvis stepped up to the window and put down ten dollars. When he said something to the man, the man chuckled half-heartedly, obligingly. Pelvis picked up a yellow ticket and sauntered back to Titania. He explained that he had just bet on Come On. "Come on" was the last thing he had said before he had entered the sanctuary, so it was a good idea to follow through and bet on a horse with that name. Playing hunches was one way, he said.

But apparently Come On needed more urging than that which was found in his name, for a few minutes later Pelvis tore up the yellow stub. Titania watched the blackboard as numbers were written after the names, then erased and changed to other numbers. Sometimes checks and exes and circles were added hastily to the front of three names as the scribbling continued across the board. It seemed as though time were more important than clarity.

Pelvis said that he wished he had bet by his numerical method, which was working from the order of the numbers in his licence plate. But when the first three numbers of his licence plate failed to show, he said he should have tried his mathematical equation. This method consisted of subtracting the weight of the rider from the reputation of the horse, then adding or subtracting his lucky number three for weather conditions: a sunny track for a mud horse meant subtraction, but a wet track for a mud horse meant addition. As the numbers cancelled themselves out, the horse with the final figure which approached zero was the one most likely to win. Titania didn't understand it, but he got the general idea that this method was all-inclusive. The direction and velocity of the wind were two variables which had to be checked at the track. Even the jockey's colours were considered important if the horse had a seeming aversion to a particular colour. Since this procedure depended upon information which was at the track, Pelvis relied upon less scientific methods. He bet on long shots to win because that was where the money was. As the afternoon progressed, he began instructing Titania on the gradual method of recouping his losses by betting in the place and show divisions. He let up only to refill his glass with whisky, never failing to include Titania's glass in his trip back to the bar.

"Have a chair," he offered on one of his return trips. "You don't have to stand 'less you want to. I want to," he said.

Titania was too tired to reassemble his bones in another position.

"See that guy in the cage?" Pelvis asked, pointing to the man who had applied for the job in Tit's cigarette ad. "He's a whore runner. Used to be. Had all he could handle and a line block waitin' to get on his list, but he quit. More legit, this is."

"He's got the looks for it," Tit admitted.

"Smart dago," Pelvis agreed.

"Let's eat," Tit said.

"Eat? I ain't hungry. After all that liquor?"

"I want to do something," Tit whined.

"Okay, wait a minute," Pelvis said, walked over to the cage, and whispered something in the bookie's ear. Titania shivered with envy. Pelvis' whole body was sheepishly intoned until the bookie disappeared under the counter and called Pelvis into the cage. Pelvis stayed only long enough to bend down and raise up again, but he waved a friendly thanks to the bookie, then motioned for Titania to fall in step behind him.

"We might as well have one last one before we push on, huh?" Pelvis suggested, then asked the bartender, "Ain't it about time for one on the house?"

The bartender ignored him.

"Hey, bud, I'm talkin' to you. I've been drinkin' in here all day, and I haven't even gotten a little common courtesy."

Pelvis leaned over the bar and watched him fill up a glass with bar whisky. The bartender took his time, set it in front of Pelvis, then took off down the bar. "How 'bout my friend here?"

"No," Tit insisted, "I don't care for any."

"Go on, take it. It ain't nice to refuse."

"No, really, I'm not thirsty."

"Well, how 'bout it?" Pelvis asked the bartender.

"He don't want none. Didn't you hear him?"

"Yeah, but we're goin' to drink it later." When his explanation didn't impress the bartender, he shoved his glass at Titania, then asked the bartender, "Where's mine?"

The bartender poured a short whisky and set it on the bar. Pelvis picked up the glass and walked towards the inner sanctum door. He stopped and motioned for Titania to follow him. Tit did, but he left the full glass of whisky on the bar. Pelvis came back, picked up the long one, then motioned for Tit to take the short one.

"I don't want it," Tit said.

"You don't have to drink it," Pelvis said. "Just hold it for me."

Pelvis downed both drinks in the inner sanctum, placed the glasses on an empty chair, and walked out.

"They're not bad guys," he said, "but you gotta be firm with 'em."

As they headed for the exit, the bartender yelled, "Hey, where's my glasses?"

"Up your ass," Pelvis said.

Outside, Titania felt the early evening dusk as a grey glove for his mood. "You were too good to them," he said.

"O, they're all right," Pelvis said as he plopped into the driver's seat.

"Where'll we eat?" Tit asked, trying to brighten his mood. "I know an Italian restaurant which serves torrone with its espresso."

"Aw, man, don't talk about food when I'm broke."

"Broke?"

"Flat, man, flat. Broken, busted, cleaned, nowhere. Over a hundred smackers smush."

"They got it all?"

"O, I got ten. I borrowed it from that dago." Pelvis slapped the gears in low. "Those dagoes are all right. They help you out when you need it, so I ain't exactly street level."

"No," Tit said, "just ten steps in the basement."

"He'll get it back, don't worry. You eat. I ain't exactly hungry."

Pelvis drove to the Italian restaurant, then plopped himself in a booth with a show of petulance which warned Titania to play the hostess with effusive charm. All through the meal Titania asked him if he didn't want anything, if he were sure that he didn't want anything, and Pelvis said "No" so many times that his voice filed the corners of the word sharply until the word severed the conversation. Still, Titania didn't feel right about eating in front of Pelvis. He thought that Pelvis' pride was stifling his appetite. In a last desperate effort to persuade him to eat. Tit shoved his antipasto towards him.

"I'm thinkin'," Pelvis said, ignoring the antipasto. Titania ordered two beers. "To lubricate your thoughts," he told Pelvis when they arrived.

Pelvis had been absent-mindedly nibbling on the antipasto, so when he saw the beer, he accepted one, but not before he shoved the platter away from him. "This stuff's too salty," he said, reaching for the beer. After gulping at the nozzle of the bottle, he brightened. "I been thinkin' about gettin' in a game over in Charley's back room. He runs a bar in my neighbourhood. I can get in with this ten and probably pick up enough spending money for the rest of the week."

"I don't play cards," Tit said.

"You could watch."

"I've been watching," Tit reminded him.

"Beer tastes good," he said. "What do you want to do."

"O, I don't know." Tit refused to offer a suggestion. He had been doing nothing for so long, all afternoon, that his mind was paralysed.

Pelvis popped a radish into his mouth, then finished his beer.

"Let's go some place else," he said.

"I was thinking about some tortoni or a little gelata, if nothing else."

"I know a place you can get that."

"Why not here?"

"I don't feel right. I don't like the feel I got when I come in here. Ain't that enough?"

His voice complained, but Titania didn't care. In fact, he was enjoying making Pelvis uncomfortable.

"I don't think this place is so bad."

"Then buy me a beer," Pelvis said.

"Buy yourself one. You got money."

"No, I ain't."

"Ten dollars."

"I'm savin' that."

"For card sharks?"

"Yeah, somethin' like that."

"Why not spend it on beer?"

"I don't want one that bad."

"Then thirst."

"I bought you some drinks this after'. No tinhorn beer neither," Pelvis reminded him soulfully.

"Did I ask you to?"

"No, so what? You didn't pass them up, did ya?"

"No, but—"

"I don't like this place."

"Why not? I don't see anything wrong with it."

"Yes, there is. I know the dago which runs it."

"So?"

"So, buy me a beer, and I'll tell ya."

Titania ordered some nougat candy, then bought two beers while he was at it.

"You've been actin' like an old bear ever since we came in here."

"How'm I 'post to act? You didn't lose your loot. Why don't you act like you're sorry or somethin'?"

"We can't both drag. We'll never get off ground." Pelvis smiled, tipped his bottle up, then killed it.

"Let's get out of here," he said.

"What about that dago?"

"He's a big fat clown. You gonna finish that?" He pointed to Tit's half-empty bottle.

"No."

"Then hand it over." After polishing off the remainder of Tit's beer, he said, "Let's breeze."

"What about that dago?"

"O, he used to run a bar down the street."

"What happened?"

"I'll tell ya in the car."

Tit sat sideways in the front seat; one knee poked the back rest while an elbow rested on top of the seat. He was hung there, his hand dangling from the wrist of the raised arm. He assumed the position in order to relieve the effervescence in his blood. Anxious bubbles, like charged water, were acting up, and he needed a spillway to stem the rising current.

"This guy is one of those gobby guys," Pelvis began, "fat like that jerkwater at the club."

"You mean Denis?"

"Yeah, all hands full. He sops up spaghetti like a pig goes to slop – until his heart went bad, and the doc tells him to get into another business, so he rents out his joint and buys into a bar down the street. Now he's always got a bottle of cheap dago at his elbow. I use to go in his joint only after I been everywhere else."

"Never seen it sober, huh?"

"I seen it all ways. I just went in to snag a couple before I called it a night. Two seamen were next to me at the bar talkin' about a girl. Big talk! And I knew, since they was on beer, that they got rolled or took and were just eking it out 'til they got back on the ship. Big talk on beer! So I start askin' questions to catch them up."

"'She let me do anything,' one says, 'and it was all pure pleasure.'

"'So what,' I says. 'That don't mean she was virgin.' He looks at me like I was nuts.

"'Could be,' the other guy says. Then they slide down the bar aways. They make me mad, the ignorant bastids. I moved down towards them, but I couldn't hear so good. Their words were strained and muffled, so I says, 'Speak up, I know –'

"'Who's talkin' to you, anyhow?' this guy barks back, and I says, 'Can't take it, huh? You don't like no back talk to your lies.'

"He turns his back on me, and that really rags me, so I says, 'But there t'weren't no blood.'

"That boiled him 'cause he went right on talkin' low like he hadn't heard, but he was red-necked mad. 'It was just as tight as you please,' he's sayin', so I come back with, 'But there t'weren't no blood!'

"'She wasn't shy, you know what I mean?'

"'T'weren't no blood!' I throws at him. I knew they were gunnin' for a fight. I could tell by the way they egged me on by puttin' me off.

"'I make like I need a beer right after, so when I look and see she ain't got nothin' cold, I breeze.'

"'T'weren't no blood!'

"The guy turns around and gives me a dirty look, then reaches for his beer. He starts talkin' low to his buddy, and I know what they're sayin' without listenin'.

"'Ya gonna shut up?' he asks, and I get ready for him. I fix my feet. But they jab me a couple good ones and run for the door. I grab the guy's beer and heave it – right when they're passin' the juke. They duck, and the juke gets it right in the glass. I explain it to the old dago, but he says he saw me, and that's that. He has me hauled in on a charge and wants thirty-five bucks for repairs.

"'I ain't payin',' I says and spend the night in the pokey. In the morning I give them ten bucks, and they let me off. That's the only time I been jailed and all on account of that dumb dago, too."

"How long ago was this?"

"Was what?" Pelvis asked back.

"This seaman and this girl."

"Just before I met them, I guess. How should I know?"

"I just thought you might. They didn't mention any names?"

"I don't remember. You know him?"

"No! No, of course not. I was thinking of a timid soul I used to know, but I probably only heard about her at the club and didn't know her at all. You know how stories circulate." Titania spoke casually, but his face spoke defiantly: strained, fixed, and intense – until he had suppressed the episode again.

158

He felt the air rush in the window as Pelvis turned the corner, and he was grateful for the distraction. The wind was strong enough to sweep the alarm out of his mind. His nerves tingled. He choked for breath, but Pelvis didn't slow down. The houses flew past, so did the stop signs, and Titania huddled with himself until Pelvis turned a corner and stopped abruptly with the car pulled up next to the kerb, neat and nice, on the wrong side of the street.

"What was that for?" Tit asked.

"A cheap t'rill," Pelvis laughed, putting his arm on the back of Tit's seat.

"Where are we?"

"I live down the block. You want to see it?"

"No."

Pelvis shifted his weight and moved closer, tapping his fingers on the seat. "I don't care—" he started to say but ducked his head and cut himself off with a kiss. Titania tightened up, tried to push Pelvis away, but Pelvis held the kiss until Titania relaxed. "You're soft," he said. "You had me guessin'. First, I thought you were. Then, I didn't know. Well, you want to go in now?"

"No."

"I got a mirror. In just the right place. Ever do it in a mirror?"

"I'm tired."

"It's just like a movie."

"I'm tired."

"How would you like that?"

"I'm tired."

"You don't want to see yourself in a movie?"

"You're deaf. I'm tired."

"You want to go to your place?"

"No, why?"

"I ain't never been. Sorta like to see it."

"Why do you keep up?"

"Why'd you say you were, then? Ya keep itchin' me. I ain't got all night, you know. I gotta get this ten in a game, and I don't have all week to go scratchin' for some. I gotta get it on Saturday night, or the week's wasted."

"What about Sunday?"

"Aw, I don't do nothin' on Sunday. I gotta get up Monday morning."

"You could, if you wanted to badly enough."

Pelvis dropped his hand behind the seat and fumbled with something which clicked a couple of times. The back rest gave way and flattened out. He started wrestling with Titania below the window level.

"I want to bad enough right now," he said, playfully. Tit wiggled away from him. He rapped Tit a couple of times on the arm. He swung and clipped Tit's jaw with his fist. Tit's teeth clicked together. He swung for his head, but Tit was ready for him and ducked, but he wasn't paying any attention to where he was sitting, so when he jerked his head, he smacked it against the window. He was furious, furious with Pelvis for making him duck and furious with himself for misjudging the distance.

Pelvis laughed in two spurts, then tried to bury his head in Titania's shirt.

"I'm going," Tit said, starting to get out of the car.

"I'll drive you home."

"No, you don't have to."

"I'd drive you home, but I don't have time. I have to get over to that game."

"Where's the bus?"

"Over there on the far corner. Any bus that way," he motioned.

160

"Thanks," Tit said, lacing the word with sarcasm.

"You mad?"

"No, I'm not mad."

"At me?" he asked again.

"No, not at you. Just sober up."

Tit dragged across the street until Pelvis was out of sight. Then he skipped the rest of the way. When the bus arrived, Titania waltzed on. He paid his seven cents with several flourishes, one flourish for each coin, then took a seat in the middle of the bus. When he noticed that people were staring at him, he passed his hand over his head in a nervous gesture, only to discover that his hair was mussed. His smug smile ignited the envy in their eyes, as they were trying to discover what all the rumple was about, but he only smiled again, this time lightly, suavely, curiously.

Titania took the glaze off his stare.

"I see the princess is back with us again," Rose announced. "Toot, toot, red carpet and all that. How was the turret this time? Had I known I'd be casting for the Lady in the Lake, I would have worn my doublet and pourpoint. Or, perhaps, a swim suit, would have done the trick – some trunks which were fashioned from some precious skin: my own."

"I'm Hector," Denis said, jogging in place, "bouncing off boulders while bound to the back of Achilles' chariot as he rounded Troy. And all on account of Patroclus, too. That selfish! "

"You just wish you were," Tit advised.

"You look like you swallowed a couple too many boulders, Hector."

"O, this? This is my armour," Denis admitted, jiggling his jelly.

"But did you have to swallow it?"

"Well, yes," Denis said, curling his hands in the air as if they were smoke caught in an updraft. "I wanted the world to bloom in wild cherries, thin-skinned but, O, so red, so gorged with blood." He opened his palms. They blossomed, all pink and white, on the ends of his arms which were stalks. Then he tightened his fists and constricted the blossoms. "I needed pits to sow," he said.

"I know just what you mean," Rose said. "You were thinking double."

"No," Denis said coyly.

"Backwards?"

"No."

"Upside down?"

"At least! And while the world was turning, too. That made it difficult."

"How ghastly, but a new position is nice once in a while."

"It strengthens the antagonistic muscles, they say," Denis said.

"Do tell us about it," Rose urged.

"Strenuous but nice, that sort of thine."

"You're impossibly vulgar," Tit told them.

"It bothers you?" Denis wanted to know.

"No, of course not!" Tit said loudly, but his conviction wobbled when he choked on a sigh.

"That's all I wanted to know," Denis said. "I just wanted to find out if you were thinking about Pelvis, that's all. And now I know. If he were thinking about Pelvis, such talk wouldn't bother him, which he has led us to believe is the case. Pelvis can't rise above the lowest common denominator of smut, so Tit should be used to it, but since he said that it didn't bother him but acted as if it did with that sigh, you may think, Rose, that that disproves my theory, but it

162

does no such thing. It doesn't mean that he wasn't thinking about Pelvis. It just means that he was out to deceive us into thinking that he wasn't. Isn't that right, sweet princess of the sigh? Ruptured thigh is more like it."

"Stop trying to muscle, Denis," Tit said, trying to counter-attack with gall.

"Who me? On that runt of a rhino?"

"Runt, perhaps, but still a rhino."

"Darling, you know I have sex on the tip of my tongue always, but, alas, hardly ever on the tips of my fingers!"

"Don't try that. Self-pity is just a ruse with you, Denis. You haven't any self."

"What do you call this?" Denis asked, flapping his flab.

"Soiled snow, dirty rain in a freeze, a lump of extraneous matter."

"I'll lump your matter," Denis told Rose.

"Don't act tough. On you it looks impossible."

"Better impossible than what it looks on you, Rose. Ridiculous!"

"When was the last time, Denis?" Rose asked.

"You all remember Daniel, don't you? Well, I suppose you would say that he was the last – steady. There's a difference."

"I meant the last one!"

"The last time? The last time I was all Valhalla at Bayreuth."

"Do tell us about Brunhilde," Rose begged.

"Well, Brunhilde was just in off the sea. I'd itemize his disasters if they weren't so tedious, but disasters in groups are so over-boring."

"You mean overbearing?"

"That, too. He had just had an operation, and he couldn't return to his ship until the incision had healed. Now isn't

163

that a fix? You can be sure that I didn't view the predicament entirely without heart. I saw a slim chance of helping this Ulysses through his nth adventure."

"You Circe you!"

Denis smiled absorbently.

"You know how some men have a certain quality in their flesh which makes it the glowing essence of virility, a manly nimbus?" Denis asked, then didn't wait for an answer. "A hard skin surface, like taut silk, which gives the muscles underneath a rippling underplay? Like muscles in silk pyjamas, you know. Well, he was one. Something shimmering about his flesh. Of course, his features were mature, yet young, not misshapen with age, and perfectly proportioned with the rest of him, and the crowning glory is always the fresh tragedy, like an operation. Misfortune always seems to set the jaw, inflame the eyes with cunning, and deepen the colours of pity by a few degrees as though the painting were touched up by Corot – one of his fresh mornings, fresh with drear – and the madness of Utrillo – shabby, bleak, grand in muddy shades of violet and sulky shades of red and blue-back. But he was a cheat, you might know. Any other time Fate would have been the personification of kindness to set such a dish before a queen, but now? Not now. When I had the chance to revel to my heart's content, Fate had to make an incision."

"The operation?"

"Yes, it was rectal."

"O, my God!"

"I had to make allowances, that's all. I couldn't let personal preferences spoil the evening. I was too far gone. I was sure that God Himself would burst from that flesh once it was ignited."

"There's something awful about it, Denis."

164

"Awful, hell, it's downright discouraging."

"Did he ever come back?"

"No," Denis said without a hint of emotion in his voice.

"I almost wish he had," Rose said. "It doesn't matter to me either way of course, actually, you understand. I certainly wouldn't want him to come back just so you could revel, but that is a shame, too, in its own small way, but I wish he would return so I could finish the dream which you started in my head. That is truly sad."

"There goes your old flame again, Rose. Always trying to fire-ize yourself, but you didn't tell me that you had converted to gas!"

"Your bitterness is total, Denis."

Titania sat in the booth, facing Rose, but, by looking around Rose, he could watch Old Pelvis at the bar and make those in the booth think that he was looking at Rose and was following the conversation. When Rose saw Titania looking in his direction, he thought that the princess had abdicated her tower, had deserted her turret. But Titania's look only paved the way for his thoughts to mature into dreams. There was nothing complete about his silence, nothing resembling solitude. His silence wasn't even quiet. It was turbulent, flopping from his likes to his dislikes of Pelvis.

Tit saw Denis' hospitalized friend as Old Pelvis, but the misery in Pelvis' eyes was not soft as it was in the other man's eyes. Nor was it tender. It was hard and agatelike from the continual rush of events which had reacted upon his emotions as water reacts upon wood. Tit applied a leisurely gait to his body, then arrested that motion by removing Pelvis to the beach with his mind. Now Pelvis was a reclining nude on the sand, etched with a few strokes of grass (he was back on the sea wall) and a backdrop of the sea, Lake Pontchartrain, a shallow slate colour which, as the lake deepened, drifted into a flat blue. A hot wind came from nowhere (from the back of Tit's mind) and freshened the landscape, giving it the apotheosis of desire. Pelvis adjusted his trunks to satisfy the severest requirements of the most avid sun bathers. He rolled them down until the top of his buttocks was exposed, then rolled the short leg holes up until a narrow bunch of cloth, almost a line, was all that remained of his suit. He faced Titania in order to use Titania's body as a shield. Titania's body was lying long like a low fence. Pelvis was not completely reft of shame as the narrow strip of cloth testified, being the length and the breadth of his shame.

After glancing in his direction, people drifted into the water or picked up their belongings and wandered down the beach. Soon, Titania realized that they were virtually alone on the beach. Wide expanses of nothing were on both sides of them.

Pelvis rolled over on his back, then squirmed. His body contracted. Solid but supple, Tit thought. He became aware of how Pelvis' body had not deteriorated with age as his face and head had. Vague shapes formed a queue across his mind in a wash of tears: Pelvis' former lovers. Then his eyes focused on the casual arrangement of hair on Pelvis' chest. Pelvis was now lying on his back with his knees bent, forming a two-sided cabana, or an arbour in a summer garden. He had flipped over to tug at his trunks. The narrow line of his suit was binding. His hair wasn't' luxurious or even ample, but it was carefully arranged in order to cover a large area with a small outlay. It curled abundantly, though, and it was black. Saying that it was black as Titania bought black was a misleading assumption. It was like mixing two ingredients which appear identical but which have radically

166

different properties. Titania's black was a stark, raving, blazing black, an effect which was achieved by surrounding the dark colour with a dead white background such as the colour of Titania's skin, a black which was the very essence of a state induced by pentathol without the enforced relaxation which accompanies it, that black transfixed with terror. The magnetism was too great, too compelling, to permit the slightest deviation from the black essence.

Pelvis pulled at his jockstrap and tried to relieve his discomfort. He rolled over on his side and faced Titania, unconfined. The supporter was flesh-coloured; it resembled an extraneous loop of skin.

"It does it good," Pelvis said. "The sun makes it tough!"

Titania would have said "The sun makes it hard." He knew that it was incorrect, but he thought, hard, anyway, to dispose of his feelings. In this way he aligned hardness with toughness (his thought of hardness and Pelvis' declaration of toughness) as if hardness thickened the toughness and gave it the dimension of depth. He knew that the toughness was real because he had felt it on those nights when he had worn the gown of the bitch, but the toughness had always been on others. Primarily, on Pelvis. As he thought hardness, his brain converted the thought into feeling. Titania's feeling of hardness was nothing more than a splayed thought which his body could sneak under and camouflage itself. His brain flowered and unfurled petals which covered him with hardness, for his brain was a stone flower. But, when he looked at Pelvis to confirm his theory of transubstantiation, he saw that his brain was unable to support the weight of his thoughts, for he was unable to maintain the hardness. He touched his skin accidentally, and it betrayed him. It contained an unsuspected layer of fatty tissue, as, at other times, when he revelled in the softness of his body, he was

167

betrayed once more by desire which intruded rigidly. But this time his thought had softened, as soft as his brain, for Pelvis had smiled a black smile, and the attraction was still there as real and as alive as ever – an electric magnetism which had the power to derealize concrete . . .

"I can't imagine what's wrong with me," Denis admitted grandly but padded his words with a dubious sincerity. "I'm overwrought, taut as a you-know-what string on a harp." Then, before anyone could hypothesize, Denis helped himself to the plethora of theory which was available. "It's exercise, I guess. I rarely admit this to anyone since the very thought takes considerable energy on my part and so liquidates my spirit, but even I contend that a little romp is good for the corpuscles once in a while. Lets them knock around a bit and stretch their ectoplasm. Really quite invigorating if you happen to have a good catalyst. By the way, Tit, have you ever thought of turning catalyst?"

"Good pay?" Rose asked.

"The pay is excellent, Rose, if you qualify." /

"What?" Tit asked, only half-hearing Denis' proposition, but he got the drift of it. He recovered his perspective and placed it in the booth. "No, not me. It sounds too much like analyst."

Rose smiled.

"Titania is not about to let her altruism run away with her, Denis. Not that she isn't generous, but she *is* selective. I always say that selectivity hangs together, being always very selective myself."

"Ho-ho," Denis spit. "You can't watch anyone bend over without getting it in your head that he's flirting with you. Selectivity, indeed !"

Titania resumed his indifference as well as his position and looked beyond Rose to where Pelvis was at the bar. Pelvis stepped back from the bar and distinguished himself from the crowd. His isolation was significant, for he waved his arms in the air as if he were demonstrating some crucial point in a conversation with someone at the bar, supposedly, but Titania couldn't see the con- end of the –versation. Pelvis' actions, stretching his arms in order to stretch his shirt across his back or shadow- boxing strenuously with an imaginary foe, reminded Tit of his preliminary sex antics when he would use his need for exercise as a feeble excuse to exhibit his muscles or a desire to wash his back as an excuse to remove his shirt while Tit was occupied elsewhere in the bathroom.

Rose, who was watching Titania but talking to Denis, smiled eagerly and misinterpreted the gaze which Titania lavished upon Old Pelvis. He leaned towards Titania and confided sweetly, "You look positively ravishing tonight, honey, and you caught me at just the right time. I knew it would show. I can't help it. I don't weigh much, and my flesh is negligible, so it's impossible for me to conceal anything. I don't really give a damn, but it brings on so many unsolicited offers which simply don't interest me – like Denis, that bloated goat. She's drooling this minute, but, as I said, you're in luck. I just happen to be free this evening."

Titania didn't answer, except to look exceedingly uncomfortable. He drew himself up into a knot, then waited for an invisible shield to drop between his body and Rose's intentions before he rejoined the group. But Denis was never at a loss for anything as easily to come by as words. He brought the issue out into the open.

"Who's gonna take Titania home?" he asked. "I don't mean to rush things, but I just thought that I would put in my bid since it is the early bird which catches the worm fresh with dew, if you like yours with dew like I do, the dew of tears for the last, late, lamented, lucky copulator."

"You flatter me, lovelies. It just so happens that I need a bath desperately," Tit said. "I've been terribly negligent lately, and I wouldn't want you to suffer that."

"Don't worry," Denis said. "I always stock detergent for emergencies."

"I'm afraid detergent wouldn't help. I need a week's soak in a hot tub."

"Don't fret. I don't mind, really. I'll just chalk it up to flavour."

Rose held back. He had been puzzling the situation for the right approach. "I suppose I could make an exception," he said, "but you understand that I only do it for special cases."

"Don't put yourself out, dearie," Denis jeered.

"O, Rose," Titania said, with his gaze flirting about looking for a means of escape. His gaze didn't land on anyone for long, but it did hesitate significantly as it buzzed over Pelvis' head. "I didn't mean a bath, exactly. It's my cavities which are giving me trouble."

"Cavities? What cavities?" Rose flinched.

"I fill all cavities gladly," Denis offered, "free of charge, sight unseen."

"I have a couple of lulus which are plaguing me with a breath which is ossifying."

"That's all right," Denis said, unfazed. "I've been bowled over before, and, if you breathe just right, we might be able to turn your misfortune to our advantage."

"You lie beautifully, Tit," Rose whispered, then turned on Denis. "Can't you see that she doesn't want to have anything to do with your fat attentions?"

"O, I don't know. She didn't say so," Denis said.

"Jealous? You're over-upholstered, Denis. You should travel in your own class."

"You mean heavyweight?"

"No, overweight!"

Titania's gaze trembled, then fled to the bar for shelter, but Pelvis still lurked as the only possibility.

"You girls know that I haven't been feeling well lately. It must be the weather and so forth and so on and so be it. You admitted yourselves that I haven't been able to keep up with the social events of the season. Why, you've hardly seen me at all. Well, I didn't want to tell you this, but" – Rose and Denis leaned forward to absorb his confidence – "my system has not been all that it should be."

"None of us is perfect," Rose conceded.

Then Titania knew that it was time to employ a last resort, for if Rose didn't mind, then no one would. He gasped as if struck by a sudden attack. "See?" he asked, fleeing to the john in a flurry of made-up apprehension. After he lost himself in the crowd around the bar and approached Old Pelvis, he steered his course to one side. Pelvis was alert but respected the deviated course. Still, he leaned into Titania's patch to provide an opportunity for grazing, but he did not insist.

Tit felt a tug in Pelvis' direction, but it didn't deter him. It just tested the ground before he stepped on it. Tit went to the john. On his way back to the booth, he collided with Pelvis, who had moved into the aisle to commit himself fully.

"Pardon me," Tit said.

"How ya been?" Pelvis asked.

"O, fine, I guess," Tit said.

"Ready for a beer? I am."

"So am I," Tit said. "Won't you join us?" He motioned towards the booth.

"I'll get the beer," Pelvis said.

Titania walked back to the booth and slid into his seat across from Rose and Denis.

"Feel better?" Rose asked, and Denis said, "I swear by Kayopectate myself. It does a snappy job."

Titania laughed, but not at the joke. His laugh bubbled up from a geyser inside him which erupted his relief.

"Well, as I was saying, the issue is still before us. Now that you've had time to caucus with yourself, what did your charming self come up with?" Rose asked, smiling sweetly.

"Well," Titania began, stalling, but he didn't have to stall for very long as Pelvis was standing in front of the booth with a bottle in each hand. Titania welcomed him, but Denis frowned and let a remark slip. "Some people don't know when they're not wanted."

Rose's hope tempered the remark. "Why, I don't believe I've had the pleasure."

"I'm surprised," Denis jeered. "This is *Old* Pelvis, and if he's not in your league, he's at least in your generation."

"O, don't mind Denis. He always has a burr up about something. Pleased, I'm sure," Rose said, extending his hand.

With a secure grip on the bottle, Pelvis waved a beer in Rose's direction.

Rose pardoned him profusely, then made little of the fact that he had bought only two beers. It was Denis who inflated the discourtesy.

"There are three ladies here," Denis said, but Pelvis slipped in next to Tit and started talking about some matter which was of little interest to any of them, including Pelvis.

Denis listened in, but he couldn't make anything out of it.

Then Titania said, "Well, it doesn't look like much is cooking tonight, so I think I'll wander on home."

"I was thinking the same thing," Denis rushed to agree. "Goin' my way, Tit?"

"I think I'll just mosey on," Tit said.

"Want a ride?" Pelvis asked, pointing his question at Titania.

"Don't mind if I do," Denis said, keeping his big toe in, which was any toe on Denis.

"Are you going that way?" Tit asked. "I wouldn't want to put you out."

"Yeah, I am. I'll drop you off," Pelvis said.

"See you girls," Tit said, drifting out the door with Old Pelvis.

"What gall!" Denis shouted.

"I'm certainly glad I'm not a tart!" Rose said.

"It just goes to show. I was right all the time. I knew they were going together, but I couldn't get Tit to admit it."

"Are you satisfied now?" Rose asked outlandishly.

"I should be," Denis said. "That little bit of foul play proves everything, but I don't feel quite right. I feel let down."

"I should think so!" Rose scoffed. "It's all your fault. You're responsible for the whole mess. If it hadn't been for you, I would have scored long ago."

"Me! What did I do? If you thought you could've done better, why didn't you try? You and your feeble agreements! Your dying insistence not to offend. You're impossibly naive for one so old. You've been fucked weary, my dear, and life escapes you as it always has."

"Go ahead, blame me! You're ignorant, Denis. You're fat enough to be impregnable, but you're not. Invincibility comes with strength, not bulk, and you're nothing but mass."

"Look who's talking. You don't have to demean yourself

for me, you know. I don't give a damn which way you point. You think I care to listen to your tripe night after night? Just talk, that's all you are. Just talk and a lot of balk. You're full of shitshat!"

"Now who's demeaning themself?" Rose asked, struggling to slip past Denis, but Denis squared away his bulk and prevented the escape.

"Going some place?" he asked snidely.

"It will do you no good, I assure you. Keeping me here against my will is no way to prove your desirability, ha!"

"Then ask like a lady."

"Where's the gentleman?" Rose wanted to know.

Denis moved as if to show him, but Rose slipped under the table and started to crawl out.

Denis kicked blindly, and Rose yelped. When Rose was free of the booth, he charged. He slapped the fat boy with wild misses. Denis struggled out of the booth and attacked with the slow moving fury of a tank. Rose tried to butt Denis in the stomach with his head, but Denis grabbed his head and twisted his neck. Rose screamed. Heads at the bar turned and focused their attention on the fight. A circle formed around the combatants, and clouds of laughter billowed up as Rose clawed and spat and Denis swung wildly and whined when he missed. Denis got it in the eye and covered his face with his hands. Then Rose pushed him over, and he fell thudding to the floor. Rose kicked him in jabbing fits. Denis grabbed Rose's foot and wrenched him off balance. He crawled on top of Rose and applied the full weight of his body. Rose struggled to free himself, but all he could muster was an awkward pelt which missed its mark. When Denis started his hips in motion, the crowd cheered.

"She's gettin' it now."

"Takin' is more like it."

"You mean he's gettin' his."

"I didn't think he had it in him."

On one of the upward thrusts Rose turned on his side and knifed Denis with his pelvic bone. While Denis howled, Rose wiggled out from under him. Rose blushed, but it was only a summons to rally his strength. He started scratching Denis, who was still puffing on the floor, trying to sit up, but he never got the chance, for Rose knocked him down, stiff-armed him, then scratched him some more. Finally, Rose shot to his feet and lorded it over Denis, who tried to grab Rose's foot and give it a

Hip, but Rose side-stepped and proclaimed loudly, "That ass! I would have won more if I had stooped to his dirty tricks, but I prefer the slim victory of a lady. Who does she thinks she's foolin', anyway?" And Rose scooted off, waving his arms gaily. Denis sat up on the floor and shook his head to shed the daze which had overcome him. He braced his hands and feet in preparation for his body to be hoisted to his feet by a group of sympathizers who were forming the derrick.

Titania wandered willy-nilly through conversation and scene as if he were propelled by an icy wind.

One night, he spoke indifferently to Rose.

Rose thought, kindly.

"I never should have come out tonight, Tit. The weather is cold and damp, and the odds are pitifully against the aged on a night like this. I should have stayed in my room and finished my dream. I dreamed that I was the Little Dipper. I was the Little Bear roaming the sky in search of the Big Bear, and when I found him, I palpitated all over the place, but when we collided, all we did was clank like a couple of empty tin buckets. What does it mean when your dreams fail to climax? It's like an orgasm without feeling. You know what I mean?"

Rose didn't wait to find out.

"The weather! Mardi Gras always has the worst weather of the entire year. It's a plague, and I know I'll miss the ball at Sparafucile's. I suppose it doesn't really matter, for the best place for me is home in bed with my afghan pulled tightly around my fading shoulders. Besides, I don't know what to come as. I've run out of ideas. But it never fails, Tit, always the worst week of weather."

"Nature has to make the decision of whether or not to be born again," Tit tried to explain. "It's the change from winter to spring, and sometimes it's a tough decision to make. One season, all winter all year, has its points. The cons for spring often outnumber the pros, for hibernating is an awful temptation, and, if the cons don't outnumber the pros, they usually outrank them."

"O, I knew that," Rose said. "I didn't think of it as a question, that's all. I don't want to ask any more questions."

Titania roamed off and left Rose with the early part of the evening, the only part which he allowed himself out of his room these days. Rose bought a beer but didn't dare drink it as it would reveal his trembling hands. He kept his hands in the pockets of an overcoat which he wore, indoors and out, to hide his shaking body.

He gazed with little wonder at the passing crowd. Some, some of the older ones, acknowledged him with a wave, a remark, or a smile, but the smiles saddened him, for they were always reft of passion.

His complexion had faded from white to too white. His pallor had deepened. He attributed it to too much

With his hankie poised in his least shaky hand, he waited for the cough. When the cough came, he rushed the hankie to his mouth and patted his lips dry, openly acknowledging the red as lipstick stains.

"I really must try some of that new, stay-put kind," he said aloud to no one.

Rose placed himself at one of the tables which had been installed for the evening. The table was nothing more than one centre leg which supported a small, unpainted, plywood top and provided room for one beer or, at the most, two. The table resembled an oversized tack which had been stuck in the floor, and Rose's beer, his lone beer, sat untouched on the head of the tack.

He watched the masqueraders as they danced and drank, pushed and shoved. He believed that it was indeed a good year. Never had he seen such loveliness. He was glad he came, after all, especially since he had missed last year's, on account of Louise, then, and he hadn't felt like coming this year because of his ceaseless hacking and that damn Yankee weather, or so he told Titania after he stopped her and said, "Tit, darling, do be an angel and help me to the john."

Titania offered his arm, then commented upon Rose's disguise, which was pathetically realistic.

"Now, Rose, really, how did you think of it?"

Rose thought that it was positively brilliant to come as an old lady, too. He wore long cotton skirts, a tignon tied fetchingly under his chin, and a cumbersome afghan draped around his shoulders.

"The afghan is part of the costume," he explained. Then, snuggling deeply into the afghan and hugging it gratefully, he cursed and complained of the cold. "This weather! Really, Tit, in all my days I've never seen it so brutally cold."

Tit nodded but fanned his face with a little parchment fan.

"It's mad, Tit, mad, isn't it? I mean, the ball."

"Fabulously fabulous," Tit said.

After they returned from the john, Tit left Rose coughing into his hankie.

The costumes were layers of silk upon silk. Salome was there. Mata Hari slinked down the bar in his work clothes: a cloud of *négligé*. Kwin-yins were rampant, and even Madame de Pompadour put in an appearance until his wig toppled.

Oliver Cromwell fidgeted with her fingers as long as she was on the losing end of an argument with the Dauphin, a Renaissance fop, and Charles the First, but she settled down and made herself comfortable after she found a niche at the end of the bar which was ideally suited for lopping off the heads of beers as they passed.

Heavy cloth introduced lesbians, and the frailer materials were manoeuvred by the truly dainty.

The cowboy mosied with his pardner, the sailor hornpiped with his gob, the lumberman drank with his jack, and the gangster plotted with his accomplice. A physical culturalist brought his shadow.

Early in the evening an Egyptian motif condescended to waltz with a robot.

Someone was dancing with Martha Washington, whose blowsy rotundness was not confined to his costume alone. His complexion was as white as his wig, and rouge had congealed on his fat cheeks like two blotches of blood which had fallen on snow, freshly fallen snow, but that was the extent of his purity, for he manoeuvred his bustle, which was large and incredibly real, like a tart, like the wanton woman he was. The broad movement of his ass might be construed as gluttony, but in a lighter and more distinguished age it would be construed as gaiety.

"You dance divinely," Martha Washington implored.

"That's 'cause I'm Christ," said Jesus Christ, a frail wisp of a man whose complexion was a deft shade of tubercular white.

The crass naivete of some of the masqueraders was appalling. It was clearly evident in the three who came as Jesus Christ. There were other Christs as well, but they were barely distinguishable from each other. Some, some of the fat ones, yellowed their bellies and came as Buddhas. But the effectiveness of each costume was dimmed by the presence of others in almost identical attire.

One poor Christ was a mess. It was difficult to tell that he was Christ at all. He had come in modern dress. He dropped benign smiles on everyone, and when he patted the Buddhas on the back, he said he didn't mind the yellow goo which stuck to his fingers. He had groomed his hair for weeks, and he carried a palm leaf which was noticeably green. His modesty prevented him from wearing anything but the most conventional attire, so he was vague, all too encompassing, and always looking ahead. No one believed his disguise. His detractors charged that his jokes were incomprehensible and had roots in the evening, so he retired to a corner and sulked out the night.

A lesbian came as a lumberjack. Her colourful red and black shirt proclaimed her lust, and her moustache was etched in bold strokes. Her jeans were skin-tight, almost hypodermic, and for a stunning effect she had strapped a banana to the inside of her thigh. She subjected Titania to the dance.

Titania was an instantaneous success. His costume was novel, ingenious, and fully realized. Sir Denis said that it was crass egotism which made him do it. Burnished Rose labelled it "Simple gall." He dabbed his lips with his hankie

179

when he coughed it. And Minerva tossed it off lightly, though a bit enviously, as, "It's psychological, my dears. He'll be couched before the evening is o'er."

Titania was pure sensation. He came as himself. He had stretched pink tulle over fine wires which had been fashioned in the shape of wings and had been fastened inostensibly to his shoulders. His wings got in his way, hindered him from moving on the dance floor, but he didn't mind, for he loved the brushing of the whirling skirts against the delicate wing mechanism. He thought that the wires were antennae which established contact with others and made it possible for him to close his eyes and still know that he was real, for he communicated with the brush of his wings. A sparkling golden tiara, as fake as his wings, was suspended over his head by a stick which was fastened to a wire which girdled his skull. He was a sensation of grace and incorporated a lightness into every gesture which hinted at things cosmic.

"I wish I were a lady with such delicate tastes and fine sensibilities," the lumberjack confessed as Titania dipped low in the dance and incited the envy of the most graceful luminary.

Someone stopped Denis to goose him with a verbal thrust.

"Hey, fart, whatever became of your art?"

"O, haven't you heard, turd? I had to give it up. All on account of that slut, Titania, and stubbornness. His! I did so want to compose an epic on his affair with Pelvis. It had such cute possibilities which swelled to the sheer and veritable immensity of life, but Tit clammed up, so I was barred from research. I would have gone mad if a new theory hadn't just happened along. I decided that one had to live fully, and, to do that properly, I had to discontinue writing. There is no time to reflect on what has already happened, living a moment twice is not for me, so writing became redundant. Your question is a bit passé, but it was nice of you to ask. By the way, are you doing anything special tonight?"

"Yeah, lookin' for somethin' special."

"O, well, just thought I'd ask. I am only fat."

And, like a bloated bloodhound, Sir Denis waddled off to the john.

Glances were exchanged, and bodies bubbled like newly popped magnums of champagne. Their breaths canted whimsy and insinuated that the world was good.

Two speculators were squeezed in next to Rose's table, so he leaned over to listen. It gave him an opportunity to prop up his head with his hands. But from Rose, subdued by the clamour of the group, came a perfect cry of pain and ecstasy. The cry was accompanied by a nauseous giddiness and announced by a trumpet cough, a spot of blood, and a single, blinding flash of light, all white.

"What did you say?" asked one of the speculators at the next table.

"I said, 'Have it your way. Shall we dance?'"

When Black and Nickie walked out of the john, Sir Denis was waiting by the door with a bottle of beer in his hand.

"Well, fuck me double," Denis screamed, "if it isn't Aphrodite Schultz, in person."

Denis poured the beer over Nickie's head and repeated the name "Aphrodite" solemnly.

Aphrodite looked up, smiled coyly, then spoke reproachfully.

"Shit, girl, that's no way to treat a lady."

Aphrodite pushed his way to the bar, nudged a butt off

a bar stool with his quivering behind, then adjusted his composure by brushing off the beer with tiny flicks of his fingers.

Some teddy bear pushed in beside him.

"How 'bout it?" asked teddy.

"Talk to me," Aphrodite pleaded.

"What's there to talk about?"

"O, I don't know, anything."

"I can't," said the great, big, beautiful man.

"Then, no! Does that answer your questions?"

The teddy bear answered his by pushing his way down the bar.

Aphrodite looked after him lovingly. He wanted to call him back, but he hung his head instead. He knew the moment had passed. That split second when two worlds meet head on and collide had been averted. The probability of a celestial merger had seemed immense, but the timing had been off, and the planets had glanced off each other. Spinning in their own orbits, they whirled into space in opposite directions, never to meet again, never to know if two lonely planets can merge and make one less lonely one.

The night raced on into the dark sky, intent only on burning itself out. Meteors burst in pure flashes of colour while stars flaunted their fiery brilliance. White against black, black against white, and all the colours in between whirled, twirled, swirled, and were consumed in their own fire: Saturn in red, Venus in yellow, and someone in blue. Planets clashed, pushed and shoved, speeded up and idled by in their celestial orbits. The more magnetic bodies attracted vagabond moons. Stealing stray moons was sport among planets. Comets fulminated and soared into the night. In their haste to descend, they glanced off one another and gave off sparks. Some were on their first flight. Others were on their last. But always the heavens were full of skyrockets.

It seemed as though Denis had just stooped over and whispered in Titania's ear, but actually it happened several days later.

"It was right over there," he confided, "some time during the masquerade."

He pointed to a spot, and Tit pictured Rose sprawled there, strangely mangled.

"But what happened?"

"During one of his periodic sweep-outs through the night, the darky found Rose among the broken glass, and, like the glass, he was unable to recognize her former shape from her present condition. I identified her from the shreds of her costume. You remember that afghan she wore? Outrageous as it was, it did come in handy, after all."

"It always was functional," Tit told Denis as he recalled Rose snuggling in it on the night of the masquerade, a warm spring night.

"Well, Rose apparently fainted some time during the heat of the ball, from some undisclosed cause, undetermined, too, and while on the floor he was trampled by different hooves, spiked French heels, not heavy with femininity," he scoffed, "but heavy with a determination towards that end. You know, the girls. Cleats also disfigured Rose. They were ragged, worn rough by the urgent necessity to sound virility. So, Rose's flesh submitted to imprint. His mouth was open, and the corners of his mouth went in the opposite direction of his eyes which went up. His nose went in, his jaw sideways, and his skull hedged, for it was both lumped and dented. Frankly, it looked as though he were trying to make a last desperate effort to escape from something which

183

was approaching from I don't know where since he tried to escape in six different directions at once, but the look on his face was the record of a frozen moment, preserved at the height of its feeling."

"Knock it off, Denis. Get to the point."

"Well, I'll rally simple words to convey the rather complicated emotion which I saw on his face."

Tit raised his impatience to a higher power.

"Well, his face reported simply that he had seen a vision but had not liked what he saw."

"Rose always did sit in his own typhoon," Tit said, then wondered if he had said Rose or himself. He wondered who had coloured the dream more, or if either of them really had; then all his thoughts were flooded off of their moorings by one big wave which inundated his conscience: flight, flee, fly . . .

Rose died, and Denis was grateful, grateful to Rose for dying, for the death gave him an opportunity to circulate, a chance to dispatch the details of a sudden tragedy. Denis even explained it to perfect strangers. He cornered a seaman at the bar, encircled him with words, these words: "Of course, we're all broken up over it, really. Quite, quite crushed. There's no explaining it. Her destiny promised so little. It wasn't even of the pigeonhole variety, let alone a hint of the grandiose. Not at all the sort of thing you'd care to sing chansons over. O, she gave nice parties in her way, when the mood struck her, and she was unselfish in a selfish sort of way, but that isn't the sort of thing which moves me to eulogy. Frankly, it's for the best. She wasted herself on her opportunities. It's about time they cleaned some of the deadwood out of this joint."

"Never knew her," the seaman said dryly.

"Well, then, it doesn't mean much to you. Actually, I suppose I was hit the hardest. You see, she was my best friend, but we had a tiff just before the accident."

"Accident?" the seaman asked. "Smash-up?"

"No, just a fight."

"Fight?"

"Yes, but you can't tell it now. Sparafucile is very tidy in those matters. He doesn't like to have personal grievances clog the vestibule."

"Don't look like no fight here," the seaman said after he examined the bar for evidence, for fresh wounds. "Not lately nohow."

"Of course not, that's the charm of Sparafucile's. You could entertain a holocaust in this joint and not know it the next night."

"I should have dropped in sooner," the seaman said, shaking his head with regret.

"Yes, it was almost like Rose refused to succumb to the Lenten season. The soufflé was her fight, her refusal to relinquish desire, even though *her* desire had become quite seedy, had there been seed, less than seedy, just chaff!"

"Sorry I missed it."

"You're just in time for the funeral, though," Denis said. "I'm going. Must. But a crew of seamen couldn't get me to touch the coffin. Familiarity breeds something,

I don't know exactly what. I'm not even going to catch the bouquet, funeral wreath, or whatever. Bad omen!"

"When did she kick?"

"Over the week-end."

"Then I didn't miss it by much," the seaman said as though the thought held some consolation for him; then he started to wander down the bar.

"But I haven't told you what happened yet?" Denis cried.

185

It didn't matter if his statement was a question or not, for it was the desperation in his voice which elevated his tone. "I thought – all the gory details . . ."

But the seaman didn't hear. Or if he did, he paid no attention.

"An event! How can anyone be so casual about an event?" Denis wondered, then drifted into a group of girls who looked appreciative.

"Rose has been satanized," he announced dryly.

Hands groped to stifle surprise or to muffle shock.

"You mean she shelved her ass?" asked one of the first to recover.

Denis nodded.

"I knew she wouldn't last the season."

"She didn't even make it to spring."

"Christ left in the spring, you know."

"So what has that to do with Rose?"

"She probably had to be different, had to make her own Easter."

"Don't worry, they'll never resurrect that! "

"Don't be too sure," Denis warned, then drifted away on the crest of his enthusiasm.

Denis spotted Minerva. After he told him about Rose, Minerva made a face which was stubbornly casual, then yawned, "So the old girl finally ran out of grit."

O, well, there's the funeral and, perhaps, a tea after; but Denis sighed as he thought this.

"The strain," he told some latecomers, "the strain is positively too much. After all, she was my best friend. It's all right for you girls to wax witty over Rose. I have to suffer. I have to bear the bereavement like a curse. On those nights when Sparafucile's is all aflame and I'm sitting here by myself, who will reach over and pat my hand?"

"O, you make me tired, Denis," Minnie lied, for he never displayed any feelings which could be construed as a desire for a bed in the presence of Denis. "Always feeling for yourself. The truth is that you never cared one ounce for Rose, and you know it! She was a drag, and you, dear child, have enough to drag without her. Why, only the other night you could have scored if it hadn't been for Rose. Some frightened little scamp was looking you over, limp-eyed and fraught, but Rose was there, and, well, who wants to mingle with a ghastly ghost?"

"Really?" Denis asked, then posed demurely just to prove that the possibility wasn't as remote as he had made it sound. "Well, in my day I had to fight them off, and I suppose I have let this thing hit me just too hard – but the harder the better, I always say." Denis giggled in tarnished coyness. "Now that you mention it, Minnie, I remember that little one." And Denis dreamed a dream, his favourite. It involved some little scamp, limp-eyed and fraught, and Denis, a mound of delight, quivering hopelessly in anticipation of things to come.

"Dead?" Denis asked a group who were discussing Rose without consulting him on the finer points. "Dead?!" he asked again, as if that weren't the half of it. "My dears, let me tell you! It takes more than a skirmish to do me in, but you know Rose. Always was weak in her joints. I had just stepped out when the joint fell apart, when the stampede turned in her direction. Fainting spells do happen, you know, and Rose had been looking like hell for weeks; so, when I came back and found her in some flatfoot's arms, well, naturally, I was curious. When I went up to see if I were seeing correctly, this flatfoot asked me if I knew the deceased. I had to go along with him. He insisted. Besides, he was cute. And then that awful sergeant at the station.

He was worse. The cop at the club at least had the decency to graze my thigh as we were getting into the squad car, but the sergeant at the station made me strip – in front of all those men, too. What had I done? Nothing. I had just come along to identify Rose and straighten out a few details – when they made me strip. It was scandalous. I shivered in ecstasy, but it didn't do any good, so I made like a mad swan. I ruffled my goose pimples, flapped my wings, and strutted around like it had all been a terrible mistake. Then I squawked and squawked, but it still didn't do any good. They were all on duty for the night. I said I had a perfect right. After all, it was Mardi Gras week, and anyone may wear a costume. I rustled my Colonial silks even though I had to walk over to the sergeant's desk in order to do it.

I flapped them coyly, then thought malicious thoughts, but the thoughts were not all malicious. Some were delicious, and the rest were just wistful. This cop's features were a pure and simple matter of conscientious beauty, evenness and restraint, but he raised himself to the nth power of contempt by being a cop. The mantle of the criminal would have become his already overpowering self, his sacred bearing, and his body! His body was an exquisite temple for the worship of strange, active, but unrecognized religions. The worship of material things, lust, truth, youth, beauty, power and reason made their points in his countenance. But, instead of a founder, or even a follower, of these religions, he was just a spoke in the wheel of the law, but the very word 'law' made him eligible for the opposition, so eligible and so opposite. Then, when he handed me my blouse, I memorized his build. He was kinda chunky but cute in his own preposterously overbuilt way. Of course, I took my blouse and said, 'Thank God for small favours,' but I wished he had handed me my skirt instead. The very idea of handing me my blouse first proved that he was up to something. What could I cover with just a blouse? I was indignant. What else could I be? I didn't know what they were going to do next. I was sheer mortified, but the sergeant dismissed me and said that a masquerade was a masquerade, he knew, but it wasn't necessary to go all the way with the costume. Then that cute one, whom I had really worked up quite a fondness for by this time, handed me my bra and undies just like he was proving the sergeant's point, lie smiled hatefully, too. Invidious, it was. Well, I just took my time dressing, I tell you! I thought I might as well show that big lug something about how a lady dresses."

Minnie loaned his presence to the booth one night when Titania and Denis were discussing funerals. Minnie was an expert on death, having died more times than he had been born, and he seemed to flutter up whenever death was mentioned. When Denis excused himself to track a hunch into the john, Minnie slid over to the wall and installed himself.

"Tit, you always seem to be here with Denis," Minnie observed. "I've seen you two sitting here lots, at least for the early part of the evening. Then you disappear for the longest time." Minnie stopped, read Titania's blank stare as boredom, then changed the subject of the conversation without changing his motive. "The club is full tonight, no?"

"Yes, brimming. There's an excitement in the air which depresses me. I'm pooped, utterly reft of reft, so reft that I don't even know what it is that I'm reft of."

"You need a spin with a new stick," Minnie said, | striking a novel pose.

Titania looked sceptical.

Denis bubbled up, threw his weight in the booth, and

gasped, "You'll never guess who I just saw!" Denis' birth must have been traumatic, for every entrance since then was nothing short of trauma.

"Who?" Titania asked.

"Sounds like it must be Achilles with his tunic askew," Minnie said.

"No, Pelvis! An old flame of Tit's."

"Stop guessing, Denis. You don't know the first thing!"

"You left with him that night Rose was sitting right where Minnie is now, and we didn't see you for weeks but to make a brief appearance at the masquerade, solo, which I can't explain to this day. I heard something about Pelvis going to his uncle's funeral, but nothing more, and I'm sure no relative of his would grease him with anything."

"He went for his mother's sake," Tit blurted. "She was favoured in the will."

"So! How do you know?"

"So nothing. You know more about it than I do."

Pelvis began his elaborate system of tailing Tit where- ever he went, of staying behind him but out of sight, behind the nearest counter in a drugstore, protected by a display of merchandise, in the doorway of the nearest bar to where Tit was drinking, behind the building on the nearest corner and so forth. Titania thought that his tactics were disgusting. An obtuse shadow, full and fat, like a runt of a rhino trailing a mouse to amuse its fat wit until the mouse was seared with fear and cauterized with terror. Then, when the rhino tired, he would conclude the game by blindly obliterating the mouse with one blow of his fist as though with one careless stomp of his hoof. The mouse decided to remain in his hole. So Tit holed up in his apartment.

But, whether his thoughts cruised frontwards or

backwards, his mind arrived at only one conclusion. Leave, he thought. Pack, cut your curls, and go.

He thought of dying his hair black, of buying a tweed suit to fill out his figure, and of honouring his fingers with rings, big solid knots which were the emblems of athletic trophies. With square, heavy-soled, box-toed shoes he would be just another Southerner in search of Manassas; the people in the South would think as the North would think, just another Yankee looking for Antietam.

So, feeling that Antietam was elsewhere, Tit packed, threw a few things together, after he snipped his ringlets to the nubbin and looked almost respectable, he thought. But there was nothing he could do about his pallor, which was a shade lighter than Confederate grey. He decided to explain it away by saying that he was South, or "*that* South!" with concocted contempt. He would cat constantly on the bus, snacks, then fill up at the bus stops, regular meals even. When he tugged at his suitcase to lift it, he warned himself to make meals a must.

He slipped out the gate and made his way through the Quarter at breakneck speed. The iron-strung balconies and the tinted façades which weather had worn to maize were only blotchy blurs. 'Scat caught up with him before lie was out of the Quarter and knocked his suitcase for a way. He wanted a drink. He was irate over something. Titania didn't pay enough attention to him to find out what it was that was troubling him. Then he was furious. Then he was gone. Titania outdistanced him as he exited the Quarter, for 'Scat hedged on Canal Street as though the street were a boundary which he dared not cross. But perhaps it was Titania's desire for flight which stranded 'Scat on the corner, looking sadly awry.

As Titania hurried towards the bus station, he felt relieved when he heard a song coming from a juke box in some bar. The singer was matching him despair for despair. "Going to the river, gonna jump overboard and drown," the singer droned as the saxes grumbled, but the advice seemed invalid to Titania, for if he deserted his body, he would combine with nothing and become less than wind.

Seeking shelter from the rain of his thoughts, he entered the bus station and hurried to the ticket window. There was a line, so he became the last link. When he noticed the man in front of him, short, broad, confident, he was reminded of Pelvis, and the thought saturated his body with excitement as though it were drenched by one rainy cloud in a cumulus sky. The man looked at Titania with casual indifference, then turned around. The point of Tit's stare stirred up something in the man's back. That something was a flurry of nervous tension. The tension, now winged, gave off gentle vibrations which attacked the stiffness in Titania's body. The stiffness was a bulwark to compensate for the man's indifference. But now Titania's body turned liquid and flowed outward. When the liquid body made contact with the vibrations, there was a soundless crash, but Titania felt the effects of the contact when a tingling sensation rippled his flesh.

The man might have been a seaman. He stood firm, resolutely stout, implacably strong in body, and he had the soft shadow of disquiet in his eyes, which proved that he was used to dealing with the infinitely vague and the mysteriously immense. He was more accustomed to fuzzy, blue, haze-ladled horizons than to the sharp particulars of a crowded city.

The seaman turned around and looked at the clock on the wall with a slow, steady, wheeling motion.

Titania's hands fluttered to his lips to prevent the escape

of his thoughts, his surprise, his pleasure, but his thoughts were too accelerated to muse. They knocked around inside his head like a rampaging parrot that, sensing the approach of danger, objected to the confinement of his cage.

"In a hurry?" the seaman asked. "You seem kinda hurried." He didn't say what it was that had given him that impression, but he smiled as though he were opening the front door of his home to welcome a guest.

Titania's lips fumbled with a yes, and the man stepped aside, executed a short bow, and offered his place in line to Titania. When Titania stepped in front of him, his nervousness affected his knees and made his reply resemble a curtsy. After they traded places, Titania noticed a change in the man's body. He realized that there was no need for his body to remain fluid since the seaman's body no longer remained compressed behind a hard shell of self-sufficiency. The seaman's body was now on the slant, tipped forward, as if reaching for something.

"Where to?" the ticket teller asked.

Titania turned around, mumbled something, and fumbled with his wallet. He realized suddenly that he didn't know the price of his ticket because he didn't know where he was going. He fumbled some more, this time trying to extract the name of his destination from his wallet. It never occurred to him that he was really going somewhere. He just wanted to transplant his person to some distant land which would avail him of a new scene. He thought, Home? A possibility. But where's home? An impossibility. Does the wind have a home?

He was about to admit that he didn't know where he was going when he said, "Chicago."

Chicago? Age-old buildings, ripe for demolition, a sooty grey black, a gloom in bloom.

"Twenty-eight, forty-three," the teller said, and Titania rummaged in his wallet, grateful for the opportunity to occupy his hands.

He stuffed the ticket somewhere, picked up his suitcase, and hurried outside where the buses were lined up in stalls. He sat on his suitcase, crossed his legs, and felt relieved as if he had confessed his crime and now only had to wait for the routine preparations of the executioner.

He mustered his mechanisms, consolidated them, then projected naturalness, but, no matter how he looked or what he looked at, he had to stare, so he focused his gaze on some distant object. He looked across the street, but the object which he selected made him start and grip his knees. That object was a man – Old Pelvis – looking absolutely garish with his eyes twinkling and his smile studded with lead stars. Every time light struck the saliva gloss on his lead fillings, a star of light was born, and he tried to appear conspicuous by veiling his body from head to toe with longing. He was unaware of the devastating effect created by tucking his scarlet shirt into his muddy-maroon trousers.

After watching Pelvis look alternately pensive, casual, forgetful, and any other attitude which justified his right to that spot without disclosing his real motives, Titania busied his gaze with the loading buses, though his stare did inch around to gaze at Pelvis regularly. Just to see that he stays there, Tit thought, justifying his occasional glances at Pelvis.

The seaman came out of the waiting room with a small suitcase and a mitty bag. Titania watched him out of the corner of his eye with an off-balance look. The seaman stopped to adjust his load when he saw Titania. He threw his bag on his shoulder and a big smile at Titania as he walked towards his bus. Titania's heart flipped once when he watched the seaman board the Chicago bus. He wrenched the thought from his mind, but not before it bloomed massively. It might be fun for a summer weekend. He looked at Pelvis to discourage the thought, and Pelvis was still standing across the street, patiently waiting for recognition with an untiring stare.

A loudspeaker announced the approaching departure of the Chicago bus. Titania shivered because he knew that it didn't matter where he sat on the bus, he would still be in the vicinity of that seaman with no recourse to action. The seaman's hair was brown and tempered with gold, his smile rich enough, and his eyes sad enough to shift the emphasis from the top of his head to his face without losing a drop of enthusiasm, and Titania would have to sit and watch his feelings stagnate, twist, and curl in place while he squelched the epitome of action with no stronger deterrents than the presence of strangers.

The loudspeaker announced the second call for Chicago. Titania stood up and glanced across the street, but so sudden was the thrust and so rapid the recovery of his sight that he didn't see Pelvis. Nevertheless, the look was meant to be a quick good-bye. Nothing more, nothing less. A fast farewell. As he picked up his suitcase and headed for the bus, he noticed a woman struggling with a bulky suitcase. She gave him a couple of pleading looks, but Titania was fighting a fluttering heart. When he bumped into her, she apologized, looked forlorn, then brightened when she noticed that he was a man. Smiling politely, she stepped back and left the suitcase in Titania's way as if she promised not to object if he would wrestle the bag onto the bus for her, but Titania pardoned himself nervously, swept past the woman, and entered the bus in a gust of trembling.

That woman! What gall! Who does she think – but he

thought this on his way out. He stepped off the bus and walked gingerly across the street. An elasticity entered his step. He had begun to thaw. He flew up on the kerb and soared into the nearest bar. Inside, there was a swirling blur, but the blur subsided when he became accustomed to the dim illumination. He ordered a beer, a fishbowl.

The next thing he knew Pelvis was standing next to him at the bar.

"O, hi," Pelvis said with bridled enthusiasm. "You drinkin' tonight?"

"Yeah," Titania said, expelling the word from the bottom of his voice box as though he were cleaning it out, ridding it of the last remnants of a former role. Then Tit basked in the beam of Pelvis' smile. The beam was a spotlight, beckoning. He pirouetted deftly at the bar, then concluded his performance by raising his arms above his head and letting them slither down below his waist where he arranged his fingers at weird angles.

Pelvis said, "I been thinkin'—" He stopped and chuckled when he noticed Titania's pose. "Gettin' comfortable, huh?"

"Yiss," Titania screeched.

"I been thinkin' a lot lately," Pelvis went on. "You wanna hear about it?"

Titania reached over and reassured him by touching his sleeve, then pitched explosively, "There's nothing I'd like better!"

"Let's go," Pelvis said, discarding his reluctance.

"Where?"

"I thought a ride, just breeze. I got my car around the corner."

"O, joy!"

"What?" Pelvis asked, then caught himself and didn't press. He finished his question with another question in order to obscure the first what. "Your hair's a mess. What didja do?"

"O, joy!" Tit said, answering the first what. He jumped at the chance to repeat his delight.

Pelvis was equally pleased. He made like a pouter pigeon. He pulled his shirt open at the neck, then pushed his belt down to give his chest unlimited room for expansion.

"Where's the car?" Tit asked, but Pelvis didn't answer. He looked straight ahead and ignored the remark.

"Where's the car?" Tit asked again.

Pelvis spoke slowly, importantly, as if to miscalculate his tone would misshape his meaning and result in a misfortune for the miscalculator. "Over there," he answered, then waited for the chill of silence to set in before he broke it. "Down the block," he mumbled.

Titania's mind took off and sailed among his memories. The memory which tacked to the forefront of his mind was the incident which had provoked his present estrangement with Pelvis.

"You know what?" Pelvis said.

"No, what?"

"I found a place where I can get fixed."

"Fixed?"

"Yeah, a connection," Pelvis said.

Once, while riding in the car with no destination in mind, Pelvis had said, "You know what?" It had been a softer what this time. He had let the word slip out of his mouth without moving his lips, low and breathy, as if he hadn't said it, so if an argument arose, he could blame it on someone else, even though there was no one else around. He could accuse the weird angle of the window vent with the wind whistling through it. "I wish I had something to lift me up."

197

Insulted, Titania had retorted, "Yeah, way up, something to jog your jugular."

Then, Pelvis had smiled, but he didn't press. He took it easy, for he knew that time and boredom would take care of things with a sludge of moments, and that way he could accomplish his objective without admitting that he was the source of the suggestion. To Pelvis, the law was a sandtrap on the way to the green. His first connection was a con man who had one stick and was hungry. Pelvis said that he could have gotten the stick off the guy for nothing if the guy hadn't been hungry. But that stick wasn't very good. It was full of seeds. They drove along the highway, puffing occasionally, with the windows rolled up, and the tobacco popped and crackled and went out. After the butt had become too small to hold between his fingers without burning them, he stuck a toothpick into the butt and smoked it all the way down.

The next connection was better, had better stuff, a Prince Albert can with few seeds. What seeds there were didn't hiss when he lit up, and there was enough for a binge. He went out and tanked up on beer, then retired to a secluded spot along the highway and threw open the car doors after he had inhaled his share, not before, for open doors created draughts which burned the stick up too fast. He took his sex as dessert to the meal of smoke, but he savoured the dessert for at least an hour, just lolling, improvising.

"It never gets soft when I'm on," he said, bleary-eyed with smoke. "The only way to die," he recommended, for he believed that death was a climax, an exclamation point at the end of a sentence and not just a period.

His concentration was immense, tightly geared, finely strung, and tuned to his strumming for one who was carelessly lolling. Careless skill was all that was necessary for desire to soar, bounding into the deepest fields of satisfaction – at least for a while, then the numerous preparations began to pall on Titania. It took most of an evening to prepare, to make sure that no intruder was around, to laboriously tank up on beer beforehand, to drive out to the rendezvous, some remote spot which was remote from everything but the fear of discovery. It took an evening to prepare for an evening. Titania held the tin by the window while Pelvis drove in order to heave it out at a moment's notice – when the squad car swerved in front of them and forced them over to the kerb. But after Pelvis was through for the night, he took the can and stashed it personally. He selected a vacant lot which looked especially vacant, then screwed himself in on the surrounding landmarks, orienting himself, before he buried the stuff under a clump of weeds which he excised carefully from the soil with his pocket knife. He arranged a few bits of broken glass or bright bottle caps over the buried tin in a pattern which was known only by him.

Once, he spent the day trying to retrieve a tin. He knew that that was the lot, and he knew that those were the bottle caps which marked the spot where the tin was buried, but the pattern wasn't his. When he saw some kids playing in a nearby yard, he thought, messin'. He told Titania that those kids had stolen his tin. But, before he could question them, some housewife barged out of her back door and screamed, "Get outta here. That lot don't belong to you. You got no business here. Gwan, git!"

He left like a chased dog, scooting, with his head down and his back up, and he drank all afternoon in a bar, the same bar, saying he couldn't do nothin' else; he couldn't keep from thinkin' about that weed; he knew it was there and unsmoked; he wasn't sure how much, but he was sure it was enough, and it was there, and it was his; those damn kids, they got no right fussin' with what's not theirs; that bitch saw him bury it and poached ; she sounded mighty het up over nothin', and she put those kids up to stealin' it; she had the quick temper of a bennyhead, all right – only to return at nightfall and light matches to no avail. The seed had been sown to the sod.

Titania's feelings had become brittle since he had started smoking. His nerves were sharpened to finely toned points by each succeeding cigarette until they quivered like arrows which shot into his brain.

"She sounded like it," Tit said, referring to a piece of the conversation which had taken place that afternoon because they hadn't spoken since, and it was now evening. Mute, intent, and singular, they concentrated on the misplaced tin.

Finally, the strain snapped the arrows. "I'm sick of it," Tit screamed, prompted by nothing, but he had been thinking about the time when he had taken too much, had drawn too deeply on the butt and had passed into a deep sleep which had pried the room from the building, but he had felt the rumble of his discontent even then, through the deep calm, so now, without the deep calm to cushion his feelings, his irritation was raw. "It doesn't work," he said, "any more. I need something stronger!"

"You don't smoke it right," Pelvis told him. "You gotta take it slow and sip it. It's the only time I get off a good dream any more."

He meant that the smoke set the stage for the play in his mind. After he had prepared for the evening, he was receptive to the dream. He giggled boyishly at nothing. Comedy was everywhere. The drama did not move through its acts realistically, for only the high spots of living were considered as apt material for the dream, had any potential for his purposes, and even the high spots had to be elevated and developed with his mind's desire in order to create the proper effect, but in his own arbitrary way he was selective. He chose an impossible suavity, a strength to equal the weight of Colossus, and a law seven times as definitive as Deuteronomy. When the world was Thebes, he was Alexander. A policeman grovelled in the dirt at his feet in an absurd position even for a lardass, but Pelvis went one better. He outdid himself. He eclipsed that miracle with another. He stuck the cop's tongue out of his jowly mug, panting.

Titania knew the principal parts of the dream from his own wanderings in that realm, but the subject and object of his dream were reversed. The smoke seemed to transport his mind over the horizon as a gas manipulates a solid, and that took power, strong smoke, but the dream lasted only as long as it took for the smoke to curl into the air and dissolve, leaving only a plaintive yearn, a pain, which was the substance of that dream.

Titania's dream: Lithely dressed in a gown of pure anguish, a sequined pain, which materialized in the dream as a fire in the centre of a circle of hairy Mexicans who had rebellion smarting their eyes, Titania waited in the wings until the fire was hot enough to slip over his head without chilling his desire. His desire was as fragile as flame but thawed things easily and scorched things just as easily. He knew that the proper timing was sometimes the difference between success and failure, so he examined the scene before he made his entrance. Six Mexicans circled the fire. They spoke unpleasantly in a vulgar patois which was girdled with grunts. Squatting on their haunches, ready to leap, they stared at the fire which kindled their discontent by crackling. As the discussion grew hotter, their desire grew likewise. Their emotions blazed, and they borrowed the characteristics of the fire, principally the heat. They were aroused magnificently and on the verge of combat. Their legs were bound in white cotton fabric, and their crotches gave a shape to their feelings despite the resistance of the taut cloth – like glutted worms struggling to burst their cocoons. Then Titania appeared as the saviour in the dream, in the form of a wraith, as a dream within a dream, when the tiny licking flames, his many tongues, wound out of the fire. He knew what he had to do. He was uncertain about where to begin.

"Aw, forget it," Titania shouted. His tone was not commensurate with the act which had incited his rage, which was Pelvis' lament over his lost stash, but Pelvis' damnation was attacking everything in sight. His beer was warm. The pinball machine was rigged with magnets for percentage payoffs. He didn't have enough money to invest in a packet of birdseed, let alone in some seed he could smoke. He didn't even get an iron claw of candy when he tried for that camera.

"That camera wouldn't work anyway," Tit said.

"How you know?"

"It was bakelite."

"What's bakelite got to do with it?"

"It's a decoy."

"Decoy, shit!"

That night Pelvis had to drum without his usual inspiration, and Tit had become accustomed to the long, winding approach to the climax of the evening, so Pelvis was rebuffed when he considered employing last resort. He knew how he could get some money quick if Tit would only accommodate his method. He might need Tit's apartment, Tit's facilities in the broadest sense of the word. His smile indicated that Tit would be more responsible for getting the money than he would, but it was still his idea. He was the brains.

"We need a hotel room and a client and a—" he interrupted himself to make his apologies early. "I don't know how much quality I can strike up for you, but I'm gonna try real hard. We're interested in what we get out of it, anyway, ain't we? But I'll try real hard. Just off-hand, I was thinkin' about that fat boy."

"What fat boy?" Tit asked sharply, and Pelvis dropped the subject.

"I was just lookin' the field over. I didn't say nothin' for real. After all, you want the stuff as bad as I do. It's what we're after that counts, not how we get it, exactly. You want it, too, don't you? Then, I can't do all the thinkin' and everythin' else, too."

Titania heard only the toos, and he didn't hear them very well, at least not well enough to be convinced. Despite what he had done in the past, and Black came to mind, immediately followed by Sovastapole Harry, despite what law he had transgressed, he had never violated his taste. Now he was being asked to forego his taste, his last surviving principle, which had remained miraculously intact. But why hadn't his taste been vitiated sooner? What was so formidable about his taste?

"Denis?" Tit asked, spitting out the name.

"I didn't say him, exactly. Now don't get your back up!"

Titania still wasn't convinced. There were words and words; some words even formed promises if they were welded together with the right amount of sincerity, but Pelvis' words hinted at nothing but poor faith. Titania didn't justify his past acts, but Denis was another story. He would be worse than prostitution and masturbation combined

203

and strangely akin to both. Does one wind copulate with another wind to produce a little breeze? Two distinct quantities were at work, air and motion, never interlocking. Air pressure and air operated independently to produce air currents, so their combined efforts did produce something: wind. Titania had eloquently disproven his own argument. The analogy was apt, not strangely inept. Then Titania decided that his thoughts were not the mental equivalents of his actions.

"But you meant Denis," Tit insisted.

"No, I didn't mean nothin'. All I said was that we could probably make an easy score with that creep. Give him a good scare and make him fork over the money without feedin' him."

"Still, it's Denis, and forking Denis without feeding him would hardly produce a sonorous effect."

"You're green, green as a mouldy dick."

"I wouldn't say that. Frankly, I'm enjoying this. You could promise me a medicinally approved regiment, and I would refuse on the grounds of sterility."

"You're nuts. You're so smart? You get the money. How you gonna get it, huh?"

"I'm not," Tit said defiantly. "I don't want any money. It's green, and I'm green enough already."

"You want a smack? You're askin' for it, you know." Titania offered his cheek.

"Quit smartin' off. You're gonna get it if you keep up, so simmer down."

Titania smiled.

"Cut that out."

"What?"

"That suffocatin' smile. I'll give you somethin' to smack your lips over."

"Please do."

"You silly-assed freak!"

"You must have more names. Next, please."

"I have, but you don't deserve 'em."

"Then think up some I do deserve."

Pelvis was silent. He didn't say anything, but he wasn't silent. He was kicking his feet around.

"Always one to oblige in a pinch," Tit said. "How about the reticent lack of putrid disentanglement?" Pelvis laughed.

"What about the concomitant epitome of lurid disenfranchisement? Or, the basal metabolism of agglutinated swivel!"

"Yeah, that one. I like that one best, that metalute swivel."

"There's still the heavenly debasement of the imperturbable fuckstick. Surely that appeals to you."

"No, I don't like that one. Let's go, metalute swivel. You're gettin' dirty now."

"Dirty?"

"Yeah, dirty. That fuckstick's dirty."

He buckled with laughter.

"I'm not going anywhere," Tit announced.

"I thought we were goin' – Well, then, what should we do?"

"Haven't you got any ideas? You're the big-brained man of the outfit."

"Let's pool our cash and see what we come up with," Pelvis suggested.

"Agglutinated swivel has three cents, two coppers and a lead."

"Dig deeper."

"He hasn't a cent. He just threw his cents out the window."

"What didja do that for?" Pelvis whined.

"To piss Pelvis."

"You're goin' to, too, if you don't watch out."

"Quaint threats just encourage me."

"Why ya keep raggin' me? Ya wanna know what I think, then ya rib me when I tell ya. Ya get your money out to give me, then ya heave it out the winda. Why don't ya do somethin' regular?"

"'Cause I'm agglutinated swivel."

"You're gonna get dropped if you keep up."

"Can I count on that?"

"Yeah!"

"Agglutinated swivel is now going to take him up on it and get dropped."

"Then settle down."

"I don't want to settle down. I just want to get dropped."

"Cut that out."

"I have no shears."

"Very funny!"

"I didn't think so, and I'm always the first to recognize a joke."

"Sez you!"

"I'm sorry, but I'm no longer agglutinated. From now on I'm just going to swivel." With these words Titania stepped out of the car and walked down the street, trying to match his step with the deadbeat tone in his voice.

Pelvis pulled his car into a driveway, backed out, then followed Titania down the street slowly, closely.

Titania saw the car out of the corner of his eye, but he ignored it. He impressed his robot voice onto his robot walk, turning the corner mechanically.

Pelvis pulled around the corner, speeded up, then slammed on his brakes when the car was a short distance ahead of Titania. He bounded out of the car.

But, before he reached Titania, Titania let out a war whoop. "You goddamn, crazy-assed queer! Get out and stay out, you hear? You queer, queer, queer!" His loudness was formidable, for Pelvis turned tail, scrambled into his car, and shot down the street in a gust of exhaust.

Titania looked around sheepishly to see if anyone had heard. An old man was sitting on his front porch, but he gave no indication that he had seen or had heard anything. The expression on his face was blank, emotionless, indifferent, and when he saw Titania staring at him, he picked up his newspaper and began to read. Still, he had been looking directly at Titania as though he had been looking through Titania at something beyond.

The delay is a simple procedure. He puts the needle and the syringe in a pan of water, first.

He puts the pan of water on the stove to boil, and lets it bubble briskly for ten minutes, like the book says. While he is waiting, he takes out a little dish and pours in the alcohol, which is seventy per cent absolute, and seventy per cent absolute is absolute enough. Then he replaces the bottle of alcohol in the cupboard. The bottle is brown, for no good reason. Next, he takes out a ball of cotton. He has to fuss with it, tear the paper casing away, in order to get at the soft, white centre, sterile and pure. He pulls off a hunk and dunks the hunk in the alcohol. Then he gets a little bottle from the refrigerator, the one at the bottom, which is kept there because the directions say to keep it away from the freezing unit. The label on the bottle is blue with green ink, or green with blue ink, he has forgotten which, but at one time, early, he knew the colours well, just as he knew what the NPH stood for, that scientific mysticism which was inscribed above the word insulin.

The needle is done, so he pours the water off and lets the needle cool until it is cool enough to assemble. The time is now. It doesn't take long. He takes the plunger and fits it into the barrel of the syringe, which has a graduated scale on one side. He attaches the needle on the other end of the barrel. When he sets it down, he makes sure that the needle touches only air. He brushes the top of the insulin bottle with the alcohol- soaked cotton. Everything he touches is so pure that he feels as if he is operating in a vacuum.

After he has inserted the needle through the rubber cap on the insulin bottle and has drawn off the correct amount of milky fluid, he bares his leg. Once again he makes sure that the needle touches only air when he sets it down, and once again he picks up the wet cotton from its crystal clear bathtub.

With the cotton he dabs his leg in the fateful area which will permit the needle to enter his leg and which will grant him life and time to see the end of the day.

He lifts the syringe, plunger, barrel, needle, insulin, and all, all assembled, above that spot. He hates that needle. He hates it with a hate which is so intense that he becomes simple about it and can only say that he hates it. His hate is unadorned with adjectives which might broaden his hate and imply more than a singular hate. The needle is small, and the prick in the skin, which the needle makes when it is inserted, is infinitesimal. Only the grief is large. The syringe resembles a tiny viper, the needle a fang, which emits a gentle venom, a life-sustaining poison. They say it's because his pancreas doesn't function properly, but he says, "Yes, I know, but what about destiny? What about when sin and salvation are one? A gentle venom?"

He closes his eyes and jabs. He sees blackness. As he

opens his eyes, the blackness turns milky white. Then, as he pushes the plunger, the milky whiteness drains to a shade of white which is as clear as the empty barrel of the syringe.

And he resumes his way of living, but calmly.

And now, in the booth with Minnie and Denis, Titania was looking that way at Minnie. His focus was somewhere beyond, on the bar in back of Minnie, and the excitement there which had no centre.

"Rose is dead, dead and gone, gone and died, but not for long," Denis sang. "I don't know what I'd do, Min, if it weren't for you. I have nightmares concerning Rose, you know. Not about what's in store for her, but nightmares of the past. I know she can handle herself in any situation, at least enough to get by. Remember that stocky little man, in grey overcoat and hat, who brushed against Rose's shoulder in a superb display of technique? So slight was the bump that the manoeuvre must have been practised, or studied, to achieve such a delicate effect. Rose thought, delirious effect. Rose and I were walking down the street, discussing the pros and cons of sailors, when this solid little man made this all too familiar gesture as we were entering the commercial district. At the moment of contact, the man tipped his head towards Rose, though his face was turned away, and whispered. Well, Rose swung around and followed him down the street with her eyes, but the man didn't look back. He didn't even turn around, so Rose arched her eyebrows with obvious disdain and accused him of trifling.

"'Why, he didn't even look back,' I said.

"'A cop!' Rose said flatly, slightly annoyed. 'He thinks he's incognito.'"

"The poor dear," Minnie mocked. "If he had been serious, he would have stopped to admire some merchandise in a window, any window and any merchandise. I've seen thugs with a purpose, an ulterior one, stop to admire perfume."

"Yes," Denis said. "It's all kinda mixed up and quaint, but, my God, their conception!"

Then Denis told about the cop who paid a regular visit to Rose's hotel room when she first arrived in the city. Punctually at ten every night, the cop made his rounds and dropped by Rose's room, shuffled his feet outside the door, and whispered 'blowjob' through the keyhole. The word implied an invitation, and the tone was vaguely seductive like the wheeze of a hippopotamus on heat. "New on the force," Denis explained. "He never heard of underworld finesse. Why, Rose told me that she never made big decisions like that until she had at least seen his face."

"A queen, a virtual queen, and she knew it."

"What do you think of that, Titania?" Denis asked.

"If they would wise up their policemen, they could eliminate some of the smut in this town."

"You can't hate them as much as I do," Denis said. "Policemen have been an awful trial in my life."

"How so?" Minnie asked, resting his gaze lightly upon Titania.

"Well, their uniforms for one thing. They do it deliberately. They have no shame. They bind their buttocks just to make people think that they are first prize in a beef exposition. I have never seen a more unprincipled lot. They act as though the law were just one more involuntary response of their muscles. Of course, they are only the representation of the law in flesh, so when their private opinions differ from the statutes, they have to disregard those opinions during working hours, but the disgusting part of it is that they act as if they never varied. They are one, a group of consolidated bulls, who are as regimented as their uniforms are full, and believe me, that's full."

"Sounds to me, Denis, like you only object to them because they have a place in space, an ordered corner."

"I have quite a place in space myself."

"Yes, but you haven't any framework."

Denis turned to Titania and changed the subject.

"I don't want to sound discouraging, Tit, but it looks like Pelvis has deserted you. Money will do it every time, not even money, just the promise of money can sometimes affects a person's attitude."

"It bothers you? Don't flaunt your motives."

"Me? You know what I think of Pelvis. He's strictly an effete geek with me."

"Then, what's the to-do?"

"I just like to keep my pairs up-to-date, that's all. When someone asks, 'Is she taken?', I don't like to give bum steers. I'll just say, 'O, that Titania! Don't muscle. She's currently engaged, if not fianceed, to that runt of a rhino, Pelvis.' And, if it's all off, I'll say, 'O, that! She's wed, worn, and widowed. You'll have to use helium to get a lift from that.'"

"You're too kind, Denis, but the truth is that I don't need any help from the court gossips."

"I agree," Minnie said. "O, look, there's Pelvis. He's hustling, drinks, it looks like."

"Ha!" Denis commented. "He's being hustled is more like it, and Tit refuses to score. She won't even cut us in on one round."

"So what?"

"So he's dumb as Adam, so what!"

"I wouldn't say that," Minnie defended.

"You mean, Minnie, that Pelvis whirls you, too?"

"No, I didn't say that. He's a little old to boil my blood."

211

"He isn't any older than you are. In fact, I'd say that he was a mite younger."

"I don't care for the muscle. At this point it just gets in the way."

"But, Tit, why don't you say something to grease the conversation?"

"It's slimy enough already," Tit said.

"Shall we leave, Titania?" Minnie suggested. "I don't care for his repartee."

Minnie started to leave, but he had to wait for Denis to let him out, but Denis didn't block Minnie's exit. In fact, he rose to accommodate Minnie.

"That's all right, Tit," Denis said. "You may go. I don't mind, really. I shall find something to do. Go on, git!"

Tit baulked, and Denis moved into the booth and propped his bulk against the wall, assuming the attitude of The Quite Contented. He toyed with the ashtray, spun it on his finger. Minnie slipped in next to Denis, waiting, declaring his reluctance to leave without Titania. When Tit started to rise, Denis asked, "What shall I tell Pelvis when he drops around?"

"O, you'll think of something," Minnie said. "If that's all that's worrying you, Tit, I'm famous for phrasing some of the shortest regrets in history."

"Such as?" Denis asked.

"Tut, tut," Minnie said as he offered his arm to Titania.

"Really, now, I find myself wanting a beer," Titania said. "How 'bout you, Min?"

"This is all very interesting," Denis said. "I didn't know I had such paralysing charm."

"Go fuck a fishnet," Minnie cooed. "There's enough holes there for an army."

"I think I'll get a beer," Titania said.

"There's no reason for you to guzzle one now. Why don't you save it?"

"Maybe if we left, we could stir up something on the way out," Minnie suggested. "We might crash something new."

"I'll tell Pelvis you willed him to me," Denis said.

"But he won't stay willed for long, will he. Tit?" Minnie said, hazarding a joke.

Titania laughed, but not at the joke. It was a mirthless laugh which gave him an opportunity to scan the faces at the bar.

"When the young thing arrives, just tell him that we send our love posthumously."

"Did the gents buy Pelvis a drink?"

"No, but one did lend him a little incense to sweeten his breath. Then Pelvis headed down the street where he could get double shots for fifty cents."

"That's probably where he is now. Tit. Shall we branch out?"

"I don't know what all the hurry is about," Tit said. "I never said anything about wanting to find him."

"No," Denis said, "but you've been looking like it ever since we came in here."

"I have not. You are more interested in finding him than I am."

"Denis, why don't you run across the street and see if he's there. Just so we can get this thing straightened out. I would go, but I can't stand the sour smells."

"I would go, Min, only that would be too easy for you. My place is here, and here is where I stay." Denis rose, then plunked down again. "If you want to go, go."

"You heard her, Tit. Want to go?"

"I haven't had my beer yet," Titania said.

Minnie rose, waved vaguely, and drifted towards the bar.

213

"She's impossibly fresh, that girl," Denis said. "I think she thought that you were interested in her," he laughed, then went on discussing this and that, here and there, ever and anon, but his words fell upon Titania's eardrums as though they were weights. Tit was being pummelled to death with words.

"I'm dreadfully sorry, Tit, but I just couldn't go over there and look for Pelvis. I can't stand that place. It always smells like someone just puked, and, more often than not, they just have. And think! they serve oysters there."

"Sounds brisk," Tit said.

"Well, I'd leave if I had any place to go," Denis said. "I've known about you for some time, Tit. About how you cavort, and, God knows, I've suspected it for even longer. I think we could have been very happy, had things been different. I just think you missed a golden opportunity, that's all. All those others! Why not me? me? me?"

Denis had, perhaps, made his most sensible proposition, but Titania was not receptive to sense. Denis pointed his finger at Pelvis, who had distinguished himself from the group at the bar. His coat-tails were flapping, and his face was swollen. The veins in his temple bulged. His blood had to make room for the alcohol in his system. His eyes were bleared, and his nose was lustrous, but the glow was intermittent as though his nose were wired on a poor circuit. He strolled towards the booth in what he thought was a leisurely manner.

"Look!" Denis shouted. "The master has not only hung one on, he has hung several on."

Denis rose, curtsied nimbly, and motioned to the vacant seat next to him. Pelvis bowed gallantly. Denis slid over next to the wall, contracting his bulk so that there appeared to be plenty of room. As Pelvis straightened up from his bow, his head wove, and he bumped it under the table.

Denis giggled an aside to Tit. "It's that bump which puts the man in humanity."

Pelvis laughed the loudest and the longest until a hiccup cut off his laugh. "I always get these damn things," he said, pointing to his mouth. He tried to snatch his finger with his teeth, but his finger outsmarted them. His other hand grabbed the flirtatious finger and held it for his teeth to sink into. He bit into his finger mercilessly until he choked it white.

Denis reached over and put his arm around Pelvis. Pelvis didn't object, so Denis let his hand slide down his back. Pelvis still didn't object, so Denis left his hand there in the shape of an empty cup, in an attitude of immense hope.

As Titania watched the proceedings from the other side of the booth, he thought that he would object to Denis' pawing, but there was no emotion even remotely akin to jealousy in his make-up.

When Pelvis leaned towards Denis, Denis brought up his arm to steady him.

"Who's your friend?" Pelvis asked.

"Don't you know?" Denis asked back snidely, then waved his hand in back of Pelvis at Titania.

Pelvis lost his balance. His elbow slipped off the table, and he became unpropped. Raising his head up and peeking over the rim of the table, he said, "Just like a bushel of new mown hay, his lap is."

"The better to cushion you with, my dear," Denis said. "Say, whatever happened to that little potato you had in your tie? Hocked it already? "

"Naw," Pelvis said, shielding his mouth with his hand. "Too many thieves." He tilted his head at Titania. "T'aint safe. But it was a beaut, wasn't it?"

"O, yes. I haven't seen the likes of it since Diamond Jim quit busting out all over."

Pelvis smiled largely, but Titania's didn't react. Every time Pelvis spoke, Titania felt an icy sensation in his stomach.

"Well," Denis said, "if you want to be impulsive, I know a better place for it."

Pelvis smiled, but he placed his hands in front of him on top of the table and folded them primly. "I'd have to be a lot drunker than I am now."

"That time may come," Denis warned. "Ever have a fat one?"

Pelvis looked at Titania before he answered. Then he refused to answer.

Tit stood up and drifted through the crowd towards the door. He felt strangely buoyant, demagnetized, because regret, like friction, was not retarding his inertia in motion.

Denis was stupefied. His torpor exploded sweetly when he closed his eyes and said, "I know just the place, a cute little, ole, abandoned farmhouse on the edge of town. You do have a car, do you not? Well, there's a litle arbour in back, just a nook, overgrown with wild roses, and But Denis opened his eyes to roll them for the crowning effect and realized that he was propositioning himself.

"I would have loved him all over," Denis said, sighing a deep, all-inclusive sigh.

Pelvis pushed outside and stumbled up the street. The air was with him, or so he thought, because his drunkenness had made him light, so the wind all but carried him up the street.

"Want a lift?" he called to Titania.

Titania stopped at the corner and turned around when he heard the shout. He waited for Pelvis to weave, stumble and grumble his way up to him.

"I parked down this way," he said, moving in the direction of the warehouses and their shadows, going towards the river. Titania followed him carelessly. Pelvis thought, obediently. Every few steps Pelvis stopped and turned his head around to see if Titania was still following him. Then he wove and tottered and started up again.

Since they were walking away from the source of tight, the shadows appeared deeper, denser and more confused. Pelvis turned around and placed himself squarely in Titania's path. He spread his feet, rocked, then produced a knife, snapping the blade with a vicious click. Titania stopped a few feet in front of him and stared at the blade.

"You're gonna leave town," Pelvis ordered, rasped out.

"O, I don't know," Titania said, trying to appear calm.

"You're gonna leave town," Pelvis rasped again.

"Why?" Tit asked. "I don't see any reason for me to leave, if I don't want to."

"I'll give you a reason," Pelvis said. He flashed the blade.

"It's a free country!"

"I wouldn't know about that, but you're gonna leave, and you're gonna."

"Why?"

"'Cause I don't like to have you around, that's why."

"Look the other way."

"If it ain't me, then I don't want to have you around remindin' me, see?"

"Where shall I go?"

"I don't care – any place. Just get out."

Titania leaned forward as though he were going to whisper, but he shouted, "Don't you think I'd like to get out and stay out? But there are no vacancies!"

"I guess you heard that I came into a tittle money," Pelvis said. "When my aunt dies, I'm gonna come into some more, get a little place back of town, and probably set up housekeepin'. Anyway, I've been thinkin' along those lines. You want to come in?"

"I tried that, and it didn't work, remember?"

"It'll give ya a place."

"It didn't work!"

"Then get out!"

"I'll think about it," Tit said and started to walk away, but before he took a step, he heard a scuttling on the sidewalk; then he saw the blade, in pieces, scoot past him. He swung around and glared. Then Pelvis charged, mumbling something under his breath. The alcohol in his system retarded his speed, and he moved forward furiously in slow motion. Finally, his fist struck Titania's cheek. Tit's cheek stung, then smarted. Before Pelvis could regain his balance, Tit poked him in the stomach. Pelvis buckled, reared back, and swung with his fist but missed, grunted, and swore. He waited for Titania to come within striking distance again, but Tit easily outmanoeuvred him. Tit faked, then stepped back and watched Pelvis strike the air where Titania had been.

"You're punching air," Tit told him.

Pelvis struggled to increase his speed and decrease his reaction time, but the effort threw him off balance, so when he lunged, Tit stepped back, shot forward, and shoved him before he was able to cock his fist. Tit laughed shrilly. Pelvis reared back to deal a death blow, but Titania stepped to one side and watched him crumple to the sidewalk. He crawled over to a street light where he propped himself with his legs sprawled on the sidewalk.

Titania leaned over him and yelled, "Can't you see I'm tired? We're through!"

"How come?" Pelvis mumbled sullenly.

"It's impossible," Tit shouted. "Impossible, you hear? No—" Then he stopped, for Pelvis seemed to be listening. Anyway, he was sitting quietly. Titania lowered his voice.

"At one time, yes, I thought it would work. I thought it was all I wanted. It seemed to answer any question I could put to myself, but I don't feel it any more. Not even a raging, ringing revulsion. It just isn't there!"

Counting points scored or number of rounds won while in the ring, Titania would have won, but he didn't feel like a winner because the submission of Pelvis was not the crown which he had been fighting for.

"Then you gotta go," Pelvis said. "You ought to know that I can't have you around if you're not goin' to be for me." He spoke slowly, softly, trying to strike the same chord of understanding which Titania had struck in him. Having tried and failed to get up, he said, "Here, give me a hand," and Tit obliged. "You're goin' then, huh?" he asked with the last flicker of hope dying in his voice.

"Just as far as money will take me – and that's pretty far."

"How far?" Pelvis asked.

"Far enough."

"Just so it's far enough is all I care."

Titania had no place to go but elsewhere. He wanted to blame his failure on something tangible, like drugs, Sparafucile's, booze, something which, if it hadn't existed, would have changed the outcome, but the feeling which overpowered him at the moment was not a disgust for these things but simply an overwhelming feeling of exhaustion.

For the first time since he had arrived in New Orleans, he went back to his apartment and slept soundly with Pelvis at his side. Pelvis assured him that he would only stick around until Titania made it to the depot.

Titania didn't object to what he would have construed earlier as a breach of faith, ruptured trust, for when he looked at Pelvis, he failed to recognize him. He did not feel a twinge of uneasiness at the thought of what a stranger might do. His uneasiness was incited by what Pelvis could do during the night, what old motives could revive him to do, but then it didn't matter what he did, for Titania felt as though he were capable of resisting anything, and anything which he could resist was meaningless to him.

The next morning they awoke to a dead silence and a sky mottled with mist. Sound was still asleep. They dressed in the same noiseless vacuum. They drank last night's coffee, flavoured lightly with milk which coloured it a gravel tone. The world had gone grey overnight. It was a morning which Titania had seen many times when he had strolled home from an uneventful evening. The sky, then as now, was the colour of his feelings.

Pelvis stood beside Titania at the station without comment. It was too quiet. At other times when there was no sound, the silence wasn't empty, for his thoughts rattled around in his head and gave the sensation of loudness.

"You ever been here before?" Pelvis asked. He cushioned his words with a whisper.

"Not like this," Tit said, feeling the alien quietness settle upon him.

"Me neither," Pelvis said.

They walked into the station and sat at the lunch counter. Pelvis ordered two coffees. Titania watched the tired sky out the window. It was replete with weariness, pebble-stoned, dapple-grey. He turned and looked at Pelvis. Pelvis must have understood, for he was sitting there wearily content.

"It's almost time," Pelvis said, reaching for the handle of the suitcase.

Titania felt a stab of pain, but it was lessened somewhat by the motion which he made when he slid off the stool. Motion seemed to deflect the pain. He stopped and gestured meaninglessly towards the door which they were passing through. Pelvis nodded, then made an equally random gesture towards the door.

They walked the rest of the way in silence. Stopping at the end of the platform, they looked expectantly at each other. Then Pelvis looked away, but nothing impressed him, so he looked back at Titania. Titania's thoughts had settled upon nothing but a plaintive yearn which refused to attract itself to anything specific, anything physical. Then it was his turn to look around to see if he could uncover some bit of trivia to break the silence.

He recalled his hate for the town, but his hate washed away in the fog. Despite his loathing for the place, it was the site of his battle, the place where he had expended his unruly energy.

He watched the mist evaporating into the air. New cloud formations collected overhead, bland, weary shapes in tarnished bleakness. He could not see beyond them. Still, a ray of sunshine penetrated the overcast. A sign of things to come, he thought, but he was not convinced. Just another one of life's mirages, he decided.

"I better get on," Tit said.

"Yeah, huh?" Pelvis asked.

"I said I better get on."

"Yeah," Pelvis said.

Pelvis handed the suitcase to the porter, and Titania gave him his ticket to check the seat number. The porter disappeared inside the train with the suitcase.

As Titania looked around for the last time, Pelvis' gaze followed his eyes until they came to rest momentarily upon him.

"I'm going in," Tit said softly, "and thanks."

"Yeah, ya better, huh? What you say?"

"I said I'm going in."

"No, not that. That other. That last."

"And thanks?"

"Yeah, that. That must have been it," Pelvis said sadly, happily, as though a new nerve had been inserted into some deep tendon.

"Thanks, anyway," Tit said, disappearing inside the train, carrying his last look at Pelvis on the edge of his mind: Pelvis standing solidly in place, looking almost peacefully proud.

As Titania made his way to his seat, he realized that he had travelled this far before – on the bus, but that time he had been unable to free his mind of Pelvis' image. Now, having dismissed him with his body, he had to dismiss him with his mind. He trembled at the thought, for his mind ran back and embraced Pelvis openly, then rushed forward, not beyond him but into him, and the world dissolved in furious motion. Muscles took on the properties of qualities: the timbre of sound, the texture of a logical proposition, always affirmative, and the social tone of eminence. But the muscles weighed lightly upon the scales of his conscience because they revealed an inner essence. They revealed their function, which was to liberate rather than to confine. But the illusion was not real. Only the intensity of the illusion was real.

He did not have to return to Pelvis in order to itemize those traits which were sacred, sacred in the sense that they implemented his salvation. Besides, those traits were indistinguishable now that a luminous glow enshrouded them. The traits were more certain than his own awareness of being on the train – blue upholstery, beige and coral walls, luggage rack, and aisle rug in its marbleized plastic deception, smooth, plain, even colours, intended to soothe, to lull on a low plane of pleasantness, which alone would have made the journey memorable.

Tit's mind reached back, into, within Pelvis where a cosmic – brace took place and refused to be broken until both parties had relinquished that which had attracted them in the first place, he strangling he, in a dance where the prize was salvation. His mind reached back, into, within, and the image rose up in all its splendour, down to the last detail of feeling.

The gaudy image was a group of characteristics which varied by the instant as if by the owner, but they varied only slightly as the essence remained constant. To wit: black hair, the curl was optional. An imposing build, firm roundness, full compactness, O, you know, he was decidedly suave with muscle and possessed the humility which accompanies such a body, a humility fostered by flattery and admiration. In short, his bones were amply covered with flesh and muscle which suggested that there must be a firm foundation to support such opulence. His modesty broke through in thrusts, outbursts really, huge and intact, which incited a feeling of helplessness in the beholder. His smile was slight, less than a ripple. As a snake weaves to hypnotize his prey, the image smiled to immobilize his victim. Nakedness became him, like so few. He was incapable of the vulgar, the awkward, or the unappetizing position as he was exempt from the vulgar motion. His face resembled a sky which was illuminated with black stars, his eyes. His agility, more grace, was too obvious to doubt. It was before the fact. And it was this image which Titania took to bed with him on nights when he slept alone. Titania offered his bed by smoothing fussily with a bit of rumpled sheet, which the image always looked askance at because it was expected of him. Tit knew that one rarely pleased an image with improvisation.

Mean-spirited, cravenly base, unflinchingly hostile was the image at his best.

Tit gave the image names. He dwelled upon the name Carabelli, which meant "dear wars" in corrupt Italian. Yet, Tit mused, it comes close to being "dear beauty," and it wouldn't have to be corrupted much more to be "the dear beautiful," but that sounded foreign to Titania, rather too sweet. Vittorio Manuel was another. For some curious reason Manuel was pronounced "manual." Vittorio, whose insertion was accomplished by one ripping thrust, had more hair on his body than was customary for an image, but it was permitted as a precautionary measure, for the springy curl was essential to his tactics. Without the spring he would have been inadvertently devoured, so powerful was his thrust.

Body heat did not have to be assigned to the image as a special trait, for Tit had to compile only a few of these traits before they became combustible – spontaneously combustible.

Once, the image turned Greek. He was accompanied by such a gross amount of humility that he was frightening. All his features were toned with a softness which radiated tenderness. Tit thought that he had accidentally wrought his own undoing, for how could such serenity be converted into sexual fire? Unwittingly, he had emasculated the image. He felt helpless and raged. He tried for a Turk, then a Hungarian, but the Greek's warmth was unassailable. The image appeared as a true eunuch until Titania surprised himself by unveiling the sex of this handsome, though kind Greek, whose tunic was trousers. Unveiled, the image was a magnificent Greek bastard. Greek because of his extraction and bastard because of his magnificence. To widen the Greek's already broad smile, Titania tacked a sign above his head ALL GREEKS PLAYING LEAPFROG MUST COMPLETE THE LEAP. As the image read the sign, his smile turned lawless. And so, the image was redeemed by the lucky revelation that he was a Greek bearing gifts.

At the base of this image, at the foot of this emblazoned structure, grappling for his own censure, was the shadow of his immortality in flesh. Revelation brightened the luminous glow. As the light becomes brightest prior to its cessation, so the image was becoming . . .

The train started to move. He felt the rhythm jogging him. It jolted him out of his mental socket, and the lulling overpowered his concentration. He was lulled into an all-pervading twilight consciousness.

He looked out the window, but a moth, which he must have flushed from the upholstery when he sat down, intercepted his view and divided his attention. The small bleached wings fluttered, beating furiously against the glass. He tried but was unable to see beyond the moth and its compulsive activity, so he concentrated on the moth struggling against that which it could not fathom, the transparent glass, which was radiant with light. As he watched the wings, he noticed how the delicate membranes flared from the thorax in splendid profusion, in excess, like the winged hips with a phantom colouring. Winged hips – phantom-coloured. A sharp pain cut him up, bisected him vertically, and he reached up and snuffed out the moth with his fingers as he would extinguish a flame. He felt nothing, nothing but a vague relief which seemed complete, no remorse, not even the substance of the moth between his fingers. He looked at the powdery remains on his fingers. The dust from the wings was some old, worn out prop from an obsolete dream, but that was all. He blew the dust off his fingers, and then there was nothing.

He looked straight ahead at a beige wall. A spot appeared about halfway down. First, it fluttered like a moth. Then it became fixed as though the line of his stare had become rigid. It relaxed him to stare at that spot. He felt hungry, but he did not want to disturb the utter calm which the spot seemed to generate, so he postponed his trip to the diner.

The calm reminded him that his impure silences were not enough. Formerly, his silences had built up a wall against situations. A layer of skin had become tougher and tougher as events had necessitated. He was encircled by a wire mesh which his emotions could slip through, or it was a blue veil, sheer knit? Sound was muffled but not indistinct. His body was a cage which he could move around in freely until he tried to step out of it. But why escape? It was warm and comfortable there, a bit boring, and it would become more tiresome all the time, but he was getting used to the void of sound and feeling. But silences congeal, and the wall thickened, receding inward, until his own feelings were in jeopardy of being locked outside the wall.

He twisted his head away from the spot in order to free his stare. His head moved but so did the spot. A rigid invisibility set in. Invisible adhesions locked his joints. He tried, but he couldn't move his body. He tried again. He felt himself relax instead of strain, but the change in his body relieved him. At least he could move his head because he recalled the moment when he had done so even though the spot had remained attached to the point of his stare. He didn't have to get up right away anyway, so there was no call for alarm. He would try again later, harder next time.

He jerked his head, tried to wrench it from its socket, but he wasn't sure if it had moved or not. He tried for alarm but materialized only a mild concern, some involuntary, muscular strickening which he couldn't name, but he didn't view his failure as an injustice because he tried for outrage and failed to materialize it. He viewed the situation in silence, in a perfectly pure silence.

There was no need for him to turn his head, for he knew that he would see that spot wherever he looked. He had finally achieved the highest of immovable states, something as hard and as rigid as stone but still breathtaking: white bronze, so now he was ready – curried, combed, clipped and cured – ready to take his place among the monuments of Twentieth-Century America.

Epilogue

"When I look at the night, I see the sea," Denis might say if I were putting words into his mouth. "Dark, rolling waves churn their discontent in a secret rhythm, and all I have to do is to touch the crests of those waves in order to feel the throbbing beat of my own pulse becoming stronger and stronger as the vibrations mingle with my trembling. My pulse is lacking in counterpoint until that fusion with night currents occurs, and the dissonance begins. Yet, the music is as endless as the struggle between moonlight and twilight in their eternal conquest of the evening. The sea toils. How can anything be so beautiful and still be lacking in oxygen which is in a usable state?"

Denis would say, "My God, the material abounds. All I have to do is to put pencil to paper in order to disgorge a bevy of thought which swirls as mightily as the sea and is as self-contained.

"My life is a dedication to all the weary travellers of the soul who have slept with Futility – not a nice lady – who forced the bud in that well-regulated hothouse calamity. Futility is a lovely rose after you have become accustomed to her face, that moss-green complexion, the backwash of sloughs. That quiet green flatters brown- drenched water.

The catfish prefers pellucid water, water made translucent with light among the muck and mud particles, but his eyesight is poor, so he relies upon feelers in order to distinguish one thing from another."

Light is an emotional redundancy. I have no patience with those who eat the marrow and leave the bone because it is harder to digest. Magnify that catfish's sensations to a brittle fineness. Swell his body with dreams, and you have a man : dream-packed embonpoint. But when that man becomes packed with dreams with no way to crystallize them, like Denis, then you have a fairy, oviparous with the ovipositor jammed, a constipated feeling, but nature is notorious for her tricks and little known for her caution, or, an even dirtier trick, with the ovipositor malformed, a *cul-de-sac*, so he swells, swollen with fetid fatness. Then he speaks from a distended point of view which verges on the unique. But don't be misled. The universe of a myopic fly is less real but no less valid than the viewpoint of an ordinary fly.

The sea abounds and enchants. Man rarely thinks so big, nor is he often content with the restless motion which confirms the eternal by affirming the endless. Cover me with the undulating sheets of turquoise on the bed of the sea, blue music, but, if you please, no seaweed. Kelp is whelp – whelped from nothing more than a misunderstanding, and when the misunderstanding occurred, the heavens convulsed and expelled a babe, but not from under any star, not so as you could notice anyway, for he was destined to be the wind made flesh.

"Mother was a lioness, Father a renovated lion. The product was a cub" (Denis smiles modestly), "a lofty conceit, a canker, which the species seems unable to transcend mutationally, for misunderstanding is a disease which is contracted easily and apt to linger, but then so is cancer, and both are chronic."

The lioness rears her lovely head which is well- fashioned, for her mane is newly done in permanent.

"Mother was a cat," Denis says. "Snarlingly defensive, but, like a lion, she could purr. She was good at purring, bather was a slob, indifferent and lazy. His mane was moth-eaten to rags and shreds of rags, overcome and tortured by a desperate lassitude. He was king before he was prince. He bestowed the title of king upon himself before he had done anything to deserve it. It was a miracle that any crown fit upon his head, for his head was constantly expanding, and the night before his coronation it became necessary for him to dream up his provinces.

"'Be like nothing,'" Denis says his mother said. "'Be like the wind, felt but never seen, felt but never feeling, an entity without form, distended motion, that's all. That way you can be as subtle as a breeze and as unruly as a storm, as formless as a ghost and as dense and gratifying as a miracle. Circle my hand like a glove, kid!'"

"'Mother, trim your claws!'"

Still, Denis rose in the embodiment of a vision, coreless, as light as music and as graceful as fat people are said to be when they are dancing, his body in air as wood in water, bobbing sweet embonpoint, but no matter how you cook it, embonpoint still boils down to fat.

"I'm a self-immolator," Denis says without being prompted. "Know what that is? A person who walks into a crematorium without being pushed, and you've got to have guts to do that, if you expect any ashes.

"'I tried with the flesh once,'" Denis thinks his father was fond of saying with his deep-rattling rib-cage sigh. "'Now I only try in my head. 'Cause I never once thought that I would conceive a pig, not even when I did, that once. I must have been thinking in generalities at the time.'"

"That's all right, Father," Denis excused. It hurt him to capitalize that word, that noun, for when he did, he felt as though he had flown from the relative importance of the word and the basic relationship between the participants. "You were no blue ribbon entry yourself, you know, Father." A stab of pain. "But the coin looks brighter when you polish it with your brain instead of with your flesh. Thinking takes on the aura of achievement, and you settle for less, thinking of the flesh that you conserved. But you gave no thought to the energy which you expended on your brain children : that child from the Lancelot line whose one flaw you mended by patching your thoughts; you second-born, Sirius, took his place in the heavens at the top of Bootes. You were proud that night. It didn't matter that he was a dog. He rose heliacally and ruled over the Dies Caniculares; and Seneca, who talked, then bade his Younger to philosophize. That younger Seneca was a son of yours. The order was there; grand, self-born, without direction. Remember your wife's bastard son? You thought he was sired by a god, you, in a moment of folly because his appearance was a joke. And remember when you were Philip of Macedonia? Then you became Alexander the Great after you threw false accusations at your son, Demetrius, and pined away with remorse while Perseus came into his own. And I was Demetrius without the remorse," Denis said, "eloquently slain while you gathered in the Greeks in splendid profusion, changing body for body, filling your head with the pride of muscle until you became me, nobody.

"I'm trying to be like the wind, see? Pine away with the coniferous scents in your head which appease the fury; but still a seed remains unsown, discontent, in dismal insistence to be more than wind.

"Under the guise of a slow, roving shadow, I emerge: a rollicking, tear-stained laugh, a catch in your voice, a gag, to be expelled only to be expelled again while I whistle around the Tower of Babel, never daring to be more than wind, so I wind through the lower halls, and I seek disturbing places, never showing myself for what I am except for a few random guesses. In the meantime, while you have been galivanting all over Greece, I have become royalty. I was Mad Ludwig of Bavaria when he lit the palace. Ten thousand candles spoke only to me from ten thousand windows which were laced in shadow.

I was Michelangelo once. I had heard of his fame, and at the time I was in the market for a sturdy body. Clothed or unclothed, I didn't care which. Either would have been an improvement. I would even have settled for an old model from an early period, but he wasn't selling any bodies that day. In fact, he wasn't available. He had become sullen and wasn't even conversing with his spirit, for he had been tossed in the hoosegow the night before for roughing up an uncooperative young prince. But, while I was he, I never saw what I painted. I may have thought that I saw it and felt it, but I doubt if I ever really saw it. The form is fluid, but the core is there. It was almost fun being Christ until the nails prickled, but, no matter who I was, I was there, felt but never seen, the hot breath of Canis stilled by ice floe, a halitosic nimbus, that of a dog."

"Be the wind!" cried the parental rule.

"I am the wind," cried the overruled, "if this feeling would only stop being obstinate, forever distilling itself into ice floe. My lunar axis does not rise heliacally."